CHARLIE COCHRANE

COUNT the SHELLS

RIPTIDE PUBLISHING

a PORTHKENNACK HISTORICAL

Riptide Publishing
PO Box 1537
Burnsville, NC 28714
www.riptidepublishing.com

Count the Shells

Cover art: L.C. Chase, lcchase.com/design.htm
Editors: Sarah Lyons, Carole-ann Galloway
Layout: L.C. Chase, lcchase.com/design.htm

ISBN: 978-1-62649-655-2

First edition
October, 2017

Also available in ebook:
ISBN: 978-1-62649-654-5

CHARLIE COCHRANE

COUNT the SHELLS

RIPTIDE
PUBLISHING

a PORTHKENNACK
HISTORICAL

For all who didn't return from WWI, and those who returned a different person.

TABLE OF CONTENTS

CHAPTER ONE

"Count the shells, please, Uncle Michael."

"As you've asked so nicely, Richard, I will. *Un, deux, trois, quatre, cinq.*" Michael Gray smiled indulgently at his nephew as he laid down each limpet shell in turn. He picked them up to lay them down again, one by one. "*Uno, dos, tres, cuatro, cinco.*"

Richard Cavendish scooped them into a pile, dropping them into Michael's hands with a plea for him to count again. Nothing changed; children throughout time must have enjoyed repetition of their favourite things. Michael tipped his hat forward, shading his eyes against a sun that was beating fiercely down on the beach and performing dazzling dances on the sea. He'd always loved the beaches on the Porthkennack headland, since he could first remember coming here as no more than a toddler. This area had always been a place of refuge, of comfort, of hope.

"Uncle?" Richard tapped his arm.

"Sorry, old man. I was woolgathering. Where was I? *Yan, tan, tethera, pethera, pimp.*" He laid the last shell down with a flourish of his hand, like a conjuror performing a trick.

Richard burst into giggles. He always liked the sheep-counting style best of all the ones Michael used. "Again, please."

"*Yan, tan, tethera, pethera, pimp.*" Michael, stifling a yawn, spoke the words slowly and pompously this time, lining up the shells like a colonel inspecting his troops. The mewing of gulls, the susurration of the waves—he'd almost forgotten how soporific sounds of the seaside could be.

"Are you tired, Uncle Michael? Is it your leg?" Richard was the only one in the family who referred casually to his wound, with a child's typical candour.

"No, the leg's fine." He'd come out of things a lot better off than many of his comrades. The thing functioned pretty well, despite being pockmarked where they'd taken all the shrapnel out, although his foot looked a mess where the little toe had gone. He couldn't—and wouldn't—complain. "Simply the effect of the local beer I had last night, making me a bit sluggish. Don't tell your mother."

"I promise I won't." Richard put his hand on his heart while making the vow. "Will you do the 'Einz vie' one?"

"*Eins, zwei,*" Michael replied, automatically. He'd known this was going to happen, and he couldn't refuse the request, not without having to tell a lie about why it upset him. Just saying he couldn't use the language of his once-enemy wasn't enough; it wasn't true, anyway. The words had acquired new connotations in his mind, over the years, connotations Richard might never understand.

Michael collected all the shells, took a deep breath, then began to lay them down one by one.

"*Eins.*"

Number one was Thomas. Thomas Carter-Clemence. *Eins.* One. The first. Never to be forgotten, even after they'd parted in such a dramatic fashion, with the mother of all rows, the spring of 1909.

"*Zwei.*"

That would be Laurence; Laurie, as Michael had preferred to call him, especially in the heat of passion, when "Laurence" seemed so ridiculously formal. Simple remembrance of those times brought a prickle to the back of Michael's neck.

"*Drei.*"

Jimmy. No, not him; Jimmy hadn't been the third. Michael had forgotten Freddie.

Freddie was third. Or maybe third and fifth, because he'd been an extra station on the line of romance when Michael and Laurence had suffered a temporary estrangement. A station which had been passed through and left behind when Michael and Laurence had made things up again, then revisited when their paths had crossed years later. He had no idea where Freddie was now, couldn't begin to say whether he was alive or dead, or whether he remembered that fleeting, if chilly, night by the river at Maidenhead or the equally fleeting, if warmer, encounter in Brighton.

Time to lay down another shell, before Richard became suspicious of the silence. He might be still a child, but he possessed a startling maturity of awareness and an unnerving habit of speaking his mind.

"*Vier.*"

The *fourth* one was Jimmy: bright, lively, and first seen pulling pints. Michael had been on a couple of days leave in London and gone for a drink in . . . What had that pub been called? Frustrating that he couldn't remember, even though he recalled every minute of the night they'd spent together.

"*Fünf.*"

Little Wilfred. They'd met in Scarborough, fleetingly, in a stationer's of all places. Shared a joke, shared a glance, shared an appreciation of a particularly fine pen. Shared a bed, sort of, briefly.

"*Sechs.*"

"There isn't another shell, Uncle." Richard shook his head indulgently, as though he were dealing with Lily, his three-year-old sister.

Michael jolted. He'd been far away, among lovers, mud, and metal shells.

"Sorry about that, old man. Got carried away. Discount *sechs.*" Lucky that Richard was too young to get the play on words. No sixth shell and no sixth bloke as of yet. *Discount sex* indeed, at least for the time being. It would happen when it happened, although how long he'd be prepared to wait was a moot point. Freddie had been an act of desperation, as had Wilfred. Always a dangerous game to play when you weren't sure of the ground you were playing on.

"Can we paddle?" Richard tugged at Michael's sleeve.

"Of course we can." Barefoot already, so they could enjoy the sensation of sand between their toes, they scampered down to the sea as spontaneous as a pair of children, to splash among the shallows.

"Do you like the seaside or the city best?" Richard posed the question as solemnly as a bishop might when addressing confirmation candidates.

"Seaside, naturally. Much more freedom here." The hustle and bustle of crowded streets no longer appealed. Not like the lapping of the waves at his feet and the mewing of gulls overhead. "What about you?"

"What a silly question. Here!" Richard flicked water with his toes as they walked along the waterline. "I wish I could be on holiday every day, rather than going to school to learn algebra and grammar."

"It's a burden that has to be borne, old man. Same for me when I was your age."

"But *why* has it got to be learned about? Do you ever use algebra?"

"Can't say I do, much. But I couldn't do without grammar. I say. What's that?" Michael stopped by a mound of rocks, where little pools of trapped water promised boyish delights. He reached beneath the surface of one to draw out something green and glistening.

"A bottle of course." Richard shook his head at such dim-wittedness.

"Ah, but is it an ordinary bottle or a magic one? If we rub it will a genie come out and grant us three wishes? And how would we divide them if he did?"

Richard frowned; clearly neither algebra nor grammar held the answer to that. "One each and one for mother," he stated, at last, and with a conviction that could brook no argument. "None for Lily because she's too young to use them sensibly."

"You're probably right." Would Richard ever regard his sister as being old enough to act sensibly? "I like that way of dividing them. What would you wish for? All the sweets in the shop?"

Richard giggled, looking exactly like his mother when she was the same age. "That's the kind of thing Lily would want. I'd wish an end to algebra or grammar lessons for any boys forever. What about you?"

"I'm not sure. You've taken care of the school stuff, already."

"I know what mother would wish for," Richard said, suddenly serious.

"And what's that?" Michael asked, attention only half on his nephew, the other half considering what *he* would do if really presented with the opportunity to make that wish. To have such power—the responsibility would be overwhelming.

"She'd wish for all the soldiers who were hurt in the war to be whole again."

"Oh." Michael, unable to say anything further, kept his gaze straight out at sea. Maybe if he concentrated extremely hard, he could keep at bay the tears that threatened to unman him.

"Yes, and she'd wish for the dead to come home too."

The only safe reply was a simple nod. Michael thought of the shells he'd just counted, the parade of names. How could he trust himself not to break down, to blurt out that roll call, then have to provide a backstory to each of them? Richard had the knack of making all his defences too relaxed to work effectively.

"Don't you think that's a good idea?"

Michael forced a reply. "I think it's excellent. What a shame it's only an empty bottle with nothing in it."

"Yes. Fairy tales never come true, I suppose."

"No. That's one of the sad things you learn in life, alongside the algebra."

Richard made a disdaining face, although whether that was at the algebra or the fairy tales, Michael couldn't tell. "It *is* sad. Otherwise we could have wished home your friend Thomas."

"Thomas?" Having just recovered his composure, Michael felt unmanned again, the waves beating more violently about him than they'd done previously—or was that simply the rushing of blood in his ears? He steadied himself with a hand on his nephew's shoulder.

"Are you feeling ill, Uncle? Come on, back up the beach." Richard took his hand, leading him like a small child.

"It's only a touch of something. Made me feel odd for a moment. Dizzy." He managed a smile. "Probably that beer last night."

"Mother says people shouldn't drink too much. So does Father."

"They're right." Eric would be giving his professional point of view, being a medical man. "And last night I was a good boy and only had one pint. I probably had a dirty glass."

"I won't snitch."

"Good man." They'd reached the place where they'd made their little camp of towels, shoes and shells; Michael settled himself on a flat rock, then took a deep, steadying breath. Caroline never discussed the war in his presence, or those who'd been lost in it, but she must be ready to discuss it with her family when he wasn't there. And mention quite freely those people she never spoke to him about.

"You've got a better colour now. You were as white as if you'd seen a ghost."

"Not quite." *Not seen, merely thought of one.* "Thanks for playing nurse. We should get ourselves home or we'll be in trouble."

By the time they'd dried their feet and got their shoes and socks back on, Michael had pulled himself together enough to ask, "How did you know about Thomas? Has your mother been talking about the time he yanked her pigtail?"

"No. Did he really?" Richard's eyes widened. "He must have been very brave to do that."

"I suspect it was a case of foolhardy rather than brave. He regretted it afterwards." Michael could just about smile again in remembrance of those fond, silly adventures from that summer of emerging manhood, when Thomas had first come to visit the Gray family and left a never-to-be-erased mark on everyone's hearts.

"Mother has a picture of you and him, at home. Did he always have funny hair?"

"He certainly did. I never knew anybody who looked more like the scullery maid had upended him and used him for a mop." Especially after they'd been playing tennis. Or in the morning, after a night in which it had been tousled by passion.

"Was he a good friend? Do you miss him?" Richard was wearing his serious face again, his ever-changing thoughts and emotions plainly displayed.

"Yes and yes." Michael concentrated on sorting out a nonexistent knot in his laces. "He was my very best friend at school. Like that rascal George you hang around with."

Richard giggled. "George isn't so bad. He has three older sisters, poor thing."

"Then he deserves a medal."

George was supposed to be with them, but a mysterious rash had struck his family and he'd been quarantined along with his sisters. Once the all clear was given, he'd be allowed to travel down, and until then, Michael was doing his avuncular duty to the best of his ability.

He held out his hand. "Come on. Home. Or we'll be court-martialled."

At the top of the trail which led up in a zigzag from the bay, a small gate gave onto a path cutting through shrubs and borders to High Top, the house the Gray family had taken for the summer ever since Michael could remember. The views across the bay were stunning, the beach close by, if a bit of a scramble, and the lawns smooth enough for croquet or tennis. There were maturer pleasures close at hand too: the twin delights of dances or dinners down in Porthkennack or Padstow, although Michael had always preferred the simpler things. Nobody could try to pair him up with an eligible girl when he was out on the rocks, sketching.

A party of females emerged from the French windows as Michael and Richard came across the lawn. Caroline, Michael's sister, holding hands with Lily, and Alice, the nursery maid, close behind.

"I was about to send out a search party, although I suppose they'd never risk missing luncheon, would they, Lily?" Caroline said, as her men folk approached.

"Not in a million years." Michael winked at his nephew. "Especially as we've spent the morning wrestling with giant squids and fending off vicious mermen. It's hungry work."

Caroline rolled her eyes. "I guess there's no chance you'll ever grow up."

"I'm afraid not. Beyond hope." Michael ruffled Richard's hair. "Let's hope this youngster turns out more to your approval. Go on, Richard. Hands to wash."

Richard surrendered to the ministrations of Alice, who whisked him and his sister off to get Lily ready to take her meal and to make her brother presentable for appearing at the table with the adults.

"I've never disapproved of you, Michael," Caroline said, once her son was out of earshot. "I wish you wouldn't say that in front of the boy."

Michael slipped his arm through his sister's. "It was in jest. Richard's used to my ways, and he knows what's meant seriously and what's just fun."

"He's only a boy."

"That's as may be, but he's a lot smarter than either of you give him credit for. He notices what goes on. He understands it."

"Does he? Then he's taking after his uncle." Caroline patted his arm. "He thinks the world of you. You'd never disappoint him, would you?"

"I'll always try my best never to let him down. He's too important to me. Nearest thing I'm likely to have to a son." Michael steered his sister towards the flower bed, which lay in full bloom by the steps up to the house, then stopped. "He mentioned Thomas."

Caroline frowned. "Did he?"

"I wouldn't have said if he hadn't, would I? Sorry," he stroked her hand, "shouldn't have snapped at you. He did. He said he was highly amused by the state of Thomas's hair in a photograph you must have of the both of us. I didn't realise you'd kept one."

Caroline, blushing, kept her gaze on the petunias. "Oh, it's an old one. I have it at home. Remembrance of when we were much younger. You and me here, Thomas at Broch, Eric at— Whatever was his uncle's house called?"

"Cataclews." It had been a ghastly gothic pile, on its last legs when Eric's family had used it for holidays. "The only good thing about it was being the vehicle to his meeting us."

"So he says, as well." Caroline smiled. "Anyway, that picture kept me going all those long days when the family waited for the next letter from you."

Michael nodded. Many a photograph must have kept families, wives, and sweethearts comforted over the years. "Not just me, I suspect. You always had a soft spot for Thomas, didn't you?"

"He was rather handsome. We all liked him."

Did she know how far Michael's liking had gone? It wasn't something they could ever have freely discussed, but Caroline was far from stupid. She must have noticed exchanges of glances, overheard whispers or mysterious laughter, wondered why Michael wasn't quite the same with Thomas as he was with other friends. Or had she simply assumed that was how men were when they had close friendships? Many people lived in blissful ignorance of what really went on between some couples of the same gender who shared a house or habitually holidayed together.

"Michael?" Caroline nudged him. "Are you feeling all right?"

"Yes. Just lost in memories. I can almost see him here, now. Running along this very lawn with that wretched kite."

"The one he couldn't get to fly?" Caroline snorted.

"That's the one." They'd have been fifteen, the family holidaying here and Michael introducing Thomas to them for the first time. He'd lived not far away, at a house called Broch, which was apparently some type of ancient Scottish dwelling and had been the brainchild of a previous, Celtic, owner of the property. Thomas had dropped in on the Grays on an almost daily basis, although nobody had complained at the intrusion. As Caroline had pointed out, he had been universally liked. It had been a glorious summer of warmth and light, the two boys teetering on the brink of understanding that their camaraderie was not like that of their schoolmates. "I was glad when that kite broke. I always felt he'd get so enthralled he wouldn't realise where he was running and he'd go down the path and right over the cliff with it."

Caroline, sly smile creeping over her face, patted his hand. "I have a terrible confession to make, although I won't do it until you swear you won't tell Richard."

"I swear," Michael promised, intrigued.

"I was the one who broke that kite. I had exactly the same concern as you did—he was so terribly reckless, so . . ." She shrugged. "I've lived with it on my conscience, but it had to be done."

"And it was well done. I was tempted to do the same, but never had the courage. I wonder if he ever suspected?" Although given that Thomas had such an open, trusting mind, that was unlikely.

"I always feel it's a shame I couldn't have taken up all those guns in France and broken *them*. Such a waste, but *you* don't need that particular sermon." Caroline shook herself. "Come on, luncheon."

As usual, any mention of the war had been forestalled, although she'd revealed more about herself in these last few minutes than she had in the year. Michael was going to have to reassess his view of his sister.

As Michael finished tidying himself up, the gong announced that lunch was imminent; he entered the dining room to find himself the last to arrive.

"Sorry to keep you. Too much sand to get off me," he said, with a self-deprecating smile.

"You're forgiven." Caroline unfolded her napkin as a sign to begin, the wonderful aroma of freshly cooked fish pervading the air as it waited to be served. New potatoes and peas gently steamed in their bowls, reminding Michael of days when he'd eagerly awaited every meal, desperate for permission to get stuck in. School days, army days, so often things had revolved around filling one's stomach.

Eric said a short grace—most likely for his son's benefit—then the maid dished out the trout. At nine, Richard was granted the privilege of taking his luncheon with the grown-ups, an honour his sister was some years short of. The Grays had never believed in children being seen and not heard, and he took his full part in the conversation. It was clear he'd already learned to moderate his talk in accord with the situation, his carefree chatter of the morning made less happy-go-lucky. He asked his father if there had been any interesting stories in the newspaper and was either genuinely interested in the response, or managed to feign a genuine interest, just as impressive a skill.

Eric gave a brief account of what might be of relevance to a nine-year-old boy, finishing his résumé with, "I saw that one of your teachers has got himself wedded."

"Mr. Grimshaw?" Richard nodded. "We thought that, although we weren't supposed to know. Not officially."

"So how do you find these things out?" Caroline gave her son a helping of peas likely far in excess of what he'd have taken for himself.

"Somebody's mother saw the announcement of his engagement. Word soon spread. Thank you." Richard gave his mother one of his dazzling smiles.

"You're like a bunch of old women for gossiping." Caroline helped herself, then passed the bowl to Michael.

The next few minutes were taken up with little in the way of chat, everybody properly appreciative of what was on their plates, albeit it wasn't there for long. The trout had tasted as good as the aroma had promised.

After the maid had cleared their plates and before pudding arrived, Richard turned to Michael and, as innocently as if asking whether they'd be fishing later, enquired, "Why have *you* never married, Uncle? Is it because you don't like girls?"

Michael, taken unawares by the question, was grateful for having raised his glass for a mouthful of water, and so had time to gather his thoughts. And to pray that his sister wouldn't leap in and make some comment which made matters even more awkward.

Rescue came, unexpectedly, from Eric. "Just because *you're* not keen on the female of the species, don't tar everyone with the same brush, young man. For all you know, your uncle has left a trail of broken hearts behind him."

"Sorry, Father." Richard sounded—and appeared—suitably abashed.

"He's under the influence of his pal George, apparently." Michael managed a grin. "George has three sisters."

"And doesn't think much of them, or so we've been told. His—" Caroline was interrupted by the arrival of the fruit salad. Once the maid had departed again, she continued. "His mother despairs of him at times. Says he'll end up as a woman hater."

"I don't hate women." Michael could say that with complete candour. "How could I have grown up with an elder sister such as you and not admire the fairer sex?"

"Oh, tush," Caroline said, with a not-hidden-soon-enough grin. "Don't swell my head."

"See, Richard?" Michael winked at his nephew. "Ladies simply require careful handling."

"Behave. That's enough about ladies or we'll turn on you." Caroline wagged her finger. "Now, tomorrow. If Lily's tooth is through and she's not as grizzly, how about a picnic on the beach for all the family?"

And with that skilfully imposed change of subject, talk turned to what were the best provisions to avoid the peril of sand with everything. Sometimes domestic talk was the only safe talk.

CHAPTER TWO

Richard wasn't too old to be whisked off to the nursery for a postprandial rest, even if he was excused an afternoon nap and allowed to spend the time reading or an equally sedentary occupation. He was likely to be the only one of the family who didn't slip into the arms of Morpheus, given that Lily still enjoyed her sleep—especially when she was teething—and the adults had reached the stage where it felt like a slightly wayward, and daringly continental, indulgence to take a siesta.

Eric and Caroline headed for the sofas in the drawing room, while Michael sought the harbour of the old orchard, where a capacious and surprisingly comfortable hammock was slung between a pair of gnarled old apple trees. He'd brought a novel, in case he couldn't get off to sleep; occasionally his leg gave him some jip, particularly if there were storms in the offing or out at sea. The book, a murder mystery, was well written, engaging, and required the minimum of intellectual concentration. He read page after page, but sleep wouldn't come, the slight twinge which had developed around his knee on the way up from the beach a touch too persistent. He wriggled, turned, wriggled again, but comfort eluded him.

Eventually, he laid down the novel and swung gently, watching the rustle of the leaves, thinking of all the times he'd lain in this spot and the wonderful afternoon when he'd shared this hammock with Thomas. They'd done nothing other than swing and chat and laugh—given the proximity of the rest of the family—but the closeness of their bodies had been intoxicating.

Thomas had stayed with them on and off that holiday, taking the other bed in Michael's room, but once he'd sneaked across when the rest of the household were tucked up. Then the young men had put into action what they'd only dared dream of that afternoon. Not their first time—that had been in the boathouse on Thomas's estate, the previous year—although every encounter had been memorable back then.

Michael's body began to react to the memories, a horribly noticeable reaction should anybody come along at this point. He turned on his side, trying to think of something that might cool his ardour, but his brain kept veering back to well-worn tracks, that list of lovers he'd run down as he'd counted those shells for Richard, and the lack of anybody to warm his bed now. He'd have to admit that he'd not met anybody since his discharge who could hold a candle to the least of those five men. Surely every truly decent man couldn't have gone the way of all flesh?

How could they have been so naïve as to think it would all be over by the first Christmas of the war? Although Thomas would have welcomed seeing that season, in France or at home; he hadn't made it through to All Souls' Day. But, then, he'd been a career soldier, giving up his studies and taking the king's shilling four years before war had been declared. He'd gone over with the British Expeditionary Force and, like so many of them, claimed a small corner of a foreign field to hold forever for England.

Michael wondered if he'd approached death with the same cheery smile he'd seemed to wear every day, the smile which had lit up Michael's school years and carried on shining through the university vacs when they'd met up. Either in Sussex or—more usually—Cornwall. Thomas's family had lived not far from High Top, so the summers had always featured him, with the Grays and the Carter-Clemences forming a friendship that had been rooted and grounded in the two boys' friendship. Michael vividly remembered the first conversation he and Thomas had had about Porthkennack, and the envy he'd felt that Thomas could live in such a wonderful place all the time. Thomas, naturally, had envied the Grays' life so close to the delights of London. The grass was always greener on the other side.

Like it had touched so much else, the war seemed to have loosened the bonds between the families, death casting a wide shadow, although the rot had set in earlier, with the terrible row he and Thomas had suffered not long before their last year at university. Without their intense relationship at the heart of the family friendship, the rest of the connection had always been at risk of withering. The others must have known that something had gone badly wrong, but they'd let it pass without comment, far too English in their reserve to make a fuss, and Michael had been up at university for weeks on end. Even Caroline had restrained her normally inquisitive nature when he'd been home; perhaps his pain had been written large on his face.

It had felt like hell—although Michael had gained an increasingly accurate impression of hell during his time in France—and now those feelings were reawakening to torment him. He'd managed to put Thomas to the back of his mind for so long, but Richard's carefree comment had brought him back in all his golden glory, brown eyes flashing in Michael's memory like dark stars. He'd never loved anyone so much, nor—he believed—would he ever love so intensely again. Lightning couldn't strike twice.

Michael opened his book and tried to read, but the dappled light through the trees played on the pages, bringing him to that comfortably drowsy stage at last. Forty winks were called for, although he felt like he'd managed less than half a dozen before Richard's voice cut into his slumbers.

"Uncle Michael, do you really think girls require . . . what was it?"

"Sorry? Can you say that again, please, old man? I was having a bit of shut-eye."

"Oh, sorry. Should I go?"

"No, I'm awake now." He consulted his watch, to find that he'd managed considerably more sleep than he'd realised. "Just as well you roused me. I could have been here until morning."

"You'd have got all wet with dew." Richard plonked himself down on the grass. "Girls. At lunch you said they required something."

"'Careful handling,' I think." Michael tried to stir up his sleep-addled wits.

"Oh yes, that was it."

It was time to cut off this particular discussion. "Talking of females, have you been let out of jail for the rest of the day?"

"Jail?"

"The nursery. I know those bars on the window are there to stop you falling out, but they do make me think of incarceration. I guess you've been let out on parole for good behaviour?"

Richard chuckled. "Only until teatime. And only if I promise not to go down to the beach. Alice says there's a running sea and it wouldn't be safe."

"Then we must heed her warning and stick to dry and sandless land." Michael grinned. "We can find plenty of mischief to get up to elsewhere."

Richard put his hand to his mouth. "I'd better not tell her you said that. Her reaction might need 'careful handling.'"

"No 'might' about it. I'd be in big trouble."

Richard nodded, then lay back, letting the sunlight play on his face. The ability to sit in—occasional—companionable silence was one of the qualities Michael found most admirable in his nephew.

"This 'careful handling' thing," the boy continued, eventually. "I wondered if that was why you hadn't bothered to marry. Because it would be too much hard work dealing with girls all the time."

Back there again. Well, Michael supposed he couldn't keep putting off the conversation; Richard was bright, as determined as a dog with a bone, and deserved an answer.

"There's probably some truth in your theory." It *would* have been hard work to force himself to go with a woman, but he could have done it if the circumstances demanded. Plenty of men did, hiding themselves in semi-platonic marriages or the like. Better to tell Richard as much of the truth as possible, despite the fact it couldn't be the whole truth at this point. Maybe it could never be the whole truth. "I have to admit I find females rather daunting."

"Maybe you'll get used to them one day. You're still quite young."

Michael grinned at the *quite*. When he'd been Richard's age, a man of thirty would have seemed almost ancient. "Maybe." He could just about conceive of a situation where he might take a wife to give him appropriate cover. At the very least doing so would prevent an interrogation such as he was experiencing.

"I won't ever get married. Not even to please Mother." Richard flipped onto his stomach, the better to idly pick blades of grass, then split them lengthwise. "Girls are so silly. Fancy having to put up with that all day."

"Are you basing your opinion of all females on your little sister? Every three-year-old, girl or boy, can seem slightly daft when you're five years older than they are, but most of them grow out of it. You did," Michael added, with a grin.

"I was never daft." Richard looked up, clearly offended. "Was I?"

"A little bit. You've matured remarkably well." Not that Michael had seen much of him back then; he'd felt rather an intruder in the days when his nephew was small, especially as Caroline and Eric had been so besotted with him. Surely every firstborn was regarded by his parents as the pinnacle of God's creation? "One day you might find that girls are the best things in the world."

Richard made a face, showing he didn't believe a word of it. "Is it five o'clock yet?"

Michael consulted his wristwatch. "Only twenty to. Why?"

"I have to go in then to get ready for tea. Alice says the cook's making some rather nice sandwiches for Lily and me."

"Is she? Then we'll keep an eye on the time—don't want them to spoil and go curly at the edges." Michael began to rock the hammock again.

"Doesn't that make you feel sick, Uncle?"

"Not really. Does it you?"

"Not when I'm watching. When I get in, it's like I'm in a boat." Richard chuckled. "I don't mind a swing, going back and forth, but side to side . . ." He grimaced as though he were about to be sick.

"Don't let your mother see you wearing that expression. She'll say it's not the sort of thing a young gentleman should do in polite company."

"That's sounds like what Alice would say." Richard rolled his eyes. The fact both he and Lily were still under the control of a nursery maid clearly stuck in the boy's unusually mature craw.

"You should listen to her. And to your parents. Listen and remember." Michael peered over the hammock, to face his nephew directly. "You'll have plenty of time to make your own judgements about what's fitting for a gentleman when you're older."

"*You* never tell me what to do and what not to do."

"Not my place." Michael swung the hammock again. "I hope your sandwiches are as good as the fish was at lunch. That was trout par excellence. As good as you'd get at the Savoy. Better, probably, and I speak from experience."

"I've heard Father mention the Savoy." Richard wriggled on the grass. "Is it posh?"

"Extremely. I'm not certain it's entirely my cup of tea. Hall in college was better—at least you're among pals there and don't have to be completely on your best behaviour."

"I like the sound of that." Richard sighed. "I have to be on my very best behaviour at tea."

"I'm sure there's a lot of latitude in that 'best behaviour.'" Michael chuckled. "Maybe Alice will let me come and keep you and Lily company this afternoon."

Richard sat up beaming, no doubt at the prospect of further time to be spent in male company. "She will if you ask nicely. She likes you."

"Does she?" Michael had only passed a few words with the girl. "How on earth do you know these things?"

"Oh, I've seen the way she looks at you. The same way that Lily looks at a plate of rice pudding."

The remark left Michael speechless. Richard was going to be an extremely dangerous quantity one day, so long as he learned when to share, and when not to share, the profits of his formidable powers of observation.

"You continue to astound me," Michael remarked, eventually, valuing that comfortable bond in which constant conversation wasn't required. He swung his legs over the side of the hammock. "Time to report for duty soon."

"Yes, sir." Richard leaped to attention, giving a mock salute.

A sudden, piercing memory of lads seemingly no older than his nephew standing to attention on parade grounds made Michael shiver.

"Are you all right? Is it that beer in the dirty glass playing up again?"

"No. Just someone walking over my grave, I think. Come on." Michael took the boy's hand. "We seem to spend all our time dashing off to report to the ladies."

"It's part of that 'careful handling,' Uncle." Richard giggled.

"I could grow tired of that phrase." Michael laughed, then composed himself for his visit to the nursery. Did Alice really look at him like that? And why couldn't she have a nice brother who'd want to consume him like a rice pudding?

CHAPTER THREE

ea in the nursery passed as well as could be hoped. Following the rice pudding remarks, Michael's strategy had been to present himself to Alice as a potentially undesirable visitor, through the simple tactic of making Lily giggle as often as possible. For some reason she found the phrase *sticky wicket* hilarious, so Michael regaled all present—including his sister—with a detailed account of a match he'd played in the summer of 1914, where rain on the pitch had made it ideally suited to the action of an elderly spin bowler.

Later, as he dressed for dinner, he took a moment to study his reflection in the long mirror, searching for what Alice might have seen in him. He supposed he was handsome enough; he'd certainly filled out again, to the point his dinner jacket hung properly on him once more rather than hanging about him. When he'd first returned from France, he'd seemed like a boy borrowing his elder sibling's clothes.

Laurie, his second love and the second of the men he'd thought of that morning, had always admired him in formal dress, saying he did proper justice to the outfit, whereas many men simply resembled either waiters or penguins. Laurie had scrubbed up well in white tie or black, despite his wiry frame. Actually, he'd scrubbed up well in any set of clothes—and out of them.

They'd been at different colleges, quite literally bumping into each other at a societies fair, but nothing much had come of it at the time apart from friendship, given that Michael had still been besotted with Thomas. Laurie's smile had been one to die for, though, and his lilting Scottish brogue had been enough to send any man of a certain persuasion into a jellied heap, even when they were simply sharing tea and toast with him. When the split with Thomas came, Laurie had provided a shoulder to cry on and a body to warm the bed. He'd never quite filled the void in Michael's heart, but perhaps nobody would ever achieve that.

Ironic that the same heart defect that prevented Laurie passing the army medical killed him while he was rowing down the Thames at Maidenhead. Michael, when he heard the full story, had wondered whether there'd been an element of a self-inflicted wound, since Laurie had been denied the chance to go to fight when all his friends seemed to be enlisting. He had been the sort who'd have wondered whether there was any point to him staying alive if he couldn't fight. If *they* were pushing themselves to the limit, then he'd have wanted to do the same.

Ironic, too, that so many of Michael's lovers had already gone the way of all flesh while he had survived. Maybe it was only an accident of statistics, a reflection of how many young men had died those four years. There had been a true decimation of chaps his age, he suspected, maybe a greater cull among the officers than among the men. He'd never been inclined to read anything which purported to count the true toll.

The sounding of the gong called his thoughts back to the present day and the fact he was hungry.

Dinner—a cold collation—passed comfortably, with Caroline relating the tale of her brother's behaviour over the nursery tea, at which point the conversation turned to cricket and stayed there for the rest of the meal, Eric being a huge fan of the sport and Caroline not far behind him. As a child, Eric had seen W. G. Grace play and waxed lyrical about the great man's abilities, albeit confessing that he hoped no son of his would sail quite so close to the wind regarding the rules of the game.

"I wouldn't be too worried," Michael remarked. "Richard has all the makings of a decent gentleman. He'll be a better man than either of us, I'm sure."

"Then he'll be a fine man indeed." Caroline beamed with maternal pride. "And Lily will be a fine lady."

"'Upon a white horse.'" Michael smiled as he completed the line from his niece's favourite nursery rhyme. Lily liked nothing better than to be bounced on someone's knee while they recited "Ride a Cock Horse to Banbury Cross."

Caroline rolled her eyes. "Just don't start that 'sticky wicket' nonsense again."

"I shall save it for her wedding, where I shall insist on making a speech. At Richard's too."

"I'm sorry he was so inquisitive at luncheon." Caroline's brow puckered in thought. "He will ask questions."

"Don't stop him. He's a bright boy, and he's better off asking than letting his questions stew." Michael cast a glance at Eric, but he didn't appear to have read anything into the conversation apart from the manners aspect. If he knew about Michael, he wasn't giving the fact away. "If he asks the right people, those he can trust, then they'll give him an answer that's right for his age."

Eric nodded. "Valid point. He can be alarmingly honest at times, though. And perceptive. Misses nothing."

Michael grinned. "Oh, yes." He related the conversation in the orchard about Alice. "Maybe you should advise him that there'll be situations where he'll need to keep his observations strictly confidential. Can you imagine if he said something like that to one of the masters at school?"

"I think he's too smart for that," Eric's concerned expression belied his words, "but I'll have a word nonetheless. Have you ever read the Saki story about the talking cat?"

"Yes. And while Richard's not in that league, it won't hurt him to learn a touch of discretion around others. He can say what he likes to me, of course. Make sure he knows that."

"I will." Eric raised an eyebrow at Caroline, who seemed to take that as a signal to rise from the table. Postprandial separation of men and women had been agreed on as being unnecessary, so all three moved into the drawing room to find the coffeepot waiting, with a decanter of brandy on the sideboard. Michael opted for one each of grape and bean, pouring out three tots of what promised to be an excellent vintage—given the colour and aroma—while his sister filled their coffee cups.

"I haven't shown you the photograph albums!" Eric said, leaping to his feet no sooner than he'd settled into his chair. "I'll go and fetch them."

"Albums?" Michael asked his sister, as they waited for her husband to return. "Why did you bring them?"

"Oh, it was Eric's idea." Caroline waved her hand. "He wanted to compare the views now with what they used to be. To reassure himself that the area hadn't all changed beyond recognition. And to show Richard what it used to be like. Your nephew is fascinated by old photographs."

"So I understand." Michael kept his voice neutral.

"He'd love to see those sketches you used to do. Have you brought your drawing stuff with you?"

"No. I forgot," he lied. "Out of the holiday habit, I guess."

"That's a shame. Maybe you could pop into Porthkennack and get some supplies. All those artists must get their stock of brushes and canvas somewhere." Caroline had rolled her eyes at the words *those artists*, clearly illustrating her opinion of them.

"I imagine some of the breed have whatever they need borne down from London on a bejewelled palanquin." The local artists' community was typical of the type, a mixture of talent and pretentiousness, true artists and dabblers. "Maybe I will go and restock my supplies. Although I'm not sure I'm ready to take up my pencils again just yet. I did a lot of doodling out in France, you know, and the activity's developed unwanted associations in my mind."

"What has?" Eric asked, coming into the room halfway through the sentence.

"Drawing. I suspect it wouldn't be quite the pleasure it used to be. Not at the moment, anyway."

"I understand. Or at least I think I do." Caroline patted Michael's arm. "You'll be ready when you're ready. Alas that none of the rest of us show any similar aptitude for the arts."

"Don't be so quick to judge. What about Eric's photography? That's as artistic as many a thing people can produce with a dab of paint on canvas."

"Thank you." Eric nodded solemnly, then added—with a wink, "It takes a true artist to recognise another."

"And Caroline shouldn't hide her light under a bushel, either. This is wonderful." Michael picked up the piece of fine embroidery that his sister had brought with her to work on. He wasn't the only member of the family who could produce something beautiful out of very little. "*And* I've seen the splashes Lily makes with her paints. Perhaps she'll take up Cubism or some such twaddle and make her way living and working with the rest of the artists here."

Caroline chuckled. "Several of her paintings are already better than theirs."

"Have you been and looked in that gallery, Michael? The one that's got a window full of rot?" Eric grimaced.

Michael chuckled. "If we pretend Lily's daubs are by some up-and-coming chap from Yorkshire, we'd sell the lot and make a fortune. I shall act as her agent."

"I've heard of money-making schemes less likely to work." Eric's grimace turned into a grin. "I suppose beauty—and true worth—are in the eyes of the beholder rather than in something's provenance?"

"Tell that to the art dealers." Michael sneered.

"If you're planning to discuss art dealers, then I suggest we change the subject," Caroline insisted.

Michael glanced up from a fresh admiration of the embroidery, wondering why his sister sounded quite so agitated. "Why's that?"

"You won't know because you were . . . away at the time," Caroline was evidently making a veiled allusion to the war years, "but Father bought a little watercolour for mother, and the thing turned out to be fake. It's rather tainted my opinion of the breed."

"I didn't know that."

"He doesn't like to mention it." Eric gave him a knowing look. "He's always prided himself on his discernment, hasn't he?"

"True."

Michael could imagine his father's reluctance to admit he'd been taken for a fool. An intensely proud man, he'd passed on that need to preserve his own dignity to his only son. That's why Michael and Thomas had quarrelled—Thomas had played some stupid practical joke on him, one that Michael had failed to see the funny side of. Like many arguments, it had mushroomed from a few harsh words to little short of a full-blown fist fight. Michael's pride, and his lover's, had combined to make any chance of reconciliation unlikely.

Ironic how so drastic a conclusion could have grown so rapidly from such a small, seemingly innocent seed.

"Michael?" Caroline's voice cut into his thoughts.

"Sorry old girl, I was miles away."

"So I gathered. I was asking if you'd fancy going to a cricket match if we can run one to ground."

"Isn't the answer obvious?" Michael grinned.

"If you got hold of a drawing book you could do a sketch of the scene, perhaps? Not that I'm trying to put any pressure on you," Eric added hastily. "Please yourself."

"Oh I will, don't worry. Please myself I mean." Michael took a deep, cleansing breath. "It's been too long since I did a bit of doodling. Maybe the time's right to change that. Now, let's see those pictures."

But the arrival of Alice, who confessed that Lily simply wouldn't settle because of her teeth and Richard wouldn't settle because of Lily, put paid to their plans. Caroline went off to tend to her daughter, Eric—who'd always taken a surprising view of his parental duties—went to read Richard some stirring Wodehouse tale of school life, while Michael opened one of the albums, decided he wasn't in the mood, closed it again, and headed up the stairs.

In his bedroom, he rummaged an attaché case from the bottom of his wardrobe, weighed it in his hands, then tentatively opened it.

While he'd not touched his sketchbooks since coming home from France, at the last moment he'd scooped them up with his drawing kit and stuffed them in his luggage. Although it didn't seem possible he'd want to make marks on paper again. Those drawings represented too many things which were conflated and confused in his mind: the war—as he'd hinted to his sister—but also his lovers, those previous holidays in Cornwall, the parts of his character that had to remain hidden.

The idea of taking pencil to paper at the cricket match held an appeal. A sporting scene would be neutral, a subject he was interested in but which held no great sentiment for him. It would be safe, with little risk of his own feelings towards the sitter or the scene shining through. But would the simple act of opening a page be a step too far?

He took from the case three books—one of landscapes made over the best part of ten years, one of portraits done over a similar period, and one covering the sparse output of the last few years, with several pages of virgin white still to be inhabited with faces or views. If he ever decided to try his hand again. He stared at them, afraid to even turn the covers, unsure of what memories might be stirred up. He'd poured his heart and soul into some of these sketches.

This wasn't an activity for nighttime, with the prospect of awakened memories denying his body sleep while torturing him through to the wee hours. If he was to take this fence, best to do it at a canter, in the light of day when nothing would seem as daunting.

He put the books away and prepared for bed.

The morning dawned crisp and bright, but a touch too windy for sporting on the beach. Caroline's plans of a family jaunt into Porthkennack to walk along the front and share that picnic, were scuppered as Lily—still teething—was tired and irritable. Alice patiently whisked her off, and Michael offered to take his nephew for a walk out along the hedgerows to see if they could forage anything, Richard being at the age when the thought of sleeping under a tree and living off the land was appealing. Eric and Caroline could picnic à deux, while Michael and Richard could stuff their sandwiches and the like into a kit bag.

"*Like Boy Scouts!*" Richard had observed gleefully.

Michael, spotting Eric's envious expression, had asked him if he'd like to come along, but he'd stated that husbandly duties took priority. At least for that day.

As it turned out, there wasn't a lot to forage, being too early for blackberries on the brambles or apples on the trees overhanging the road, but that hadn't mattered. They'd picnicked by some old standing stones, about which there were some gruesome local legends, although Michael didn't wish to share any of these with his nephew until the lad was older. It was exactly the kind of carefree day Michael had appreciated when he'd been Richard's age: a piercingly blue sky, fragrant aroma of grass and flowers, and the lazy humming of bees. Thank God he'd had the opportunity to return and drink it in again.

Once they'd had their fill of sausage rolls, ginger beer, and a fierce sun that threatened to burn them, they began to wend their way home along mercifully shaded country lanes.

A distant hum attracted Michael's attention, the noise familiar but not one he could place immediately. As it increased in volume, he logged that it was a motorbike, high powered and likely going at a speed unsuited to the road it was travelling on. He spotted the metal beast as it rounded a sharp bend, the man at the controls seemingly unaware of their presence. A patch of something on the road—oil, mud?—caught the rider unawares, sending the bike into a skid. This was no time for second thoughts: Michael grabbed Richard by the shoulders and flung him onto the grass verge, behind him.

"Oi!" Richard shouted. "Be careful, Uncle."

"I'm not the one who needs to be careful." Michael eyed the motorbike, which had come to a halt some three yards away. He turned and bent down to inspect his nephew, who'd fetched up against a bush. "Are you all right, old man? Sorry I had to manhandle you, but needs must. I had to get you out of the way of that death trap."

"I'm fine." The tremor in Richard's voice belied his words. "Mother's going to be cross about the state of my shorts, though."

"Not when I explain how you might have been hurt otherwise. She'd prefer seeing you dirty to seeing you . . . well, she'd prefer it to that." Michael put his arm round the boy's shoulders.

"That strategy may work with Mother, but what about Alice?" Richard, voice still tremulous, appeared to be putting on a brave front, although he seemed more horrified at the prospect of the nursery maid's wrath than he'd been at the prospect of his mother's.

"Given the circumstances, if she gets cross, she'll have me to answer to." Like the motorcyclist was about to have to answer for his sins. He jerked his thumb over his shoulder. "Excuse me for a moment, I've a bone to pick with that fool."

Richard, steady on his feet at last, broke into a nervous grin, as though torn between fear at the likelihood of a fight and delight at the same thing.

Michael shook his fist in the direction of the helmeted and begoggled figure, who was now setting his machine upright. "Why the hell can't you watch where you're going? Idiots like you shouldn't be allowed on the roads."

"I'm sorry." The motorcyclist took off his gloves and pointed along the lane. "There's a patch of oil or something over there. Sent me sideways."

"Couldn't you swerve to avoid it?"

"I thought I had. The blo—" the man caught sight of Richard, "The wretched thing spread further than I'd anticipated. Sorry I scared the boy."

"I wasn't scared," Richard insisted. "Only surprised."

"Then I apologise for surprising you." The motorcyclist took off his helmet before removing his goggles. His face was ashen, but he held his hand tentatively out to Richard, although before the boy could shake it, Michael's stifled shout of, "No!" made them both spin round to face him.

Michael raised his hand to his temple. "Forgive me. I thought I'd seen a ghost. You remind me so much of an old friend."

The motorcyclist opened his mouth, but before he could speak, Richard exclaimed, "Thomas! Is that who he reminds you of, Uncle?"

"Yes." Michael could barely get the word out.

"I knew it. You look just like Thomas in the photograph. Hair and all!" Richard added gleefully.

"What photograph?" The cyclist, smoothing his hair down to what must have been his normal state, seemed taken aback.

"The one Mother has," Richard stated, as though that were explanation enough.

Michael, composure recovered at last, explained, "Richard's rather taken with a photo of me and my friend Thomas together. Something about the unruly state of his hair fascinates him."

"Ah." The stranger nodded. "That accounts for everything. If you're thinking of Tom Carter-Clemence, then I've been mistaken for him before." He solemnly offered his hand to Michael. "I'm Harry, Tom's brother."

"Harry? Never. The last time I saw you, I swear you were no bigger than . . ." Michael held his hand six inches above his nephew's head. "That was years ago."

Harry laughed. "It must have been for me to be that small. Surely I wasn't so young when last we met, Michael."

Michael laughed, unsettled by how nervous he felt. "It's my memory playing tricks. Harry, let me introduce you properly to my nephew, Richard. And make it plain we're talking about the same man. Tom to your family, Thomas to ours for some reason."

"Probably his cheeky character. Nobody in our family could seriously call him Thomas." Harry quickly hid the expression on his face—whether surprised or amused, Michael couldn't quite tell—beneath a suitably sober smile, then held out his hand for Richard to shake. "Pleased to meet you. Your uncle and my brother were great pals. He still evidently thinks I'm aged about thirteen."

"Not quite. But you always seemed so much younger than us."

"I know. Those four years felt like a gap which could never be closed." Harry turned to Richard again. "They were always telling me off for being such a nuisance, trailing after them."

"Really?" Richard frowned. "Although I suppose I wouldn't want Lily trailing after me and my pals. She's my sister. She's only three."

"Harry always thought we were having much more fun than he was back then. We never were." Thomas had been the elder of the two. Four years, an age difference that seemed an unbridgeable chasm in those days, on both sides. In manhood, the gap was almost imperceptible. This young man with a motorbike could have been Thomas returned from France, the resemblance was so striking.

Michael became aware that he'd stayed in his thoughts too long. "We were thinking about your brother only yesterday. It must have been a terrible shock for the family."

"Yes." Harry wrinkled his brow in the same way his brother had done. "Mother took it very hard. She still has me, and Olivia, but I don't think the pair of us combined match up to him. Tom was always the favourite."

Michael nodded, choked up again. "How is Olivia?" he managed to say, eventually.

"Blooming. Expecting her third, believe it or not. I never imagined I'd be an uncle, and not so many times over." He produced a quirky smile, which made Michael question whether the remark was meant to illustrate that he knew his brother hadn't been likely to produce an heir. Thomas had always voiced the same opinion of the female sex as Michael: they were pleasant enough as friends or relatives, but he wouldn't have wanted more than that, no matter the pressure.

"I wondered whether I should call on your mother while we were here, but I've not had the chance yet, given we've only been down a few days." Michael felt exposed under Harry's keen, quizzical gaze. "And I've not summoned up enough courage, I guess."

"Would it be that arduous?"

"Not for me. I'd love to see Broch again." When had it become so easy to lie? Going there once more would be as painful as opening the sketchbooks. "I was concerned for your mother. I'd hate her to be upset."

"She'd be pleased to see you. She always enjoyed your visits—I think she regarded you as a good influence. But you'll have a long way to go to see her."

"Oh?"

"She's living up in Yorkshire, near Olivia. After Father's death, she couldn't bear to be here on her own. Broch's a big responsibility."

"I didn't realise." At least distance would mean a legitimate excuse to avoid such an awkward visit. "I mean, I knew about your father. Saw it in the *Times* when I was home on leave. I'm sorry for your loss, especially coming so hard on the heels of Thomas. Please pass that on to your mother when next you speak."

"Thank you. I will." Harry's brow puckered. "She very much appreciated the letter of condolence the Grays sent. Especially as we'd not been in touch that frequently."

"I know." Michael sighed. "That stupid quarrel I had with Thomas spoiled everything. I was thinking of it only yesterday, how it had affected the whole family. Both families."

"I never really knew what that argument was about. No," Harry raised his hand, then lowered it with a wince. "Don't tell me. Not here, not now. This should be a time for happy reunions and putting the past behind us for a while."

Michael nodded. "I say, are you hurt? Did you land on that arm?"

Harry's right sleeve was scuffed, from where he'd come off the bike. "Just a knock, that's all. Nothing a good hot bath won't solve, although I suppose it'll be black and blue come morning." Despite his jollity, Harry's face had drained again.

"Are you sure you don't want me to give it the once-over? Or get you to a doctor?"

"Don't fuss!" Harry drew back, then raised his hand again—the left one, this time—in apology. "I'm sorry. It's all been a bit of a jolt to the system, what with taking a tumble and then being mistaken for a ghost. I'll take it slowly on that bike in future."

"Please do. We wouldn't want to lose you as well." Michael felt a tug on his sleeve. "Yes, Richard?"

"May I say something?" Richard had put on his most serious expression.

"Please do." Michael inclined his head and suppressed a grin; he needed to match the solemnity and not make the child ill at ease. Richard *was* only a child and had received a nasty shock. "I'm sure Harry will understand that you share your uncle's habit of asking too many questions."

"I understand entirely. Ask away."

"Will you come and see the family? Mother would be so pleased." Richard tugged at Michael's sleeve again. "Would that be all right if we invite him along? He *is* an old friend, after all."

"He is indeed." Michael, in the act of giving Harry a wink, logged the fleeting concern sweeping across the bloke's face. For all the mention of happy reunions, there was bound to be pain in any meeting. "But, you know, we'd have to check with your mother. We can't simply drag every waif and stray off the street and into the dining room."

"But Harry isn't a waif or stray, is he?"

"You didn't see him when he was your age. That's how your mother might remember him." Michael grinned. "She might think he's going to climb up the curtains or make forts under the dining table."

Richard chuckled. "You do make me laugh, Uncle."

"He used to make everyone laugh." Harry gently cuffed Michael's sleeve. "He was always the life and soul of the party. Anyway, I shall await my invitation and won't feel snubbed should it not arrive."

"Where should we send it to?"

"To Broch of course. It's mine now. I'll be around for a few weeks, so don't feel you have to rush." The warm smile on his face hardened. "And I meant what I said. Don't feel obliged to send anything at all. Too easy to stir up unwanted memories these days."

"True." Michael nodded, although was that a valid reason for not attempting a reconciliation between the two families? "But we mustn't evade our proper responsibility regarding hospitality for old friends. Oh, Lor,'" he scratched his head, "I sound like a pompous ass. We'd love to have you to dinner, and I'm sure Caroline and Eric will feel the same."

"And I'd love to be there if you could bear to put up with me." Harry gave him a wan, almost nervous smile.

"It'll be a pleasure."

They shook hands all round, exchanging awkward words of parting, Michael keen to get away and martial his thoughts into some kind of order. Harry gingerly mounted his bike again, started it up, gave a final wave, and headed off—slowly—back down the lane.

"Wasn't that wonderful, Uncle? Your old friend." Richard took Michael's hand as they set off for home.

"It was. Don't you think it was extraordinary, his riding along the same road that we were on?"

"Maybe it's the genie."

"Sorry?"

"The genie who wasn't in the bottle we found." Richard giggled. "Maybe it was a magic bottle and he'd just popped off somewhere for a moment. Probably to make Harry drive down this very lane."

Michael had to laugh at the wonderful logic working itself out in his nephew's mind. "He should have made sure we weren't nearly killed."

"Perhaps he did. Perhaps that was the second wish, that he made sure the bike didn't hit us." The determined set of Richard's mouth would clearly brook no argument.

"And what will the third wish be?"

"We've already had that one, as well. In a way. It's Mother's wish." Richard swung his arm back and forth, taking Michael's along with it. "She wanted the soldiers to return from the war unscathed. The genie isn't powerful enough to do that, but meeting Harry is like having Thomas back, isn't it?"

He let go of Michael's arm and skipped happily ahead, leaving a trail of emotional chaos in his wake.

Michael would never get Thomas back, and Harry's presence could only remind him of that at every turn.

CHAPTER FOUR

When they reached High Top, there was no containing Richard.

"Mother!" he shouted, scampering across the lawn and almost colliding with Lily, who'd toddled over to meet him. "Oh, hello, you. Teeth all better?" He took his sister's hand, leading her back to where she'd left her beloved toy dog. "We've had such an adventure."

"Involving mermen and sea serpents?" Caroline smiled indulgently.

"No. This is serious. We were nearly hit by a motorcycle, weren't we, Uncle?"

"We were indeed," Michael replied, breathlessly, having walked faster than he cared for the last half mile and being more aware than usual of his leg as a result.

"Dear me." Caroline's horrified expression belied the mildness of her words. "Did anyone get hurt?"

"Thank goodness the only thing hurt was our dignity. We've got mud and grass stains everywhere. Don't go telling the lad off for the state of his shorts." Michael poured himself and Richard a glass of lemonade from the jug on the table. "He survived his ordeal heroically."

"Thank you." Richard took a long drink. "You'll never be able to guess who the motorbike rider was."

"I suppose not, given your excitement, although I'd like to have a stern word with him." Caroline, still pale from the shock, was evidently putting on a brave front. "Was it King George?"

"No. It was Thomas's brother. Uncle Michael's friend Thomas, who was killed. *His* brother."

If Caroline had been pale before, she had turned ashen now.

"He was everybody's friend. All of the family." Michael felt the need to point out, and not simply on his own account. Caroline clearly needed a moment to compose herself.

"The brother's name is Harry," Richard carried on blithely. "He's ever so polite. You'd like him."

"I'm sure I would," Caroline rallied, "so long as he's matured. Although if he's haring around the country on a machine like a mad thing, then maybe he hasn't changed that much."

"He always was a bit nutty." Michael sipped his drink, then let Lily clamber into his lap. He addressed her seriously, as he might were she a fellow accountant. "Now, missy, here's some Gray family history, mixed in with a touch of the Carter-Clemences. There were five of us, altogether. Your mother, your uncle—that's me, remember?"

Lily squealed, "Silly nuncle," delightedly.

"Thomas and Harry had an older sister, Olivia," Michael continued. "She'd be a touch older than your mother."

"Quite a lot older, actually," Caroline pointed out. "There was a good eight years between her and Thomas. I sympathised with her. I only had one younger brother to deal with. Two must have been a sore cross to bear."

Michael, smiling, dandled Lily on his knee. "We were all wonderful, as snotty-nosed boys go. Well, maybe not Harry. He always used to traipse around trying to get in the way. Wanted to play with the older ones and got cross when he wasn't allowed. You'll be the same, missy." He gave Lily an enormous bounce into the air and brought her gently down again, inducing a fit of giggles.

"George's sisters do the same." Richard pointed out. "We'll be trying to settle down for a game of draughts, and they come along and insist I help them learn to play."

"That's because they like you very much. It's how girls show the fact. Your mother used to insist that your father—long before he became your father—teach her how to play chess properly." He gave Caroline a wink. "All went well until she started winning every time."

"More, Nuncle." Lily tugged insistently on Michael's sleeve.

"See? You women are all tyrants." Still, he complied with the request, propelling his niece into fits of giggles again.

"Can Harry come for dinner, please? Or luncheon, because then I can be there?" Richard asked, in his most cherubic manner. "He's just as nice a person as George is."

"That's a high recommendation, then. George is really quite a civilised boy." Caroline gave Michael a brief glance, which he answered with a nod. "Yes, I suppose we should invite him here. For old times' sake, at least."

"Smashing!" Richard leaped up to give his mother a hug. "Thank you."

She ruffled his hair. "Thank you for suggesting the idea. Our two families . . . rather drifted apart. Perhaps it's time to mend the fences."

"I think you mean bridges." Michael grinned.

"I have no idea what I meant." Caroline laughed, then poured herself a lemonade. "There'll be a lot of news to catch up on."

"There will. Say when will suit and I'll send Harry a note. He's still at Broch. Only him though, as I understand it. His mother's gone to live near Olivia somewhere in the north." Michael felt himself gabbling but couldn't stop. He wanted to get all the information out in one fell swoop and not face any questions at present.

"Is Broch a big house?" Richard asked.

"About the size of this place, or maybe a touch more." How to describe such a place in purely objective terms? "Larger grounds, certainly. And a lake."

Caroline nodded. "Harry will feel like a pea in a barrel rattling around there on his own. Does he stay there permanently or is he only visiting?"

"I got the impression he's here on and off." Michael bounced his niece again. "You'll have to ask him for the details when he comes to dinner. I'm sure I remember something about the land being entailed and everything tied up. Thomas bored me with all the details once."

"I can't imagine Thomas ever boring you." Caroline's eyes met Michael's as he turned to her, aware of her change of tone.

She knew.

She knew about him and Thomas and had probably known for a long time.

He rallied. "Oh, he could be tedious when he wanted. Playing his stupid practical jokes, for one thing."

"Oh, yes. I'd forgotten. Poor Harry and Olivia usually seemed to be the butt of them."

Richard piping up, "What did he do?" led Caroline into recounting a story involving a bucket of water and the door to the stables. And gave Michael a little much-needed thinking time.

Caroline had always been so perceptive, so aware of the realities of life, rather than being the sheltered hothouse flower some of her contemporaries were. How could he ever have doubted that she would see what was going on and put the correct interpretation on it? He remembered how she'd never treated Thomas in quite the same way that she treated Michael's other friends; would she have treated a young lady he was courting in the manner she treated Thomas? He would never know, as that theorem would never be put to the test.

He gave her another long look, but she was so wrapped up in her storytelling that she didn't notice his attentions. Michael had to give her credit for not letting her knowledge affect their relationship. Many a woman might have rejected her brother had she known of his predilection.

At the end of the tale, she turned, smiled, and said, "It all seems so long ago. Did I get the details right?"

Michael, who'd hardly heard a word, simply nodded with an "Every single one, down to the last drip."

"It sounds wonderful." Richard's eyes glowed. "Please may Harry come to lunch? Please?"

"How about tomorrow?" Caroline suggested. "Our plans might change later in the week should George get the all clear, although I suppose we could suggest Friday as an alternative date if tomorrow's not convenient."

Michael eased his niece off his knee, much to her annoyance, and rose. "I'd better send him a line now and take it over."

The sudden appearance of Eric—who looked like he'd been taking a nap—prompted Richard and his mother into recounting the events of the day and let Michael escape to his room.

It was surprisingly easy to write the words, jotting down a friendly letter, and extending an invitation to lunch. Easy, too, to do all the mundane jobs of blotting and slipping it into an envelope. So far so good, but it was the delivering of it which would present the challenge.

Should he take the invitation in person? The thought of visiting Brock again terrified him, in a way that going into action hadn't. The odds had been simple then; you'd either survive or get killed or get a Blighty one. He wasn't ready to face his own past and go back to those places which had meant so much to him.

Thomas had never been far from his mind these last few years, and this holiday, he'd become an almost ever-present spirit. To revisit the haunts they'd walked together would be a bridge too far at the moment. These things had to be handled in small, manageable steps, like the nerve-racking journey into no-man's-land.

But could the post be as reliable as it had been in the prewar years? Would it get to Broch early enough tomorrow for the invitation to be accepted? Could his own reluctance be allowed to override a social necessity?

In the end he settled for a semicowardly solution—he'd go down into the town and find an errand boy he could pay to drop the invitation off. The time he'd be away would suggest he'd made the delivery himself, and nobody would be the wiser.

Tomorrow he'd be going over the top and would likely pass a hell of time in between now and the moment he'd be facing Harry across the table and thinking only of Thomas.

CHAPTER FIVE

Michael woke with a start as the dawn chorus sounded through his open window. He'd been dreaming he was back in France, his sleeping mind metamorphosing the noise of the birds into something sinister. He turned in the bed, then turned again, unable to get comfortable. Eventually he gave up all idea of returning to his slumbers, picked up a book, and went in search of somewhere comfortable to read it. A window recess in a corridor at the back of the house seemed like a perfect place to settle down and try to leave the past where it belonged.

The clopping of hooves and chinking of metal from outside brought sounds from his dream back to mind, so vividly that he had to look outside and reassure himself this noise wasn't from a gun carriage. Only the dairyman making his daily delivery, a cheery redheaded man, who was flirting outrageously with the maid by the look of it. A charmingly bucolic scene, with an innocent quality he'd always associated with the Porthkennack of his childhood, even if the place had acquired more adult connotations as the years had passed. The dairyman and the maid used to flirt back then, just as such flirtations must have been going on up and down the country for years.

Michael watched the cart pull away, the man having discharged what appeared to be a ridiculously vast quantity of dairy goods for such a small household. Perhaps all that milk ended up in the nursery, in Lily's beloved rice pudding. The carthorse, which moved with a slow, elegant plod, bore a scar on his flank; maybe he'd seen action abroad and returned home battered but alive. Maybe he wondered where his mates had gone—horses or drivers—and tried to work out why.

Jimmy—number four in the sequence of shells—had been a driver, swopping the brewery cart of London for a gun carriage in Belgium. Michael had met him in a pub, when the lad had been back home for a while recovering from trench fever. At the time, Jimmy had been helping out his father, the landlord, before returning to the front and his beloved animals. It had been a long while before Michael found out what had happened to him, Jimmy not being the type of casualty to find his way into the columns of the *Times*. Michael had got the news from a friend, who'd happened to have dropped into the same pub and heard from the innkeeper's widow that she'd lost son and husband hard on each other's heels. Michael hoped Jimmy had come to rest somewhere with his horses, man and beast lost together in the mud.

Another one gone. Such potential cut off in its prime.

Jimmy had been bright, cleverer it seemed than many of Michael's fellow undergraduates at Cambridge, but fate had put him in a situation where his formidable wits found little outlet. He'd wanted to write a book about life in London, something he'd told Michael all about when they'd shared a cigarette after their brief, stunning coupling.

Michael either attracted or was drawn to the literary type, no matter what the external indications suggested: you could tell neither book nor man by their cover. Little Wilfred had proved that—what a wealth of talent turned out to have been wrapped up in his uniform, talent that had been obliterated so bloody near the end of all the fighting. So unfair, but nothing about the war had been fair.

Michael—newly demobbed and trying to pick up the piece of a normal life again—hadn't been able to stop crying when he'd heard the news of his last lover's death, many months after the event. Caroline, with whom he'd been staying, had been there to witness the scene, but he'd blamed his overreaction on a general sadness for men he'd served with, how this one death had seemed to represent them all which, in a way, it had.

He glanced down at his book, struck by the irony of it being a collection of war poems, picked up from the rack in the half-light by mistake, in place of the detective novel he'd intended to grab. Caroline must have left it for him, thinking it was the type of book he might appreciate. He left his seat, hurriedly stuffing the volume into one of the bookshelves in the hall, and returned to his room to get ready for the day.

He needed to calm down, to stop thinking of the past, to put on his best bib and tucker and a brave face to top it all. He was surprised to find that it mattered greatly that Harry shouldn't see him in such an emotional state.

After breakfast, a car arrived to take Caroline and Lily to Porthkennack to find something to ease the child's gums, while Eric set off with his fishing rod. Michael was left to fulfil a promise he'd made to fly the rickety old kite with his nephew—almost as old as the one which Caroline had broken—which they'd found among a mass of old junk down in the cellar.

Those plans had to change when the weather turned suddenly, as it so often did on this headland, the bright blue of the sky darkening within minutes to the colour of lead as a bank of cloud rolled in from the west. Luckily they'd only made it as far as the end of the garden, so Michael hurried them indoors, away from the trees, as the first blast of thunder echoed like a monstrous cannonade. They'd just made it through the French doors when the heavens began to dump their contents.

"That was a close shave." Michael drew the windows to behind them. "Another minute and we'd have been soaked. Or fried. Never stand under trees in a storm. Better to lie on the grass and take a bath."

Richard eyed the water as it hit the panes. "I'd prefer that to taking a bath at home. Alice always makes me scrub my neck."

"And quite right she is."

The boy pulled a face. "Maybe I should bring some soap next time the sky turns grey."

Michael flicked a stray drop from his sleeve. "It was as well we hadn't got anywhere near having the kite airborne. Kites in a storm— more dangerous than trees. Or nurses bearing scratchy flannels."

"What shall we do, then?" Richard stared out of the rain-lashed windows. "I don't fancy a jigsaw or another puzzle. I can do those at home."

"What about looking through the photograph albums your father brought?"

"If you want to." Richard didn't appear enthusiastic.

"What else do you suggest. Draughts? Chess?"

"I guess so." Richard glanced at the rain, which showed no sign of relenting.

Michael remembered the disappointment of rainy days when you were a child condemned to return to school soon and wanting to make the most of your freedom. No greater love could a man show for his nephew than face his own fears. "Hold on. I've got a better idea. If you clear that little table in the drawing room, I'll be right back."

He dashed up the stairs to his room, picked up a case, then hared down again, afraid that if he slowed he might lose his courage. If it wasn't yet time to venture a visit to Broch, he could at least deal with this other problem. He dumped the bag on the floor of the drawing room, opened it, and drew out one of the sketchbooks.

"What's that?" Richard asked.

"It's where I put all my thoughts."

"A diary?"

"No. I rarely put thoughts down in words." Michael placed his hand on the cover; now or never. He turned the first page, to reveal a view of the bay as seen from half a mile along the coast. That was a safe place to start. "Look."

"Cor."

"Don't be common," Michael responded automatically.

"Sorry. These are amazing. May I?" Richard turned the page. "Did you draw them?"

"I did indeed."

"You're very clever." Richard glanced up, unquestioning admiration on his face.

"Not clever." Michael felt uncomfortable under that piercing gaze. "It's nothing to my credit, really. I guess I was born with the knack. You should praise your grandparents for giving it to me."

They worked through the album, all of which were landscapes, Richard trying to recognise the places concerned before reading the captions at the bottom.

"Do you only draw on holiday?"

"No, although that's when I began, I suppose. This is my Cornish book." He hadn't brought the little album he'd taken across the channel and filled with less pleasant views than this one contained.

"And do you only sketch places?"

"No, I draw people too. Or should say *drew*. I haven't picked up a pencil in ages."

"That's a shame." Richard flicked back through the book again, studying each sketch in turn. "Maybe you'll start drawing again this holiday."

"Maybe."

"Perhaps that's why you brought them. Just in case."

"If that's so, it wasn't intentional." Michael wrinkled his nose. "Do you remember that old bear you used to drag around?"

"Nelson? Of course."

"These sketchbooks feel like him to me. It's a comfort to carry the people and scenes." Time to take another fence. "Would you like to see some of the portraits? I keep them in a different book."

"Oh, yes, please." Richard beamed. "Do you have lots of sketchbooks?"

"Quite a few." One of which he couldn't share with his nephew. That album he never carried with him; it was kept locked away, pictures not to be shown to anyone but the sitter. Their content was far too incriminating, even if the subject matter itself wasn't obscene. It would count as artistic—as innocent in its way as any of Rubens's voluptuous ladies or a statue of Antinous in all his graceful beauty—but the meaning behind them seemed unmistakable.

He produced the portrait book he *could* show the lad, steadying his hands as he offered it for him to open.

The first portrait was of Caroline when she was eighteen, the work of a fledgling artist, trying his hand at something different. Later portraits were more self-assured.

"That's nice. Would you say Mother was pretty?"

"I think she is. I guess you and I are both too close to have an objective judgement." She'd been self-conscious at this age, though, and what the Yanks he'd met during the war might have called camera shy. "It might be fair to say she was no great beauty between about ten and seventeen. And that's not the voice of a brother like your pal George speaking."

"I can't imagine Mother as anything but lovely." Richard sounded both amazed and indignant.

"People change, though you don't always notice because it's gradual." Michael studied the sketch, seeing in the face echoes of his niece. "The same will happen to Lily. She's a pretty baby, but at some point she'll grow out of her face and then into it again. That's the great point about photographs, like your father takes. They provide a record of what things were really like, not how we remember them."

Richard nodded, took another long look at his mother's portrait, then turned the page.

"That's Thomas!" he squeaked delightedly.

Michael forced himself to view the picture. "It is indeed. Well done for spotting the likeness."

Richard shook his head. "I'd have known anyway. His name's at the bottom."

"So it is." Tiny letters, as carefully crafted as the sketch itself, reflecting the wealth of love that had seeped onto the page. Michael hadn't often put a name to a picture—the one of Laurie which Richard would come to soon remained anonymous—but Thomas had been different. Special. Unique. The first and never to be forgotten. Perhaps one day Michael could have an avuncular discussion with his nephew about the joys of first love—and what he'd believed to be true love—but that conversation was years in the future.

"This one's much better than the one of Mother."

"Thank you. I guess I got better the more I did. Although these are my special books. You wouldn't want to see my practice books. Some of the stuff's pretty poor." Michael became aware of an aching sense of loss, not for people this time, but for the act of creating images. He'd not felt this way in months.

"Alice always says that practice makes perfect." Richard went back to carefully turning the pages, sometimes with comments or questions, sometimes simply with an appreciative smile as he came across another portrait of his mother or grandmother. "Who's this?" he asked suddenly.

"That's a chap I knew at Cambridge. Laurie." Caught sitting on a windowsill in college with the sun on his face. "He really was clever. Frighteningly so."

"George is like that. He loves algebra. And he always knows when *i* goes before *e* and when it goes after." Richard bore a look of pride in his friend's achievement.

"And yet you still like him? He must be a special boy for you not to want to punch his nose for being so bright."

"He is. And he needs good male friends with all those awful sisters to contend with." Richard crinkled his brow. "I hope Mother doesn't have any more girls. I like Lily, but one girl in the house is quite enough."

"I shall remind you of this conversation, and others like it, when you first bring your sweetheart to meet me." And perhaps that sweetheart would turn out to be a boy. There was capacity aplenty for innocent ragging, although if the person concerned did happen to be male—maybe the oft-mentioned George—then Michael wouldn't be making that wedding speech he so looked forward to.

"Why has Laurie got that oar on the floor by him? Was he a rower?"

"Yes, and a jolly good one."

"Father used to row. He's got an oar in his study," Richard said, with a touch of smugness. "I'm going to row one day. When I'm big enough."

"Make sure you eat more rice pudding. Laurie used to be very fond of that too. Especially if it had a skin on top." It was easy to discuss old lovers with Richard. The boy was too young to see anything but friendship in Michael's relationships with these men, which meant he could express his feelings with a candour he couldn't achieve with anybody else in the family.

"He was sensible. That's the best bit." Richard studied the sketch, then turned the pages through to the end. "Are there any more?" he asked, wide-eyed and puppylike.

"Just the one book. Not much in it, though. I sort of lost enthusiasm." Michael fished out the third album.

"Thank you." Richard opened it. "Oh. Did you do these in France?"

"Ah. Not that first one. I have a feeling that's during training." The men—a couple of privates—looked too hopeful and cheery to be other than new recruits.

"Were these men in your platoon?"

"I think so. Difficult to remember." Difficult to want to remember, at times. Still, he studied the portraits. These were men he hadn't known as well as Laurie or Thomas, but that had been no bad thing at the time. These sketches had been meant to capture something different, a band of brothers joined together for a common cause. As the war drew on, the nature of the portraits subtly changed, reflecting a loss of innocence and the growing realisation of what going to war meant in a modern, dug in, trench-bound era of automatic weapons.

Caroline might not have approved of showing the boy these pictures, but Caroline wasn't going to know, for the moment.

"I told your mother a bit of a white lie." Michael carried on despite Richard's shocked expression, using another white lie to cover the first. "She thinks I left these at home. I wasn't sure whether I'd get them out again and didn't want her to be upset at the most recent stuff. Not given what you said yesterday about her wishing everyone home safely."

Richard nodded, conspiratorially. "I won't tell her. May I tell Father, though?"

"You can, with all that I've told you. Only ask him to keep it to himself until I'm ready to broach the subject with your mother. I've never felt good about fibbing to her." No matter how much practice had been forced on him over the years.

"I feel very honoured that you let me see them." The serious expression belied Richard's tender years.

"You should. I've not shown these military ones to anyone else. Except the subjects themselves."

"Did they like them? I would hope they did."

"I think so. And if they didn't, they were too polite to tell me." Michael grinned. "Sometimes I did a copy of the original for them to keep, but I insisted on having the masters. They feel like they're part of me."

Richard, frowning, was evidently giving that some thought. "Like your children or something? You couldn't give those away, could you?"

"No, indeed. And yes, I suppose they do feel like they're my offspring. That's probably why I could never chose a favourite from among them, either." Michael smoothed the paper between his fingers, savouring the texture. Irrespective of how much he missed the act of sketching, he also missed the sensual feel of the paper, of the pencil in his hands moving across the page.

"Would you do a sketch of me, Uncle?" Richard's voice cut into his thoughts. "Or me and Lily together?"

"I'd love to, but the prospect's a bit daunting. I've never tried my hand at picturing a child before. Only as little figures off in the distance."

Richard pouted. "I'm not a child."

"My apologies. I'll rephrase that. I've never tried my hand at picturing such a young man." Michael had to counter his nephew's obvious disappointment, though. "I'll tell you what. You can sit for me on your eleventh birthday. And Lily can sit for me when she's eleven, so you're both treated equally. Even though I don't do sketches of girls, either, your mother excepted."

Richard considered for a moment before nodding and holding his hand out to be shaken. "Agreed. I can wait, and Lily will have to, as well."

"Good man." And that would give Michael ample time to summon up the courage to try drawing again. At least one element in his reluctance was the fear that he'd lost the knack.

Upstairs, while getting himself ready for lunch, Michael glanced out of the window to see that the rain had eased, lessening the chances of Harry appearing at the door in the shape of a bedraggled rat. No doubt he'd have brought the motorbike with him; hopefully the man wouldn't take another tumble on the wet roads. A sea change had occurred in Michael's emotions while they'd been looking at the sketchbooks, his dread shifting to slightly nervous—but not unpleasant—anticipation. He wondered whether he should be at the door to greet their guest, or whether that was properly Caroline or Eric's prerogative. He wanted to appear neither too eager nor too diffident.

As it turned out, for all his fretting over the social niceties, he missed the moment Harry entered, having spotted a knot in his shoelaces and having to retie them. As he came to the top of the stairs, the sight of the visitor in the hall brought a fresh wave of qualms; in a suit, Harry bore an even closer resemblance to his brother. And while Michael had always thought him a funny-looking little boy, he'd matured into a handsome man: the straw-like colour of his hair had turned a tawny gold, the face had filled out, and his jaw had a fine masculine set. He'd make somebody a good-looking husband—probably already had a string of girls hanging on his coattails. Eligible men were in short supply these days.

"Caroline!" Harry held out his hands to take hers. "You don't appear a day older than when I last saw you."

"Oh, don't talk tosh." Caroline, blushing, was clearly delighted at the compliment. Harry wasn't just eligible but charming, Michael noted.

"It's only the truth." He turned to Eric. "Pleased to meet you. Your son does you great credit. What a delightful boy."

Michael registered a suppressed noise at his side: Richard had escaped from Alice's efforts to make him look presentable and had heard the compliment.

"He's right, you know," Michael whispered and led the boy—who seemed to have been overcome with an attack of shyness—down the stairs.

The initial awkwardness was soon eased, Eric being his usual self. Either the man was a genius of diplomacy or he possessed an accidental but effective facility of putting people entirely at ease and edging conversations and situations around dangerous corners. It was a true gift. Eric kept the discussions purely local over a preprandial sherry—apple juice in Richard's case—touching on places they'd all known prewar and whether they were different now. Harry reassured them that Broch had remained a bastion against all the machinations of change. When they sat down to eat, he edged the conversation onto their families, and how their respective parents were adjusting to the time of life when things slowed down.

During a lull, Richard finally found his voice. "Harry, did you join the army, like Uncle Michael?"

"No. Like a fool I went into the navy, and I say 'fool' because I wasn't a great sailor in any sense of the word. Stick to dry land, young man." He gave Richard a wink.

"Was it that bad?"

"Only when I felt seasick. By the time I realised I had very little in the way of sea legs, it was too late."

"Did you have a girl in every port?" Eric asked, then looked mortified. Perhaps he'd been going to add, *and a port in every girl*, before remembering that his son was present. Or maybe he was simply reacting to Caroline's glance of disapproval at what might be perceived as an insult to their guest.

"Alas, no." Harry didn't appear bothered by the question. "Although there was always good clean, honest fun to be had ashore. Excellent ice skating in Edinburgh, for one. Nice girls too." He addressed Richard. "The sort you'd bring home to meet your mother."

"I wouldn't want to bring home any girls to meet Mother." Richard frowned. "Not even my chum George's sisters."

"No doubt he depicts them all as scabrous." Eric explained to Harry, "Richard's opinion of women will no doubt change as he and George grow up."

"What's 'scabrous'?" Richard asked his father, with a birdlike tip of his head to one side.

"Having a rough, scaly surface. Like a lizard."

"Some can be too much like hard work, as Harry no doubt found when he tried to partner them on the ice," Michael chipped in. "Your mother, as I've said before, is an exception to the rule." A warm glow suffused him that wasn't entirely due to the excellent wine. For some reason he needed to demonstrate to the world—in the form of Harry—how much he valued his family. "When she was your age, she demonstrated all the qualities a girl should possess yet so rarely does."

"Your uncle's right," Harry agreed. "I would have preferred Caroline to Olivia as my sister." Was Harry flirting? Was he revealing some long-held tendresse for a girl he might well have admired in his formative years or simply being amicable with an old friend?

"An excellent choice," Michael said. "Nothing to Olivia's discredit, but Caroline was always happy to play knights in armour when we were young, and never insisted on being the damsel in distress."

"That would have been boring." Caroline flushed with evident delight. "And I suspect I would have had no choice in the matter. When there was only the two of us playing, you insisted on your choice of game."

"I didn't know about any of this." Eric raised his eyebrows. "You'll have to give me a full report this evening, Michael, when Caroline's putting the children to bed."

"I will leave no *t* uncrossed. Including an account of the occasion when she beat me with her wooden sword."

"Michael!" Caroline shook her head disapprovingly but couldn't hide her grin.

"Can you deny it?"

"Well, no. But I'm sure I must have been provoked beyond all reason." She turned to Richard. "Please don't encourage Lily to play such rough games."

"I won't." Richard, wide-eyed at the revelations, clearly had no intention of fighting his sister, even with a wooden sword.

"I'm beginning to see quite a different side to you, my dear." Eric patted her hand. He'd always been besotted with his wife; Michael was certain it would take little short of Caroline turning out to be a mass murderer to shatter her husband's faith in her.

"I shall confess all," she said in theatrically serious tones, with her hand over her heart. "I was envious of all the fun boys seemed to have. They would let me play tennis with them, or cricket, both of them being pursuits suitable to the gentle sex," she rolled her eyes at the words, "but I was never allowed to kick a ball or play any of their make-believe games. You can imagine how cross that made me."

"Indeed," her husband demurred.

"So you really rather liked me forcing you to play *my* games?" Michael had always suspected so, despite his sister's protests at the time.

The arrival of an apple tart rendered all conversation superfluous until it had been despatched. When it had been cleared away, Harry turned to Michael. "I've been trying to work out how long it was since we last met. I make it ten years."

Michael nodded. "That sounds right."

"Ten years seems an awfully long time to be away from Porthkennack. I couldn't manage it."

"Neither could we," Caroline replied. "Eric and I brought Richard here the summer he was three, but even with my parents, it wasn't quite the same, so we holidayed in pastures new from then on, although the last few years . . . Well, this year felt like the time to try again." She looked to Michael as if for confirmation. Coming back was clearly significant for them all, in different ways.

"Yes. And so far, so good. The sea's as bracing as it ever was. The beer's as tasty—I happened to drop in to the local for old times' sake, you know." Michael gave Richard a conspiratorial wink.

Harry nodded. "Shame your parents couldn't be here with you."

"Indeed. It's sad to see them slowing down quite so much. They both suffered so much from the influenza." It had taken its toll on them, more than the other privations of the past few years. "They survived, thank the Lord, but the stuffing has been knocked out and not even the prospect of a holiday in their favourite place has been able to reinstall it. Maybe they'll come next year."

Maybe.

"Lily misses them," Eric stated. "Her first word was 'Gammer,' apparently, as she worships the ground her grandmother walks on. Richard pretends he's not fussed, don't you?"

"Only a bit," Richard confessed. "I do wish Grandfather was here too. He's the best at kite flying."

"See, Michael?" Eric grinned. "No matter how much he worships you, he has twin gods."

"I gladly accept the division of affection." Michael had been luckier than many men in his parents, with a loving father who valued both his children's achievements and a mother who only gave counsel when the time was right. Caroline seemed to have found the same qualities in her choice of spouse. "You've a wonderful pair of children, Eric. They're a credit to both of you."

"I can't help but admit that I think you're right. Better than many of the little oiks we come across. But then I suppose one always thinks one's children are superior to other people's."

Caroline remarked, "Richard takes after you, though. Him and his love of photographs."

"Father has some super ones. Cards from all over the world." Richard smiled. "The Taj Mahal and the pyramids and everything."

A loud knocking on the door interrupted all discussion. The maid informed them that a telegram boy had arrived and was asking if he should wait for an answer. The message she handed to Caroline said, in many fewer words, that Richard's pal George had been given the all-clear and would be coming down by train the next day, accompanied by his mother, who'd then leave him to the tender mercies of the Cavendish family. Caroline excused herself from the table so she could send a confirmatory response.

"Richard will be disappointed George isn't bringing his sisters with him." Michael grinned.

"Uncle!" Richard pouted. "Say that was a joke. Please."

Michael touched his forelock. "I apologise for jesting over something so important. I hope you and your partner in crime have many happy, girl-free hours over the next few days."

In theory he'd be able to enjoy the same thing, left to his own devices for a while until the novelty of George wore off his nephew—if it did—and he was dragged along once again to his avuncular duties of flying kites or making sandcastles.

"Will you be all right when George is here?" Richard looked concerned. "Are you sure you won't be lonely?"

"No," Michael said, airily—more airily than he suddenly felt, faced with filling the days. "I might even pick up my sketchbook again. And I suppose if I were stuck for something to do, I could see if Harry wanted to go for a pint."

"Why don't you all come over to Broch for dinner tomorrow? Let me return the courtesy," Harry suggested.

Eric considered this for a moment, gnawing his lip. "Would it be awfully rude to defer the offer for a few days? It would be nice for young George to settle in without us haring off straightaway. And his mother might stay over if she's fagged from the journey."

Harry nodded, a wisp or two of blond hair escaping from the uncharacteristically neat coiffure. "Very wise. Perhaps you could come over for lunch, Michael? Given that you'll be at a loose end tomorrow with young Richard occupied."

Michael swallowed hard. Another fence to be taken and one he couldn't avoid without being downright rude. Perhaps it would be better to do it now, with no risk of Richard tagging along. The boy would have to be shown the place one day, no doubt, given his fascination with past holidays, but the first return had to be a step Michael took away from the scrutiny of others. "Yes, I'd like that. Thank you. It'll be good to see the old place again."

"Skeleton staff, I'm afraid, so don't expect anything as magnificent as you've given me today." Harry shrugged. "My man can turn out a decent omelette or a cold collation, and the ladies who come to clean sometimes bring a cake. Bachelor's rations."

"That sounds perfect." Michael gave Harry a smile, one which was returned dazzlingly.

By the time Harry was ready to leave, the sun had dried up most of the rain, promising a glorious late afternoon and evening. Caroline and Eric made their goodbyes at the door, while Richard came out to be shown the motorbike close up. Its gleaming metal glory was enough to excite a boy of any age.

Michael watched his nephew and old friend as they purred over the machine as a mother cat might purr with pride over her kittens. The first steps of rapprochement between the two families seemed to have been successfully taken. And, despite having spent the previous night worrying about this reunion, Michael was now reluctant to have it end. After the initial shock of seeing Harry in the hall looking so much like his older brother, he'd found that the spectre of Thomas had gradually departed the feast. Harry was his own man, and a damned attractive one to boot with the sun glinting off his locks.

Visiting Broch with Harry as host would have its pleasant moments; and maybe with this newfound ally at his side he could cope with the memories that house and grounds held in store.

CHAPTER SIX

Next morning: Broch being about a mile and a half distant from High Top, Michael dithered between walking and arranging for a car to take him there. Walking risked him arriving in a sweating heap, given that the day was already abnormally sultry by nine in the morning—and that same mugginess threatened another thunderstorm later. But to take a car felt both lazy and pretentious. Eric had mentioned something about a bicycle in an outhouse, and rummaging there produced a machine that seemed as if it would be serviceable once it had been cleaned up and given a spot of oil. Richard, who was rather lost until his pal arrived, helped to get the thing ready, then saw him off with a cheery wave.

Michael took the journey at a steady pace, the air flowing past keeping him cool. As he neared Broch, the pace slowed, all his old trepidations returning. Every room in the house, every part of the grounds, had associations with a former and happier time. He pedalled up to the lodge, where the gamekeeper had always lived, but nobody seemed to be around, which was just as well given the sluggish speed he was going at. Through the open gates and onto the drive, with his heart pounding; the expanse of the estate lay before him, tugging at his heartstrings. Broch had been as much a part of Michael's formative years as High Top had been, perhaps more so because of its associations with rites of passage.

He and Thomas had made love there: in the boathouse, up in the house, down in the depths of the woods. While swimming naked in the lake by the light of the moon and stars, bodies gliding against each other, finding release in the cool contact. Any and everywhere they'd been able to get away with it, especially the week one summer when they'd had free run of the place.

They'd been young and reckless, in love with being in love, and damned lucky not to have been caught. Maybe if they had been found out, they'd have got away with it, of tender enough years then for such things to have been passed over as youthful indiscretions, a not-uncommon consequence of attending boarding school and being surrounded by other young men all term long. Not everyone who had a taste for other boys in his early days retained that desire into his mature years. Sometimes it was simply a matter of an oasis in the desert.

He stopped the bicycle halfway along the drive, drinking in the view; there was something unreal—and vaguely unsettling—about how little the house seemed to have changed. It remained a bastion of Edwardian values standing firm in a changing world. Even the layout of the grounds was exactly as Michael remembered it: there the orchard where they'd slung a hammock and swung in the bee-loud summer sunshine; there the shrubbery where they'd played hide and seek; there the path down to the lake where they'd indulged in more worldly pleasures.

This was much harder than he'd feared. Every part of these grounds, every inch of that house, felt awash with connotations of what was and what would never be again. It seemed as though he might at any moment turn a corner and see Thomas's bright smile, feel the touch of Thomas's hand on his arm or the softness of Thomas's breath of the back of his neck. The appearance at the door of a waving figure made Michael reel, before he reminded himself that this was no ghost, just Harry. He took a deep breath and cycled on.

"Hallo!" Harry called, walking up to meet him. "Lovely to see you. I was afraid you wouldn't come."

Michael, slightly taken aback by his host's perspicacity, forced a smile. "That would have been unforgivably rude."

"I'd have understood. This house must bear a weight of memories for you. And for your family." Harry cuffed him lightly on the shoulder. "We all miss Thomas."

"He was such a good friend. Even though we argued, and everything got spoiled, it . . ." Michael pulled himself together. "I'm at risk of spoiling things. Forgive me."

"Nothing to forgive." Harry smiled. "Talk about him if you want, don't if you don't. I understand."

Did he? Had Harry, like Caroline, worked out the nature of their relationship? Had Thomas confided in his brother? That barely seemed possible. Harry had always appeared so young, tagging along, forever wondering where Michael and Thomas were going and what they were doing. Thomas, exasperated, had told lie after lie because often the truth had been unable to be spoken.

"Let's find somewhere to put that, then we'll get a sherry into you." Harry led the way.

Michael studied his host as they parked the bicycle and went down to the lawns to take their drink. It was so difficult to shake off the notion that Harry was still only eleven or twelve, a not-unpleasant boy, simply an intruder on Thomas and Michael's precious time together. But he was now a fine young man, handsome and kind, and the gap in age meant little. He and Michael had both served their country, both suffered loss, both returned to a changed world.

"Penny for them?" Harry asked.

They were sitting on the edge of the lawn now, under the shade of a monkey puzzle tree, although he couldn't remember how they'd got there nor how a glass had appeared in his hand. He must have sleepwalked through the last few minutes, lost in thought. "Sorry. Wandering through those memories you referred to."

"I suspected that was the case. Or that maybe you were sizing up the view for your next sketch."

Michael sipped his sherry. "I don't think I ever drew the house or grounds here. Maybe I should."

Harry nodded. "Feel free to bring your stuff next time you drop in. I won't bother you with inane questions while you work."

"It sounds like you know what you're talking about. Do you draw or paint?"

"Heavens, no! Art's not my thing, given that I have ten thumbs. I prefer music."

"Music?" Michael raised an eyebrow. "Don't those ten thumbs inhibit you?"

"Not when you're singing. I've been told I have a very nice voice, but how can I tell?" Harry twirled his glass. "Did your men used to sing a lot?"

"Sorry?"

"In France? Your platoon."

Michael tried to hide his relief. Why the hell had he read into the simple question something that clearly wasn't there? "Only when we were back from the lines. Too much chance of Jerry finding us otherwise. You can sing on ship, I suppose, unless you're running a blockade or something?"

"And dance a hornpipe on the fo'c'sle?" Harry laughed. "We did sing, actually. Had quite a decent choir one way or another."

"Were you really such a bad sailor?"

Harry shrugged. "The bit about being seasick is true. I wasn't quite as useless as I made out yesterday, which you've probably already guessed. I can't be doing with this 'heroic service' stuff, especially in front of youngsters. I went, I served, I came home. Plenty of better and braver men didn't. Sorry," he held his hand up in apology. "You're one of the people least likely to need that sermon."

"No need to apologise." Michael took another drink. "I'll not ask about the rest of it. You'll have times you were proud of and times you weren't, like all of us."

Harry nodded. They sat in silence, enjoying some respite from the hot sun the tree provided them. The growing sense of relief, that he'd managed this visit so far without making a fool of himself, emboldened Michael.

"What about those girls in every port?" he asked. "Was that answer bowdlerised for Richard's benefit too?"

Harry stared into the distance. "I hardly think he'd want to hear about what some of the lads got up to."

"Very true." Although that didn't answer the question, and his host's closed countenance suggested it wouldn't be worth repeating it. The arrival of what must be Harry's manservant to announce luncheon interrupted the increasingly awkward silence.

Once in the dining room, and with the servant having slipped away again, Harry apologised for his rudeness. "It's just that I don't want to talk about the war, even peripherally. I saw too many good men lost. Maybe in five years' time when it doesn't hurt so much, then we can have this conversation, but not now." He looked up from his plate, straight into Michael's eyes. "Do you understand?"

"I do." Michael bit back his frustration. On occasions he wanted to talk about the war with somebody who really comprehended. He could have talked to Thomas or Jimmy or Wilfred if any of them had survived, but death had sealed their ears and that was all there was to it. "Let's draw a line under things and stamp them *paid in full*."

Harry narrowed his brow, as though about to argue, but the frown turned to a laugh. "God, you've got that right. Paid in full, with more on top. Come on, Goode's put his best efforts into this meal. Let's not disappoint him."

The food was excellent, and so was the conversation now the air had been cleared.

"How is Olivia?" Michael had only the vaguest recollection of what she looked like: a female version of Thomas, perhaps, but he hadn't had an eye for girls then. Or since. She was slightly lame in one leg, the result of a childhood accident—he certainly remembered that, because it had led to her being fussed over and protected by her parents. In his mind she was always "poor Olivia" but perhaps that had changed.

"She's blossoming. One of the few for whom the war brought a bit of good." Harry's sardonic look contrasted the fond tone of his words. "She persuaded Mother to allow her to do some nursing. It's been the making of her. That's how she met her husband—a doctor, like Eric—hence the move to Yorkshire, where he hails from."

"That's good to hear." Funny how the females of the family seemed to have been the ones favoured by fortune, if good luck could be judged by having met someone to settle down with for the rest of their lives. After discussing Olivia and her family, they turned to Mrs. Carter-Clemence, then found themselves walking down the lanes of memory, along byways such as the present doings of old Mrs. Tregowan, who'd been the cook back in the days of their youth. Naturally conversation turned to the Grays, and by the time their recent family history had been catalogued, any lingering atmosphere between Michael and his host had eased.

"Thank you," Michael said to Goode, when he came to tidy away the remains of an apple tart. "Every bit as good as one of Mrs. Tregowan's."

"High praise indeed." Harry grinned.

"Coffee, sir?" Goode, clearly pleased at the compliment, inclined his head.

"Maybe after I've had some fresh air. That suit you, Michael?"

"It would indeed. I'd like to see round the old ancestral home before the rain comes."

Harry pushed back his chair. "Then we must make it so."

Walking the estate again was like walking through a dream. Places that Michael had only travelled to in his thoughts the last few years were under his feet and at his fingertips afresh. Yet it all looked even lovelier than his mind's eye had painted it. He'd had a concern, cycling here, that all would have changed for the worse or—perhaps more disconcerting—that his memory had been coloured by association of the estate with the man and that he would see the place for the first time in its true colours. That turned out to be a needless worry, at least as far as the grounds were concerned. The place was still as near perfection as could be; there'd always been a touch of heaven on earth about Broch.

Harry clapped him on the shoulder as they headed down towards the lake. "I do so love this place, despite the fact there are times it wrenches my heart in pieces."

Michael avoided his eye, keeping his own gaze fixed on the view. "I can easily believe that. It's hardly changed, has it?"

"I daresay you're right."

"As though it's been preserved in aspic. Sorry, that's unkind." Michael raised his hand, emphasising his apology. "That sounds as if I meant everything has stagnated, but it hasn't. Strange as it may seem, it's more alive than ever."

Harry favoured him with the kind of smile that could warm the coldest of days and melt the hardest of hearts. Perhaps Broch still felt so alive because he had a living, breathing, suddenly exuberant Harry at his side. As Eric at lunch the previous day had eased them through the two estranged families meeting once more, so Harry had eased *him* into reacquaintance with Broch.

Maybe the stand of trees on the way to the lake had thinned out a little, victim to high winds or wood management, but the greenery at the water's edge seemed lusher than before. Back then, he and Thomas would have welcomed the extra privacy it afforded.

Harry swished at some rushes. "I used to get so jealous of the pair of you. I often wondered what you two used to get up to for hours on end. I imagined you playing the most exciting games."

Michael gave Harry a sidelong look, but the remark appeared to be innocent enough. Their games had been more than exciting, but not fit for the eyes of any younger brother. "Oh, what we did wasn't as thrilling as all that," he replied, airily. "Chatting about school, planning what we were going to do at university, idling away time with everything and nothing."

"Put like that, it *does* seem a bit dull."

"What on earth did you think we were doing?" Michael regretted the question as soon as he'd asked it, but Harry seemed to take it at face value.

"Playing soldiers. Or scouts. Anything that would have been fun to join in, the more so because I knew I'd never be allowed."

"When you're young, everything you're not allowed to do seems wonderful. Even enlisting. Sorry." Michael winced at the pained expression on his host's face. "I forgot."

Harry shrugged. "It's probably a vain hope that the war doesn't ever get mentioned somehow or other. You're forgiven," he added, with one of his dazzling smiles.

It wasn't just the humid air making Michael hot under the collar now. Those smiles, in this setting, were proving disquieting and not only because of connotations of the past. Harry was every bit as attractive as his brother had been.

They walked out onto the little jetty, where Michael and Thomas had dabbled their feet in the water and made plans for a future together, just like any couple walking out. But that's what they *had* been. A couple, as much as Caroline and her Eric and unlike Michael and any other of his lovers.

Lowering clouds from the west—and an increasing mugginess—threatened an imminent storm, similar to the one of the previous day, so Harry suggested they head in the direction of the lake, given that the house was likely too far for them to get back in time. Summer storms here rarely lasted, blowing themselves out with the clouds scudding east to both the environs of St. Enodoc. If they needed to take refuge in the boathouse for ten minutes while the rain blew over, so be it; both knew from experience that the place was weatherproof.

Their timing wasn't as good as Michael and Richard's had been, the heavens opening while they were some fifty yards short of shelter.

"Hell," Harry said, shaking himself as they at last reached the safety of the boathouse. "The one thing I never miss about this place is the weather. It can't make up its mind."

"It's only water." Michael looked about him. "You've not still got that old green canoe? I'd have thought that would have been condemned years ago."

"That would be an act of sacrilege." Harry moved over to stroke the canoe lovingly. "I learned to paddle in this. As long as we can keep patching her up, she'll be here."

"And what about when she's more patch than boat? And none of them working?"

"Then I'll set fire to her and we'll dance round the flames. Like mad Vikings or something." Harry patted the hull tenderly. "But that won't be for a while."

"Will you be able to keep the estate on?"

"I have little choice, given the complicated arrangements in my father's will about keeping our inheritance for the next generation." That didn't appear to be too great a burden. "Luckily he had a good head for business. Broch should be proof against the 'slings and arrows of outrageous fortune' and all that."

That was no surprise. Sir Anthony Carter-Clemence had always struck him as shrewd, and he'd heard from Thomas how the man had a broad portfolio of business interests, including the firm of lawyers in which his younger son was learning the ropes.

"I need to put an efficient steward in place. Ypres took the previous one, and while his father picked up the reins and has kept things ticking over admirably, he wants to take a well-earned rest." Harry caressed the canoe again. "That's one of the reasons I'm here. Got some chaps coming down at the weekend for me to interview."

"I hope you find the man you want."

"Oh, I think I might have already found him."

Michael had realised the double meaning of the question as soon as he'd posed it. Had Harry? If so, he gave none of the usual indications.

Probably Michael was too aware of the resonances of this place—he'd taken Thomas in that very canoe—and that consciousness was making him too ready to see and hear what was unlikely to be there. "Rain's stopped," he remarked, looking out of a cobweb-laden window.

"So it has. Let's get back to the house before the next squall blows in."

As they walked up to the house, Michael turned the conversation back to the upcoming interviews, but if Harry had picked a front runner from the two men he was putting through their paces, he didn't make it plain. As they reached where they'd parked the bicycle, everything on that subject seemed to have been said, and Michael was none the wiser about what the comment in the boathouse had signified.

"You'll come back again?" Harry asked. "Now that you've visited once, the second time should much easier."

"I believe you're right. I will come back. Thank you." Michael extended his hand for his host to shake.

"I'd offer you lunch again tomorrow—you'll need a respite from Richard and his friend—but I've house and business stuff to deal with. Got Father's money man coming down to earn his crust." Harry rubbed his strong, supple hands together. "We'll be done by late afternoon. Would dinner work?"

"It would." The speed of the repeat invitation had to be a positive sign.

"You could come earlier if you fancied making the most of the afternoon light to try your hand at sketching."

"I could. And I'd best book a car so that I don't have to cycle back in the dark afterwards."

"Oh, don't do that. I can get Goode to run you back in the motor. Or," Harry wagged his fingers, "better still, you could stay over. This house feels awfully large when it's only me here. You'd be doing me a favour by keeping me company."

"In that case, I'll stay." Michael tried to surreptitiously study Harry's face, but the man had turned away, to manoeuvre the bicycle from where they'd wedged it behind a large flower tub. "I can pack up my stuff in a kit bag."

"And 'smile, smile, smile'?" Harry chuckled. "I need to keep an eye on you. You've got me casually making jokes about the war. You're dangerous."

Harry had spoken those last two words with an unfathomable expression in his eyes. Michael, transfixed, had to force his gaze away.

"I'm as harmless as a lamb," he managed, at last, but anything else was left unsaid. Goode had appeared to inform Harry that he was wanted on the telephone and—after another handshake and a brief "I'll see you tomorrow"—he was left to make his way home with thoughts tumbling round his head.

He felt himself falling, but couldn't be clear of his motives. Was it just that he fancied Harry? There was certainly an aching gap inside him created by the long absence of a lover. Surely he could allow himself the indulgence on either count.

How to proceed? As he'd always done, letting out his own subtle signs, as men of his nature had to learn to do in any age and in any situation. Looks, words, actions, capable of bearing several interpretations. An experienced practitioner in the art would recognise them, while an unsuspecting man would remain in blissful ignorance.

Harry had produced indications enough of his own that afternoon, so maybe he was testing the waters as well. All that was needed was a degree of subtlety; if Michael had read the signs wrong, then Harry mustn't know. He couldn't risk another breakdown of relations between the two households.

Irrespective of whether he thought he had any chance of success if he made a subtle pass at Harry, there was more holding him back, sufficient qualms over his motivation to wither any potential romance in the bud. Was he looking at Harry and seeing Thomas, thinking that to make love to him would be to somehow replicate those earlier days? If so, he simply couldn't trust himself to do it.

CHAPTER SEVEN

Michael managed to get back to High Top without anything descending on him weather wise worse than a shower of drips from a low branch he'd cycled under. He was also spared a deluge of questions, given that George and his mother were both present and were—quite rightly—the centre of attention. George proved to be a pleasant boy with alarmingly red hair. Apparently his sisters were all blonde, so this proved more ammunition for the war between George and them. He and Richard seemed to have the right balance between admiring each other and insulting each other, although Michael suspected the insults had been toned down for the company. George's mother didn't look like she approved of even the mildest affront to her son.

As the time came to dress for dinner, Michael passed the bookcase where he'd stuffed the poetry book the previous morning; he'd meant to ask Caroline about that, so went to catch her while she was alone.

"Still decent?" he enquired, knocking at her door.

"Yes. Come in." She was seated at her dressing table as he entered, with noises from the bathroom suggesting Eric was taking a plunge.

"I wanted to ask. Did you leave that book of poetry for me?"

Caroline glanced up from where she was sorting through her jewellery. "What book of poetry?"

"There was a collection of war poetry on the mantelpiece in my room, among some other stuff."

"Not me." Caroline frowned. "There were lots of books here when we arrived. More than I remember from when we came prewar. I didn't touch any of them before you came. Apart from removing a few unsuitable ones from the nursery. Why do you ask?"

"Oh, nothing." Michael squirmed.

"Nothing?" Caroline raised an eyebrow.

"Why can I never deceive you? I was planning to give you a wigging for being a touch insensitive, but clearly I was wrong."

"I'd have removed the thing as being unsuitable for *you* if I'd known. I'm not that tactless." Caroline, with an ironic grin, laid the jewellery down, bar a selection of earrings she'd picked out. "Did you know Broch was used as a convalescent home for officers?"

"I had no idea. Harry didn't mention it. Mind you," he added, "Harry doesn't like to mention the war at all if he can help it."

She held an earring to her earlobe, then discarded it. "Did lunch go well?"

"Yes, thank you. I'd been rather dreading going back there."

"So I'd guessed." She turned, taking his hands in hers. "I won't ask how you felt. There are too many memories tied up there."

Michael nodded, then squeezed his sister's fingers. "But Harry's astute—he knew there'd be ghosts to lay to rest. And I'm glad there's been a rapprochement between the two families. We should have done it long ago."

Caroline wrinkled her nose. "Perhaps. Events kept intervening, I expect."

"Indeed. Now, I have a confession to make. I said I hadn't brought my drawing things with me. I have." Michael wondered if his sister had guessed that too, but she appeared genuinely surprised.

"Oh. Then why not say?"

Michael shrugged. "I suppose I didn't want to be pressurised into drawing again. Not until I was ready to. I feel a bit of a fool about it."

"You're forgiven. For both the lie and the foolishness." She tried another earring. "Eric reckons some of the medical staff may have been billeted here when they used Broch as a hospital. The lady who owns High Top apparently insisted she did her part."

"Well, well. That might explain that poetry book. And some of the others I've seen about. Distinctly different from the ones that used to be here."

"Yes, definitely some unsuitable titles around." Caroline grinned. "That's why I had to attack the nursery before I could let Richard loose in it."

Michael thought of when he'd taken a cup of tea with his niece and nephew, of the bars on the window and the lock on the door. Had only medical staff stayed at High Top or had some enterprising doctor found those adaptations of particular use in housing patients with shell shock? There was a nursery at Broch too, that would be similarly decked out.

Caroline laid a hand on his arm. "Are you feeling quite well?"

"Yes." He patted her hand. "Just thinking about some of the poor souls who'd have been at Broch and what they might have suffered. The stories these walls could tell if they had ears and tongues, eh?"

"I'd rather not hear them." She picked up another earring, one that seemed to be more to her liking. "I can understand Harry not wanting to discuss that wretched war. I want to look to the future, not into the past."

"We need to understand the past to shape the future." Michael couldn't ignore the distaste on his sister's face. "I know, I sound horribly pompous. Forgive me. Again."

"You're forgiven. Again. Only please don't talk about those days, or about friends we've lost. You're not the only one who finds it painful. Oh!" She dropped the earring as a bright bead of blood appeared on her finger. "Stabbed myself with the thing."

"Butterfingers." Michael took his handkerchief to dab at the blood, then used it to wrap her finger tightly. "Don't get that on your dress."

"Perhaps it was some heavenly being jabbing me with the end of the earring. Serving me right for being so self-centred."

Michael smiled. "I hardly think the Almighty organises his angels' workload around you."

Caroline sniffed back a tear, then smiled. "It *was* hard, you know, here at home. For those who waited and wondered what was going on, even though it couldn't have been as hard as it was for you. I'm not silly."

"I know you're not. Come on." Michael took her in his arms. "You daft old thing. I promise I won't go awakening old memories. Not for either of us."

Caroline nestled her head on his chest. "It's been a horrible few years, hasn't it? Do you think we'll ever find the same happiness we used to have here?"

"I doubt it. You can never turn back the clock." He stroked her shoulder. "But we'll find a new and different happiness."

Caroline gave him a final hug, then wriggled out of his grip. "Gosh, what would Richard say if he heard us? He'd think we were talking a load of rot."

"He would indeed." Michael kissed the top of her head. "I'd better go and get on my best bib and tucker. Can't let George's mother down."

"Louise. Her name's Louise." Caroline grinned. "You can't call her 'George's mother' all evening."

"Better than calling her 'mother of George's awful sisters.'"

"And don't you mention that either! Or them. She's awfully proud of those girls."

Michael touched his forelock. "I promise, my lady."

He went off to change, before facing dinner with the family and their guest. Louise seemed pleasant enough, and if they could keep the conversation on topics which didn't touch him, he'd be fine.

Still, he had a habit of wearing his feelings on his face at times, so would have to actively restrain his mind from wandering down the road to Broch and its master. Harry was a problem for solving in the light of a new day.

The next morning, Michael's mind was no less of a whorl, not least because of another vivid dream, this one involving Thomas, the boathouse and an excess of sex. When he'd woken, it was with Harry in mind, though.

He couldn't manage much in the way of breakfast and had to endure an interrogation from Richard about what Broch was like and when they'd all be allowed to go there. He'd promised to tie Harry down to the date for their visit, although he wanted to use those days in between to clarify what the ties between him and Harry might turn out to be.

Afterwards, as he packed his clothes, he felt possessed of fourteen digits, all of them thumbs. Thankfully, most of the other occupants of High Top had gone off to the station to see Louise onto the train, which meant he could suffer his nerves away from their attentions.

When his packing was done, he took a book out into the garden, to read in the sunshine, but found it hard to concentrate.

As he might have expected, no sooner had he got his mind calm enough to consider the adventures of Sherlock Holmes, than the arrival of two noisy boys broke the tranquillity.

"Uncle Michael!" Richard shouted as he and George sped across the lawn. "George won't believe me."

"What about?" Michael, defeated, laid his book in his lap. "Mermen?"

"No." Richard frowned disapprovingly at the notion he might have been discussing such childish matters. "Mother. Did she really beat you with a wooden sword?"

"I'm afraid she did. Several times. Mercilessly. Although," Michael wagged his finger at George, "this was in her younger days."

"Coo." George looked impressed. "My sisters would never dare do that."

"Better not encourage them, just in case. I only had one sister to deal with." Michael turned his finger towards Richard. "And you'll have to be careful if you encourage Lily to play rough games. That decision may backfire. The tendency to putting up a stiff fight may run in the family."

"Did you fight Mother back? I can't imagine brawling with Lily." Richard, wrinkle-browed, seemed horrified at the notion of fighting with "the weaker sex," despite admiring his mother's fighting spirit.

"I'm afraid I had no choice. I had to protect myself. Your mother can be quite formidable at times. We could have done with her in France. She'd have put the wind up the Kaiser."

"Mother doesn't agree with war," George remarked; it wasn't clear whether *he* agreed with her notion. "She says it's a terrible waste. She hopes I'll never have to fight."

"I hope so too. I wouldn't want either of you to have to sign up." Michael eyed the two boys, both of whom were quite tall for their age. Some of the lads he'd seen in France had been scarcely a hand's breadth taller and had appeared to be almost as young. "Although mankind doesn't seem to have worked out a sensible alternative yet for overcoming the invader."

"Mother says we should settle disputes by negotiation," George countered, his expression at odds with the notion.

"So does my mother." Richard nodded.

"Negotiation is an excellent stratagem, but it relies on both parties being reasonable and having the time and patience to go through the process. Unfortunately, life isn't always like that." Michael glanced from one boy to the other, both of whom had drawn brows, as they might over an abstruse piece of algebra. "Just think of this. If someone suddenly reared up and attacked Lily, you or I would want to go to her aid and we might have to take up arms in order to make her assailant stop."

Richard, evidently glad of Michael's support, bounced on his toes. "That's right. That's exactly what I said to Mother, only I talked about somebody trying to steal Lily's toys or money or something."

Michael smiled. He should have expected the boy to have made such a response, with its strange mixture of maturity and naivety. "What did she say?"

"She said if such a case occurred, I would have to firmly persuade whoever was doing the attacking to do otherwise." Richard rolled his eyes, dismissively. "That wouldn't even work on some of the chaps at school, let alone a grown-up robber."

"He's right," George said, as though he'd never thought of things in those terms before. "You can hardly ever talk somebody out of fisticuffs."

"Very true. And strictly between you and me, my lads, if somebody really was hurting Lily—or either of you, come to that—I bet your mothers would forget about their principles pretty quickly. I'd not want to be the person doing the attacking, believe me. And don't you dare tell either of them I said that."

"We won't," George promised.

"That assailant would be black and blue all over!" Richard chortled. "Did Mother beat your friend Thomas as well?"

Michael, startled, dropped his book, then bent to pick it up again, buying some time to compose himself. "Not that I'm aware of. I think she'd grown out of playing knights in armour by the time we met him, given that she's older than we were. It seemed like a great gulf back then."

"I guess so."

Michael peered closely at his nephew. "You seem to be full of odd questions lately. Why did you want to know that?"

"There's a picture of them, together. In one of our albums. She looks like she's ready to thump him."

"Is there? Does she?" Michael felt at risk of gabbling, his brain and mouth having gone in opposite directions. What picture?

"Would you like to see?" Richard jerked his thumb behind him, towards the house. "It's in some special books that Father put together months ago in preparation for this holiday. The one that's got all the old views and the like."

"Ah, yes. I was supposed to see those, but Lily's teeth played up and we never got round to it. I'd certainly like to take a peep." Not least to work out why this particular snap should feature with the others. There had been plenty of pictures taken of Michael and Thomas together at Broch or High Top, albeit some of those making for slightly embarrassing viewing, the affection between the two young men obvious to those who knew what signs to look for. There had also been various group scenes of the two families together—or ones with Thomas interloping among the Grays. But a picture featuring just Thomas and Caroline, he couldn't recall.

Eric was happy to produce the albums once more, regaling George with the stories behind the photographs he'd taken himself and getting Michael to fill in the details of those he hadn't. The albums appeared to be well thumbed, and the ease with which Richard talked about the pictures—all of which predated his birth—suggested he'd gone through it on many occasions with somebody on hand to provide names for the faces.

Michael didn't have to feign interest; this was a well-chosen collection, one that evoked a host of memories and produced a warm glow of nostalgia for those far-off days.

The albums, like Michael's sketchbooks, were separated with views in one and people in the other, but apart from that there seemed to be no particular organisation, so snaps of Michael at thirteen were alongside those of Richard as a baby, the family resemblance shining through. These latter proved a great hit with George, naturally.

"What an ugly baby you were," he said, gleefully. "Worse than any of my sisters, and that's saying a lot."

"I always forget what a ghastly baby you were, when I see what a fine lad you've turned into." Eric grinned.

Richard chuckled. "I really was an awful dribbly thing, wasn't I? Mother says I was a pretty baby, but I suppose she's obliged to say that."

"She is," Michael agreed. "It's a rare mother who can see the imperfections in her own child. Grandmothers are even more blinkered. Yours used to say you were the bonniest baby on God's earth, but you were her first grandchild and therefore bound to be prodigious."

"My grandmother thinks my sisters are the most perfect beings in the entire universe." George rolled his eyes.

Michael, who'd had a sufficient diet of those girls and their perfections from Louise over dinner the night before, had developed a huge degree of sympathy for George.

Richard, poring through the collection of views, turned up one of Broch. "Did you take this, Father?"

"No. It's a postcard view. The family had them done one year, I believe?" Eric turned to Michael for verification.

"That's right. Postcards were all the rage at the time, although they always struck me as being too formal. The house looks awfully stuffy compared to how it really was. Is," he added. "It doesn't seem to have changed too much, apart from the odd accommodation that must have been made when it was a hospital."

"Will we be allowed to visit if we're very good?" Richard asked.

"I can't make promises on Harry's behalf," Michael replied, "but I will talk to Harry about arranging a visit for all the family at some convenient time, and while George is still here."

"Thank you," the boys chimed in unison, before bursting into giggles at the fact.

Eric rolled his eyes. "People change more than places. The gardener's boy who was always here, for example. Do you remember him? Bright ginger hair. Brighter than George's."

"Can anybody have hair brighter than George's?" Richard got a punch for his quip, then the boys started giggling again.

"I do remember. Mother wouldn't let us play football with him. Not in the garden, anyway. We sneaked out and bashed the ball about on the beach." Eric, glad to get away from Cataclews House—and to be near Caroline—had dropped in to play sport as often as he could when their holiday dates coincided, but he'd never been as much of a pal back then as Thomas had.

"I used to play cricket with him. Equally clandestinely."

Michael nodded. For some reason Thomas had never wanted to join in those games with the gardener's boy; probably his father wouldn't have approved of him playing with a mere servant. The Carter-Clemence family had always been proud of their position in life. "I've not seen him about, this time. I guess . . ."

"He signed up?" Eric nodded. "Luckier than most, though. Only lost part of a limb. Funnily enough, I treated him, on his return to Blighty. I think he was amazed I recognised him, but who could forget that mop of hair?"

Michael hadn't forgotten the lad, either—he'd had fine, sharp features and a ready smile. Not unlike Thomas, but Michael had habitually compared everyone to Thomas back then, and searching every face for elements reminding him of his lover.

"He won't be able to tend the garden now, will he?" George looked suitably concerned. "What will he do?"

"I believe he's turned his hand to carpentry," Eric confided. "I suppose if you're willing to take your chances and not let that kind of misfortune define your life, then there are still opportunities aplenty."

"Very true." That was the maxim more people could do with living by. "You have a remarkable knack for finding out these sorts of things. Is it the Hippocratic network?"

"No . . ." Eric made a vague gesture. "I met a chap when I was out fishing, and we got talking, as you do. Turns out he'd had him working at his house. Did a nice job."

"I'll bet. He was always hardworking." While the older generation discussed local news, the boys kept poring through the pictures. At last they came to the one which Michael was particularly intrigued by.

"Here it is!" Richard nudged George, then pointed at the snap. "That's Mother and that's our friend Thomas. Harry's brother. Harry who lives at Broch."

"Coo." George's eyebrows shot up. "Look at that hair. Mother would be horrified if I went out like that."

"Thomas's hair seems to be a major talking point for this family," Michael remarked, as airily as he could. Why had he never seen this picture before? "Perhaps they'd been out in the wind, although Caroline looks as neat as usual."

Thomas had his tennis flannels on; they might have come straight from a game, given that had been a common holiday pursuit.

"He certainly seems like he's been running about," Eric observed. "Caroline doesn't appear any too happy. Perhaps he beat her in straight sets."

Caroline was indeed frowning at the camera, but that wasn't unusual. "I don't think my sister has ever been entirely at ease with having her picture taken."

"That's quite right." Eric grinned. "Even on our wedding day she hardly mustered a smile for the camera, no matter how many she had for everyone and everything else."

"Here they are again!" Richard chirped delightedly. "He's brushed his hair for once."

This other picture was casual, taken after Caroline's marriage, the pair of them along with Eric in the garden at High Top, chatting.

"Who took these?" Michael asked, more aggressively than he'd intended to, although the others didn't seem to have noticed. This must have dated from the summer of 1909, the year he'd holidayed with Laurie up in the Peak District, as far from Cornwall as he could get. He'd not at that point told his family about the disagreement with Thomas, and clearly Thomas had kept up the facade. The autumn had seen the start of Michael's final year at Cambridge, so he'd been busy with his studies; perhaps that was why he'd missed seeing these photographs. By the next summer, everyone had known about the argument, and Richard had made his appearance, both good reasons for abandoning any idea of a trip to Porthkennack that year.

"Grandfather took the photo, I think. Is that right?" Richard consulted his father.

"I believe it is. And if your mother says so, then it certainly would have been." Eric smiled indulgently.

Richard's brow wrinkled. "I would have thought Mother would have dressed herself up for that picture."

"You might expect the same of me." Eric chuckled. "I seem to be in the most hideous pair of trousers."

"You were on holiday," Michael remarked. "Not having tea with Queen Mary."

He studied the photos again. Thomas seemed happy enough, despite their falling out, but then Michael had also been happy at the time, with Laurie to brighten his days. And nights. Probably Thomas had found another man to satisfy him; there'd been somebody in London, where he'd been studying, who'd apparently kept trying to proposition him. No doubt the offer had been taken up.

"Mother never plays tennis now," Richard observed. "Not properly. She'll tap the ball over the net for me to return, but she doesn't seem keen on sport of any kind."

"True," Eric agreed. "Maybe when Lily can pair up with me, the four of us can play doubles. And now," he held out his hand for the albums, "time you made yourselves respectable for lunch. Alice will want to brush *your* hair."

"Does that include me?" Michael asked, with a grin. "If so, I'm locking myself in my room until the gong goes."

CHAPTER EIGHT

$\mathcal{L}$unch passed pleasantly enough, the conversation revolving around the fact that Alice had picked up a tick when taking Lily out for a walk that morning. All methods of avoiding such unwanted visitors were considered, as were the best way of removing the little blighters.

Michael appreciated the bland domesticity of their chatter; it kept his mind from the butterflies that were increasingly causing mayhem around his midriff. He imagined Caroline—or one of George's oft-referred-to sisters—feeling flustered like this when going courting for the first time, all churning stomach, no appetite and prickly sensations around the neck. He forced himself to eat, but each mouthful of the succulent food was like hard, dry bread in his mouth.

How could a man who was so experienced, who'd taken love where and when he'd found it through the years, work himself into such a lather over a meeting that might not come to anything?

At last, lunch was finished and the family insisted on seeing him off in style. Caroline made them find a basket to attach to the bicycle, apparently convinced that if Michael tried to ride while loaded down with both overnight bag and case full of drawing materials, he'd be sure to come a cropper.

Richard and George made noises about how they had a very exciting afternoon ahead of them at the beach, evidently trying—without much success—to demonstrate they weren't envious of Michael's return visit to Broch, which had now acquired a rather mysterious, almost mythical status for the boys.

As he finally turned out onto the lane, thoughts of the previous day resurfaced, the mixture of emotions welling up again. He could deal with the risk that he'd misinterpreted Harry's signals, as that was the kind of social situation he'd dealt with before, but the ghost of Thomas had returned to haunt him once more and was proving difficult to lay to rest.

In just this way he'd travelled to Broch from the train station, years ago, that glorious summer holiday he'd spent alone with Thomas. Most of the staff had gone with the Carter-Clemence family to the Lake District, so that week they'd had the place pretty well to themselves, apart from a valet to tend to their needs, a maid and the gardeners tending to the house and grounds' equivalent. And what a week it had been, both of them at the age when their minds had been permanently in their trousers. An endless diet of sex, fishing, sex, eating and drinking, sex, swimming, and sex. They'd done it everywhere they could, every way they could, believing each time they'd broken new ground; Michael had found out later that there had been nothing novel in any of it, but at the time it had seemed extraordinary. If it turned out that Harry responded to his advances, then almost anywhere *they* made love, Michael would have made love with Thomas previously. Unless they were below stairs or in their father's study.

Or in Harry's bedroom, of course. Michael grinned at his own dim-wittedness. That had been a place only visited to put hairbrushes in the poor lad's bed.

Michael had returned from that holiday experiencing a strange mixture of exhaustion and elation, although they'd soon had to deal with the practicalities of everyday life. Thomas had been at a different university, so they'd mainly only seen each other during the vacations, snatching contact—bodily and social—whenever they could. It had been wonderful while it lasted.

The end of their relationship had come out of the blue. One particular Easter vacation Michael had gone back to Emmanuel for some extra study—he couldn't even remember what it had been about—and Thomas had come to stay with him in his college rooms, exploring the pleasures of Cambridge when Michael was hard at work and exploring the pleasures of *him* when he wasn't. They'd fallen out, over a trivial and stupid thing, one whose effects reverberated down the years to the present day. Michael—shaking—slowed his bicycle, suddenly in a cold sweat in recollection of the day his world had fallen apart.

One morning he'd found a note in his pigeon hole inviting him to the master's lodge for sherry and biscuits that same afternoon, in recognition of the sterling work he'd put in on an essay. An essay that Thomas had helped him to write as the subject had been one he hadn't quite been able to grasp. As a piece of erudite explanation it had been magnificent, although Michael's contribution had been minimal. He'd worked himself into a lather in case this chicanery came to light over the light refreshments, and ruined three ties and one shirt in the process of getting dressed.

When another note had appeared under his door advising that the invitation was cancelled as his misdemeanours had come to the master's notice, he'd had the worst minute of his life up until then, visions of being sent down and subsequent disgrace flashing through his brain. At which point, Thomas had burst through the door and revealed himself as the author of both of the communications and all the anxiety. No amount of love had been able to overcome Michael's desire to beat every trace of smugness from his face; only the thought of being sent down for fighting restrained him. The whole thing had escalated, as only an argument between lovers can, until words had been said—shouted—on both sides which couldn't be taken back. Thomas had stormed out of Michael's room, his college, and his life.

That had been the last time they'd spoken, the only further communication being a curt note from Thomas asking for the return of the items he'd left behind him, with a postal order enclosed to defray the costs. Michael had bundled everything up and sent it on, although he'd ripped the postal order into pieces, not wanting to be beholden to his ex-lover for anything, even a few shillings. That bold gesture hadn't stopped Michael torturing himself about whether he should try to re-establish communications, and rebuild the burned bridges before their very foundations crumbled away, although in all honesty he'd been too full of his own stubborn pride to make the attempt.

Later on, when he'd found out—weeks after the event and through a mutual friend—that Thomas had left university and opted for taking the king's shilling, Michael had known he'd missed any immediate chance of reconciliation. It wasn't just a case of Thomas having made an irrevocable change to his life; how could Michael have written a candid letter to him that might have gone under a censor's beady eye? What he'd wanted to say couldn't have been voiced on paper in those circumstances.

He took a deep breath, trying to shake off the weight of past mistakes once more, then got his head down and pedalled on.

Turning into the gateway at Broch lifted his spirits afresh, although it also rekindled his disquiet, especially when he spotted Harry's motorcycle parked by the front door of the house, something his father would never have countenanced. A car stood beside it—probably belonging to the man Harry was meeting—so Michael skirted the building, heading for the gravel path down to the boathouse and a chance to sketch in peace. Like that first visit to Broch after such an absence, taking up his pencils anew had to be done alone.

As it turned out, he couldn't face drawing. He got himself comfortable on a sloping patch of grass, facing the boathouse, but the thought of opening his sketching case was too daunting. Better to lie back, enjoy the sunshine, and think of nothing.

"Hallo!"

Michael jumped at the loud voice. He must have dozed off, under the sleep-inducing influences of lunch and warmth. He found Harry standing over him, looking concerned.

"Sorry. I should have been more thoughtful." Harry was perhaps afraid that Michael, like so many old soldiers, was liable to react at the slightest noise, especially when asleep.

"Don't worry. I was having forty winks. Just as well you came along or I might have been so far gone I'd have ended up sliding into the water. I'm sure I'm feet away from where I actually sat down." Michael leaped up to shake the hand Harry had offered him. "Very soporific spot, this."

"Yes." Harry glanced down at the drawing cases. "Not too productive on the drawing side of things, though, by the look of it."

"True." Michael felt obliged to offer an explanation. "I've been lazy, given that it seemed too nice an afternoon to spoil with effort of any sort."

"You're lucky. Still, I've got all my business done early, like a good boy. Time for pleasure." Harry plonked himself down on the grass, so Michael joined him.

"It *is* a nice afternoon," Harry continued, lying flat with his hands behind his head and starting to whistle "The Man Who Broke the Bank at Monte Carlo," singing the words once he got to the chorus.

"I haven't heard that in ages," Michael confessed, when the rendition was finished. "Makes the day feel even better. There's nothing like an old song for raising the spirits."

"The power of simple music. Like medicine." Harry turned onto his side. "Do I get to see these sketches of yours?"

"It would be a pleasure." Now that Michael had shown them to Richard, he had few qualms about sharing them again. He took the books from his bag and, when Harry had sat up, opened the one with the views, as he'd done for his nephew.

"But these are wonderful," Harry exclaimed, wide-eyed. "When you said you sketched, I was afraid they'd be amateur dabblings and I'd have to pretend they were good, for politeness' sake. But I don't. You've got the knack."

"Thank you." Michael gave a self-deprecating smile. "Although it feels like a hundred years since I did some of these. Or maybe it feels like they're the work of another man. I'm not sure I'd know how to approach the process anymore. Maybe that put me off trying, more than the sunshine."

"I daresay you're right." Harry grinned. "Anyway, why not give it a try? I can find some spare paper for you to make a start on, rather than risk spoiling these books with doodles, if that's a concern."

"Do you think my efforts would be that bad?"

"Don't be daft." Harry cuffed his arm. "But you'll need to find your feet again. Like getting back on a horse when it's bucked you off and you've taken a nasty fall. You'll be shaky until the natural feeling returns. Simply start drawing and trust your hands. They'll remember what to do."

Michael glanced at Harry, in case there'd been some half-hidden meaning in the words—but the man was still studying the pictures, poring over the places he must have recognised. Michael glanced down at his own hands, fingers now rougher than they'd been when these sketches had been made. Would they really remember what to do, whether with a pencil in hand or a lover's flesh?

"What's in the other book?" Harry's voice cut into his thoughts. "More views?"

"People," Michael said, simply, before opening the sketchbook and putting it in Harry's lap.

Harry slowly turned the pages, studying each sketch as he came to it. "Well, what can I say?"

"Are they that bad?"

"Come off it. They're even better than the views. You don't just capture a person's appearance. You get to the essence of their personality." Harry looked up, smiling; Michael could only bear that bright glance—and all the promise it might or might not hold—for a moment. Then he had to turn away.

"Thank you. You'll find one of Thomas in a moment. I'm not sure it's the best likeness of your brother, but . . ." Michael shrugged, waiting while Harry found the page.

"This is stunning." Harry turned the picture one way and another, carefully examining it at different angles. "It's the real him."

"I'm glad you think so." Michael had always worried that too much of his fondness for the sitter would seep through, but he wasn't concerned if Harry spotted that affection there. And Harry was accurate in what he'd said: a hidden depth to Thomas remained outlined in the sketch, something about him that even Michael hadn't been able to put a name or meaning to, that only appeared under the scrutiny of the pencil. "Could I try a sketch of you? Now? The light's excellent, and you would be a good subject to get me back into the flow of things."

"I'd be honoured." Harry beamed. "I've not sat for a portrait before. What am I to do?"

"Just sit still and be natural, if you can."

The pencil felt strange in Michael's fingers, and the blank page stared at him accusingly, as though remonstrating that this book had been left for so long untouched. But once he'd started, the outlines came easily, in part because Harry had lain back to take up a pose which was languid and flowed from eye to paper without difficulty. The distraction of Michael's thoughts—spinning around what he'd like to do to that body right now—allowed his fingers to get on with their work automatically, until he suddenly found he was drawing again with a freedom and skill he'd feared lost.

Still, Michael wasn't going to attempt anything too ambitious for this first outing, just some simple shading to suggest the cut of the model's shirt, the way it folded and creased along his body, the elegant line of his trousers. A suggestion of grass and flowers behind him.

In the end, the thing came out quite detailed, Michael having surrendered himself to the movement of what his hands demanded.

"Am I allowed to see?" Harry asked, as Michael brought his pencil to a halt.

"When I've done." He fussed about, making miniscule adjustments, reluctant to share the finished product. Finally, he could beat about the bush no longer. He turned the book to face his model.

"That's beautiful." Harry, shaking his head in wonder, extended a finger, then drew it back, evidently scared to smudge the drawing. "More beautiful than the model."

"If you're fishing for compliments, you'll be waiting a long time for your float to bob." Michael grinned. "I'd like to sketch you again if I may. This is only rough work, and I could do better."

"Rough? Who's fishing for compliments now?" Harry studied the sketch afresh. "Your ability to capture depth is hardly rusty. In fact, one might say that this is better than some of your earlier work. It has a harder edge, if that's the correct word. Truer and less romantic."

Michael considered his efforts in the light of those words, then nodded slowly. "You could be right. Even my drawings haven't escaped the effects of the last few years."

"Do you ever draw any classical poses?" Harry asked abruptly, and with a suspiciously offhand tone.

"'Classical'?" Michael looked him steadily in the eye, aware of a glint which hadn't been there earlier.

"Yes. Like one of those statues they cover up the bits on when maiden aunts are around." Harry held Michael's gaze.

"Oh, *classical*," Michael replied, with a smirk. "Sometimes. I don't keep them in with the others, though. I have a separate book, in case there are any maiden aunts in the vicinity. They might mistake classical for pornographic."

"Indeed." Harry stretched, pushing out his chest. "I've always fancied having a statue made of me in a heroic pose. Hercules wrestling or some such tosh. Little chance of it happening, though. Perhaps a sketch would be the next best thing."

"Perhaps. Although best not to do it here or we'd scandalise the county should they be out and about."

"Very true." Harry leaped to his feet. "Let's take your stuff indoors. We can find sketching paper if you're still willing to give it a go."

"I am." Michael, hands trembling, packed up his books and pencils, then accompanied his host on a slow walk back to the house. Anybody observing the pair would have had no suspicion that this was anything other than two friends enjoying a stroll, rather than two men possibly taking the first steps towards something of significance. Because, unless Michael had lost all his ability to interpret the relevant signs, Harry had extended a clear, if unspoken, invitation.

They reached the front door still chatting casually—the conversation now centred on the estate business Harry had dealt with earlier—then climbed the stairs to Michael's room, where they stowed his overnight bag.

"My dressing room catches the afternoon sun," Harry said, in an overly matter-of-fact way. Perhaps one of the albeit skeleton staff was at risk of overhearing their plans. "The light should be good for drawing there."

"I'll cast my expert eye on it." Michael grinned. "If it doesn't work, we'll have to try elsewhere."

As it turned out, both the setting and the light were perfect. Michael arranged his materials on a small table while Harry rummaged some suitable paper out of the bottom of a cupboard. Once the dust had been blown off, the stuff proved serviceable.

"We should start with you sitting on the window seat, I think. And seeing as it's a long time since I've attempted flesh and muscle, a brief preliminary sketch would be best."

"You're the artist. Tell me what to do." They shared a lighthearted glance as Harry's hands went to his shirt buttons.

"Slip that off and sit by the window. Leg up on the seat and elbow on your knee." So simple to ease back into old habits of arranging a sitter in exactly the right pose.

"Yes, sah!" Harry unbuttoned his shirt, easing off both it and the thin silk vest beneath, before arranging himself as instructed. "Will this do?"

"Admirably. If you could just turn slightly to your left. The sun isn't quite as bright now—yes, that's spot on." Michael took a long, appraising look at the wiry frame, with the eye of both artist and aspirant lover. There was strength there, and good muscle tone, like a runner might possess. He could imagine Harry depicted as a messenger of the gods. "Hold the pose as well as you can. It'll do nicely."

He let the words hang in the air as he got his head down over the paper once more: Harry would indeed do anyone nicely. As Michael outlined the form of the muscles on his paper, a pleasantly warm sense of anticipation settled into his stomach before edging lower.

His glance flicked between sitter and paper, resting briefly on his own hands, which were working with the old confidence now. Like Harry had said, all he'd had to do was trust them. Those fingers had proved themselves on five bodies and none of the men had complained, none of them had professed themselves to be less than satisfied or in any way distressed. Michael knew of people for whom the act of love became one of pushing boundaries, of letting oneself go entirely into a lover's power, or exercising that power over someone else. His tastes had never run on those lines. As far as he was concerned, pleasure should be shared equally, willingly, and with tenderness rather than force. All his previous lovers had shown similar inclinations, and he hoped Harry—if they got that far—would be the same.

The man concerned, who'd been sitting patiently gazing out of the window, occasionally humming a tune, asked, "How long will you be? My arm's getting cramp."

"Oh, sorry. You can relax now. Just some finishing touches due." Michael corrected a bit of shading which wasn't quite as he'd intended, then turned the paper. "I'm rather pleased with this."

"You should be. You've flattered the sitter again, but there's no doubt that it's me." Harry came over, then took the portrait back to the window to study it more closely in the light. "I could even show that to my maiden aunt. If I had one. Very tasteful."

"That sounds perilously close to damning with faint praise." Michael chuckled.

"It wasn't meant to." Harry returned the sketch. "I really do appreciate your efforts."

"It's my pleasure." Michael smoothed out a virgin piece of paper. "Shall we go for something you couldn't show that mythical aunt of yours?"

"Why not?" Harry took off his shoes, then stripped off the rest of his clothes, revealing a firm, well-toned body, the tawny brown of his forearms contrasting with the marble white of chest and thighs. Just the sight of him stirred sensations Michael hadn't felt in a long time, his body reacting in the obvious way.

Harry clearly knew what exactly he was doing. That fact was evident from the manner he subtly flaunted his body to best effect as he sprawled on the window seat, the high surround of which meant that the most delicate parts of his anatomy couldn't be seen from outside. That he hadn't locked the door suggested either Goode was unlikely to drop in on them accidentally—perhaps he'd been given the afternoon off—or that the man was perfectly aware of what might be going on and would keep a discreet distance.

Michael started his sketch, although with less confidence this time. How could he concentrate on drawing while fighting his rising excitement? How could he ignore the fact that Harry was aroused? Michael soon reached the point where abandonment was the only option: he put aside his equipment, crossed the floor, and sat on the window seat, where a place had been made for him.

Harry eyed him up and down, grinning—quite possibly at the noticeable bulge in Michael's trousers. "Given up on the job so soon?"

"Got a better one to do." Michael took Harry's face in his hands, then slowly brought it closer for a long, lingering kiss.

"Hmm. Nice. I imagine you're even better at this than at drawing," Harry murmured, before returning the kiss with a heightened degree of passion.

"I try my best," Michael countered, when they at last broke to take breath.

"You've certainly got the knack of getting me all worked up. I hope it won't be for nothing."

"If it's in my power, nothing is the last thing it'll be."

"That makes no sense, but I think I know what you mean." Harry rose from the seat, taking Michael's hand to pull him up and towards what must have been the door to the bedroom.

"I promise my actions will make more sense."

Harry's bedroom was cool, a gentle and most welcome breeze wafting through the open window. The bed was cool too, firm and comfortable; Harry's body was equally firm and comfortable. There was something ridiculously exciting for Michael about bare flesh rubbing against his clothed body, but he soon forewent that pleasure, especially when Harry's insistent fingers started working on his buttons.

And, if being dressed next to an unclothed Harry was stimulating, then being naked next to him proved to be even better.

"You have a magnificent body." Harry, taking a break from exploring Michael's frame to compliment it, ran his hand down from sternum to crotch. If he was bothered by the scars on Michael's leg, he wasn't letting on. No doubt he'd seen much worse. "You'd not disgrace any classical statue you sat for. Might shock the ladies who saw it, though, given the size of this." He edged his fingers around Michael's groin. "It would take a hell of a big fig leaf to cover that up. Especially in *this* state."

Michael laughed. "I'll confess I've never had a complaint about the service it provides."

"I'll give you my appraisal when I've seen it put into action. Or felt it," Harry added, gently stroking the part under discussion.

The conversation halted for the next few minutes—unless sighs and groans could be counted as conversation—while they took the journey of discovery into what pleased each other. Michael had always regarded this as one of the particular joys of sex: two men finding their way through the maze of delight, with the constant risk of turning a corner and finding a dead end adding to the sense of danger. All the time creeping closer to the centre of the labyrinth, the ultimate goal of ecstasy.

"I've wanted to do this for so long," Harry confided, as he moved his hand up to draw slow circles on Michael's stomach. "When Tom first brought you home, I may have been young, but I already knew

I preferred men, and you were the one I'd have preferred above all others at the time."

"I had no idea." Michael didn't want to think about Thomas, or the past, just the wonderfully unexpected present.

"I know. And I didn't have the subtlety to make you understand. In my imagination, you were going to be the first man I ever had sex with. Reality turned out differently, but we got there in the end." Harry, in one easy movement, brought his head against Michael's, kissed him, and smiled. "Thank God we met again."

"Amen to that." Michael returned the kiss. "And perhaps it's better we meet now, with no illusions about what went before."

"At least we've had plenty of practice to perfect things." Harry's fingers, groping lower again, were proof of his words. Practice had given him incredible adroitness.

Michael wanted to simply get lost in the moment, but an element of unknowing had come to bother him. Every first—or in the case of Jimmy, unique—encounter with his lovers had been subtly different, from adolescent, inexpert fumbling to a skilled coupling. While Michael didn't expect anything clumsy from Harry, he wasn't sure what the man would prefer. *Par main*, as the doxies in France were said to offer to those who valued their marriage vows? *Par bouche*? *Complète*? He'd just have to play this passage by ear.

He inched his hand down Harry's back, across his buttocks, between his legs, and over the soft skin there.

"Don't stop," Harry moaned. "Just there. Keep stroking that very spot."

Michael obeyed instructions, delighted that the simple movement of his fingers appeared to be bringing such pleasure.

"Actually you *had* better stop." Harry gasped. "Or else I'm going to make a mess all over your arm. Liable to spray everywhere."

"And do you think that would bother me?" Michael settled his hand in the place that made his lover moan the loudest.

"Probably not." Harry nudged Michael's fingers back into action. "I've looked forward to this moment for years."

"So I'd guessed." And how had it taken so long for the light to dawn? How could Michael have been so blind as to what had been going on back then? He'd ragged Richard enough about George's sisters and how they only tagged along because they liked the lad so much. He should have realised Harry had been in the same boat.

Michael brought him off, enjoying his lover's ecstasy almost as much as if he were undergoing it. It wasn't long before he experienced his own climax, a desperate urgency overwhelming him as Harry skilfully used his hands and mouth. Michael resisted the urge to shout, pressing his arm to his mouth as he'd done so often before to ensure discretion.

"Good?" Harry sat up, grinning, once it was over, although he kept his hand where it could wreak havoc afresh should he desire.

"Exceptional." Michael extended his arm, encouraging his lover to come into his embrace. "Thank you."

"It's been a pleasure."

They might have been awkward words, but this was potentially an awkward moment. To say, *I love you*, would have been a palpable lie. Silence might have proved uneasy. Harry, perhaps equally aware of the difficulty, began to hum a tune, some love song from a musical comedy which Michael couldn't quite put a name to. Light, airy and perfect, just as the act itself had been.

Michael snuggled against his lover, and tried to think of nothing but the pleasure still rippling through him. Sex, *sechs*, the sixth lover. Would Richard notice if the shell counting game now always went on from five to six? And what word followed "*pethera, pimp*"?

CHAPTER NINE

The prosaic business of getting washed and dressed again completed, Michael put away his drawing equipment, on the understanding that the half-finished sketch would be resumed at some point when, as Harry put it, they could complete the thing without having to break off to devour each other.

At the present time, all they wanted to devour was dinner, their bedroom romp having left them famished.

One of the ladies who came in to clean—a woman of French extraction married to a local soldier who'd somehow found time to woo her while serving—had prepared them a pot of cassoulet, which had only needed warming through by Goode. Served with fresh bread and a bottle of good, honest claret, it was a meal fit for a king.

They finished with cheese, port, and a cigar, taken out in the garden where the warmth of the day had hardly abated. That night promised to be sultry, perhaps in more ways than one. Harry was humming to himself again as he poured the port.

"What *is* that song?" Michael asked. "You keep singing it to yourself."

"Sorry. I wasn't aware I was. Only something the lads used to sing on board. I can't get it out of my head." He handed Michael a glass. "It's a love song. I must have romance on my mind."

"Not just on your mind." Michael's body reacted in both recollection of the afternoon and anticipation of what the night might bring. "Some of those old, cliché-ridden songs have a remarkable potency."

"Some of the ship's officers used to have special songs—the bigger and harder the man, the more mawkish the ditty I found—to remind them of loved ones." Harry lit his cigar, then sent a thin stream of smoke into the evening air. "Toasts to home and beauty and all that. Never far from their minds."

"Yes, I can understand the appeal. Songs are safe."

"That's an intriguing statement." Harry looked at him sidelong, as his tutor might have done back at university. "Care to expand on it?"

"I'll try. What I'm attempting to say is that it's difficult enough to show how much you care for—and miss—someone who's miles away, without making an ass of yourself in words. I suppose a song can express all sorts of things you wouldn't necessarily express in a conversation, or even in a letter." The most virile men would put up with lyrics that were a damn sight soppier than the expressions they'd naturally use.

"Ah, yes. That's an excellent point. Songs are useful smokescreens too." Harry produced a thin stream of smoke. "Do you know, I had a lover who used to woo me quite openly, when others were in the offing, simply by sitting down at the piano and striking up a song? People would think he was addressing some young lady, one of those present or perhaps some fair beauty far away, and they'd get quite teary-eyed about his rendition, amazed at how much emotion he was investing the lyrics with. Not knowing, of course, that the object of his affection was standing right in front of him."

"How clever." Once, Michael would have felt a pang of jealousy at the mention of a lover's other men, but he was beyond that now and could appreciate such an unpretentious yet bold stratagem. He'd certainly used his pencil to express his own affection, be it hidden or overt, for people and places.

"We thought so." Harry nodded. "And I could return the compliment, answering him with complete candour in another song. I used to assume that we'd been terribly innovative, coming up with that scheme, but I guess there's nothing new under the sun. Somebody, somewhere had no doubt already come up with it."

"Shakespeare and his sonnets, maybe?"

Harry sent another stream of smoke towards the stars. "The Bard and his beautiful boy? Doesn't he make his intention clear?"

"Don't you remember the way we were taught at school? Old Troughton made it plain all the sonnets which expressed love were addressed to women." Michael flicked ash from his cigar. "Anybody could start spouting about 'If I could write the beauty of your eyes' and plenty of folk would assume they had to be talking about a girl."

"Point taken. And I remember Troughton clearly. He was the dreariest old bore in the whole of Christendom." They smoked in silence for a while, before Harry resumed the thread. "Here's a point to think about, should Britain ever find herself at war again. What if men of our kind volunteered to take up espionage? Wouldn't we be highly effective, given that we're used to communicating in code and making ourselves unnoticed?"

Michael laughed. "I guess we've had the perfect preparation for such a career. Although too open to blackmail to be entirely successful, I suspect."

"Oh, don't let squalid reality get in the way of a great plan. It's too depressing." Harry sighed, before taking another long draught on his cigar. "I sometimes think the love that dare not speak its name nowadays will never be able to, not openly."

"I suspect you're right. Not until we get a new heaven and a new earth, anyway. I always hoped that if that wretched war achieved anything it would be to change people's minds about what really mattered. It hasn't. Sorry." Michael raised his hand. "Not much fun to talk about the war."

He drained his port, then tipped his head back to admire the existing—old—heaven, which seemed perfect enough on such a warm yet clear night as this. Maybe it was only people who made the old earth such an awful place at times.

Harry's voice, warm and rich as the stock-scented night air, sounded an invitation. "Will you sleep with me tonight? We can rig up something to look like your bed's been slept in, so as to fool the skivvy when she comes to do the room."

"I'd like that very much." Michael reached across, taking Harry's hand to caress it. "I'm so pleased we met again. You've been like a glass of cold, clean water in the desert."

Harry rubbed his thumb over Michael's knuckles. "I'll take that as a compliment."

"It was meant to be. A good man isn't easy to find."

The bed had been made up afresh—no doubt the work of the marvellously discreet Goode—and looked just as welcoming as it had that afternoon. Harry slipped his arm round Michael's waist, kissed him, then excused himself, heading off to use the lavatory.

As Michael waited for his lover's return, he took the opportunity to strip down to his underwear, oddly shy about taking off his clothes while in Harry's presence. Why was he experiencing such skittishness when only a few hours before they'd seen every inch of each other's bodies? Perhaps because this occasion seemed more calculated, and so potentially more awkward, than their wonderfully spontaneous lovemaking of some hours earlier. They weren't yet at the stage of having a comfortable knowledge of each other to ease them over such moments, but hopefully that would come with time, if they let the relationship develop. And develop it could, given that Harry was based in London and within easy reach of Michael's home; this wouldn't need to be a holidays-only affair.

He was getting ahead of himself. For now, Michael had another romantic encounter to enjoy, and if it was anywhere near as pleasing as the afternoon's had been, he'd be more than satisfied. Assuming that Harry didn't simply intend that they shared the bed for companionship. He pulled back the covers, ranged himself on the cool sheet, and waited.

The twinkle in Harry's eye when he returned from the lavatory, fly buttons still undone, settled the matter. Just sleeping wasn't on the agenda. He eyed Michael head to toe before divesting himself of his trousers.

"You dress very well." Harry started on his shirt. "But you strip even better. The sight of you lying there could get any man's heart racing."

"Not *any* man." Michael chuckled. "I suspect you do me too much credit if you think I could tempt most men off the straight and narrow. I've known plenty who'd have shot me rather than kiss me."

"You're right, as ever." Harry grinned ruefully, having discarded his shirt but pausing before setting about the rest of his clothes. "Easy to forget the world isn't like boarding school."

"Quite." What had been an expedient solution for many a young man when their sexual appetites had been burgeoning and the only opportunity to exercise them was in an exclusively male society, had become anathema to those same men as they'd grown older. Maybe it was putting away childish things, as the epistle had it, although there was probably an element of shame at what they'd done. Hypocrisy always found places to thrive. "Did you do *it* at school?"

"Oh, Lor', no. I was too scared of being caught, for a start. Don't you remember my housemaster was red hot on stuff like that?"

"Ah, yes. Puritan Peters."

"That's him. He made sure the head of house and his gang were ultravigilant for anything which might cast a spot on the house's reputation." Harry rubbed his chin. "Tom used to call them a pack of evangelical old women, rooting out sin of any sort, even if it was just overindulgence in buns from the tuck shop."

That sounded like Thomas; he'd hated to be constrained by petty and seemingly pointless rules. That had been one of the reasons Michael suspected it had taken something earth-shattering to make the man accept the king's shilling. Army discipline and Thomas didn't seem likely to be good bedfellows.

"You? Was your first time there, I mean?

"No. I was too scared, as well, despite the fact our housemaster wasn't quite as obsessed with sins of the flesh." He and Thomas had been in Treadwell's, while Harry had been in Peters's; the variety of ethos to be found in boarding school houses was something he'd never fathomed. Treadwell himself had been avuncular, full of common sense, and kindness and that culture had pervaded his domain. He'd been made headmaster of the school when he'd returned from Belgium, with half his leg gone and a Military Cross in return for it. Hopefully Richard would benefit from his wisdom if family tradition prevailed and he, too, had his education there. "Do you ever pine for school days? I've never understood the appeal of the whole 'best years of our lives' nonsense."

"I do not." Harry sat on the bed. "The only bit I really enjoyed was playing cricket. Hated the footer and all the rest of the sport. Am I the only one who thinks it took place every afternoon, day in day out?"

"I think you're deluding yourself. It wasn't as bad as all that."

"Perhaps not." Harry grinned, then once more got to work stripping. "The thing I did enjoy—apart from cricket—was seeing you at a distance. I pined for you terribly, like the soppiest sort of schoolgirl."

Michael hid his delighted smile. "I'm ashamed to say I never noticed. I do remember your batting, though, in the house matches. Your straight drive was a thing of beauty. I was quite envious."

"Alas. I am misused." Harry, back of his hand on his forehead like a swooning maiden, rolled his eyes theatrically. "He only wants me for my batting, not anything else."

"Idiot." Michael pointed at Harry's magnificent anatomy. "Why don't you come over here and show me what you can do with that piece of willow, then?"

"Which one?" Harry asked, mock insouciantly.

"The one that's sticking in my direction."

"Oh, *that* one. I've got stuff to do with it that would knock a cover drive into a cocked hat." Harry edged closer, flaunting his body—and its increasing arousal—as he did so. "Would you like a demonstration?"

"Do you think I'm going to say no?" Michael slipped off the bed and into his lover's embrace, pressing body against body, lips against lips. Harry tugged off his vest, so he could smother Michael's chest with kisses, then removed his pants, favouring the rest of his body with the same service.

"Steady on," Michael gasped. "You've got me all of a lather. Can we take it a bit slower now?"

Harry removed his mouth from where it had been causing such a commotion. "Of course. However you'd like it is fine with me. We have all the time in the world."

"And thank God for that." Among the other things the last few years had taught him was to appreciate the gift of time and the bodily vigour to enjoy it to the full. Michael had promised himself he'd never again take anything for granted, not even the simple pleasures of waking in a clean, comfortable bed, or slipping his feet into warm, dry socks.

It was only right to indulge in another simple pleasure, kissing his lover and letting himself be kissed in return. Harry's body was as clean and comfortable as any bed, his embrace warm and welcoming and far better than a hundred pairs of woollen socks. He'd also so far proved a gallant and thoughtful lover, giving and taking enjoyment equally. If there were time enough granted to them, Michael would relish exploring all the incarnations of love with this man.

He wouldn't delude himself with notions of *forever*, in the way that Caroline and Eric appeared to be joined. Thomas and Laurie and the rest of them had taught him the folly of planning too far ahead. He'd take each day as it came, and hope each was as glorious as these last few days had been.

Harry squeezed his shoulder. "What's up? You seem miles away."

"Sorry. Lost in thoughts. Good ones, though." He ran his hands through Harry's hair. "Don't stop."

"I won't. Would you like it if we went the whole hog?" Harry, voice gentle and soothing, whispered against Michael's neck. "I know some chaps don't like the notion."

"I'd like it very much," Michael confided. "Don't worry about what suits me and what doesn't. I'll tell you soon enough. And, to be frank, I don't suppose there's any way I haven't done it over the years."

"Spoilsport!" Harry nipped his shoulder this time. "I hoped I'd bring something new to the menu of delights."

"I have no doubt you will, if this afternoon is anything to go by." Michael slipped his hand down to caress the "willow" he'd so admired. "And taking this into account I'm going to be astonished."

"'Astonished'?" Harry chuckled. "You'll be pinned to the bed and pounded if I have my way."

"Then have your way, Harry." Michael brought their mouths together for a long, slow kiss, while their bodies slid hankeringly against each other.

Harry's skin—smooth, soft, and sensitive to the touch—was a pleasure to explore. Such a fine body, such admirable curves and lines, with an unusual amount of well-defined muscle on his stomach. Plenty of those classical statues possessed such definition but, in Michael's experience, very few living men. Not many classical statues were as well-endowed as Harry, though; perhaps men had been smaller in those far-off days or the sculptors had been reticent to depict the truth for fear of scandalising their maiden aunts.

"Admiring my bat again?" Harry chuckled.

"Why not? It's worth admiring. And there isn't often the opportunity of telling the owner of such a magnificent anatomical item how attractive it is. Nor what one wants to do with it. I'm taking my chances while they come."

"You can be sure there'll be a lot of coming."

They put aside all talk and jokes for the next few minutes, letting actions speak instead, until Harry—breathless—murmured, "Do you really want me to have my way?"

"I'm a man of my word." Michael kissed him again, then let him out of his grip, knowing what essential, if unromantic, actions had to come next. As Harry adroitly—clearly a practiced hand—applied some Vaseline to himself, a memory flashed through Michael's mind of Thomas doing much the same thing, before their first time. Thomas hadn't been quite as adept, only having heard from one of the chaps at school and not the most reliable source, that this was what you had to do. It hadn't turned out to be one of their most successful moments, although practice, of which they subsequently had plenty, had made something like perfection.

He was confident Harry was going to put in a much more competent performance.

"Ready?" Harry, slick with sweat and primed for action, wore an incongruously shy smile.

"Ready and willing." Michael squirmed in anticipation. "And more than able."

It had been such a long time since he'd gone this far, and there'd been moments when he'd worried that he'd never go so far again without paying for the privilege, a course he was loath to steer. To find another opportunity so unexpectedly was beyond everything he could have hoped for. Earlier in the year, he'd contemplated refusing to come to Cornwall again, dreading the re-igniting of memories, but how wrong he'd been. He shuddered at the thought of having missed out on this.

The moment of union proved to be gentle, practiced, and almost unbearably exciting. The act had been a success and surely would be again.

"Bloody hell." Michael held on tight as his exhilaration subsided. "You've certainly got the knack."

"Glad I haven't lost it," Harry rasped. "A short innings, alas. But better than the old bat not producing an innings at all."

Michael chuckled. "Next time, maybe you'll get through to your century."

CHAPTER TEN

After a perfunctory attempt at cleaning themselves up, they put out the lamps and lay on the bed, Michael curled into the crook of his lover's arm. The night breeze from the window gently wafted across bodies which were descending to the plains of normality from ecstatic heights. Harry reached over, groping on the top of the bedside table, evidently trying to find something or other. His hand landed on a silver box, where he must have been looking for a cigarette.

"Fancy one?" Harry asked, once he'd found his goal.

"I'll share yours, if that's all right. I hardly smoke these days."

Harry groped around again, then swore. "I'll need some light to *find* a light. Can't see a thing in here now."

"Go ahead." Michael listened to Harry moving round, rustling and rummaging, stubbing his toe and swearing once more before lighting a small candle.

"Thought I'd never find the matches. Somebody hides them, I'm certain."

"The same person who hides the scissors when you want them." Michael admired his lover's frame as the light flickered over it, wondering whether he'd be lucky enough to sample that body another time before he had to return to High Top.

"Every house must have one of them." Harry slipped back into the bed, offering Michael the cigarette, which he accepted, taking a satisfying pull before returning it. "Thanks."

Harry took a long drag, blowing a thin stream of smoke towards the ceiling. "Do you still think I'm a glass of clean water? I haven't gone stale on you?"

"You never could." Michael snuggled closer, resting his head on Harry's arm. "I'm grateful to whichever angel decided to put you on the right road at the right time. Our paths might never have crossed, otherwise."

Harry shrugged. "They might, but not under such strangely fortuitous circumstances. It was a hell of a shock, seeing you there."

Michael thumped his lover's chest. "It was a hell of a shock you nearly running us over."

"Don't remind me." Harry pulled on his cigarette, attempting a smoke ring and failing; a sharp tug at Michael's heart in remembrance of Thomas performing the same action, in similar circumstances, down in the boathouse. Although Thomas's attempt at smoking—his first and nearly last—had ended up in a violent bout of coughing.

Thomas. Michael had managed partly to put the man out of mind these last few hours, all qualms about making love to Harry and thinking of his brother while doing so having been overcome. But in this blissful postcoital haze, the shade of Thomas seemed to want to make its presence known. Michael reached for the cigarette, taking another drag, but it tasted bitter and unappealing. He swiftly returned it, as though the thing stung his fingers.

"Do you know," Harry continued, clearly unaware of Michael's distress, "when I came off my bike and saw you there, I assumed for a moment I'd been killed outright and been transported to heaven."

Michael chuckled. "Am I so angelically beautiful?"

"Silly sod. No, it was because I thought you were already dead. Somebody told me you'd bought it in France. They'd evidently got their facts mixed up."

"I could easily have bought it, and anybody could easily have made a mistake. You have no idea what a mess it was. You know for yourself that people disappeared and there wasn't always a body to identify." Suddenly cold, Michael pulled the cover over himself. "Why didn't you mention that before now?"

"I didn't want to make a fuss. And I wouldn't have said anything at the time, in front of the boy. Didn't want to upset him."

"Richard's a surprisingly mature soul. He'd have coped." Michael snuggled down into the warmth of the cover and his lover's embrace. "He'd have probably thought it a great joke and made a note to tell George."

Harry took a last pull of the cigarette, then stubbed it out. "Sounds like he's his father's son. Anyway, it's no laughing matter. I was shaken out of my wits, not only at seeing you but at Richard being there as well. Still, if I ever do get to paradise, I hope it's like Cornwall."

"Daft beggar." Michael chuckled. "I remember wondering why you looked quite so aghast. I assumed it was simply horror and guilt at what had nearly happened."

"Surprisingly enough, guilt didn't hit me until I got back here and considered the consequence of ploughing into you both." Harry squeezed his shoulder. "Glad I didn't. Obviously. Then to cap the shock of seeing you with Richard climbing up out of the grass . . ."

"I can imagine. Nearly hitting a child must have made it worse."

"Especially when it turned out to be that particular child." Harry pulled Michael closer once more, smoothing his hair and caressing his temples. "Just like seeing *two* ghosts."

"Two? I'm not sure I follow."

"The boy. Tom's boy."

"Tom's boy?" Michael felt suddenly heavy-headed, obtuse. Had indulging in sex after such a long period of abstinence fuddled him to the point he didn't know what Harry was talking about?

"Oh God. You don't know, do you?" Harry groaned.

"Don't know what?" Michael slipped out of the embrace, leaning up on his elbow to look Harry in the eye. "What on earth are you talking about?"

"I'm so sorry." Harry, pale faced, seemed mortified at whatever faux pas he'd committed. "I had no idea you weren't aware. I shouldn't have been the one to tell you."

"For God's sake, can you make it clear what this is about?"

"There's no easy way to tell you this." Harry laid his hand tentatively on Michael's arm. "Richard is Tom's child. My nephew as well as yours."

Michael opened his mouth, but no words came out. No bombardment of shells could have rocked him so effectively. "You're joking. Tell me this is the kind of tasteless practical joke that Thomas would play."

"I swear to you I've never been more serious in my life." Harry shook his head. "That's why I thought I saw another apparition rising out of the grass. Richard looks so much like my brother when he was younger."

"No. It can't have happened. Their resemblance has to be a coincidence. You said yourself you were shaken up. That accident made you see things that weren't there." A tightened grip on Michael's arm halted his protestations.

"Hush," Harry crooned. "You're going to have to face this. Caroline and Thomas had a brief affair, ten summers ago."

"That can't be true. It can't." The walls seemed to be closing in on Michael, crushing all his previous certainties.

"I'm afraid it is." Harry kept his voice calm. "Caroline's a lovely girl, but for whatever reason she played Eric false."

Just Eric? She'd played her brother false, as well. Michael threw back the covers, freeing himself from Harry's touch and from his bed.

"Where are you going? You'll catch your death!" Harry's voice sounded behind him, evidently heedless of the risk of Goode hearing him.

"I need to think." Blindly, Michael flung himself towards the door, gulping for air like a drowning man. Only his collision with a chair slowed him enough for Harry to catch up and block his route.

"We should go and get you a nip of brandy." Harry grabbed at his arm.

"I don't want brandy." Michael threw up his hand, as though warding off a blow. "I need to keep a clear head. Tea, coffee, that would be better. Anything to help me think."

Harry finally managed to lay his hand on Michael's arm. "You're right. We should get something warm into you. You're freezing."

"I'll be fine," Michael lied, trying to control his shivering. "It's just the shock."

"I've seen men die of that. Wait here." Harry, more solemn-faced than Michael had ever seen him, opened the wardrobe, bringing out two thick woollen dressing gowns that must have been put away as not needed for warmer summer nights. "We'll put these on, then we'll go down to the kitchen. I used to sit by the stove when I was younger. They always kept it burning low, and there'll be hell to pay and no pitch hot if they haven't kept up the tradition."

As they dressed, Harry kept fussing over him, probably trying to ensure he didn't slip into a proper state of shock or a mental slough of despond; Michael felt like fobbing him off, but gave in to his ministrations. Why not let himself be looked after?

As they made their way below stairs, the candle in Harry's hand to light the way, Michael's thoughts wouldn't stop whirring. Those pictures of Thomas and Caroline, taken that summer he hadn't been in Cornwall, following his and Thomas's argument. They must have dated from eight or nine months before Richard's birth. Was that when the deed was done? How could Thomas have been such a heel? Had he been taking revenge on the family for his and Michael's estrangement?

The kitchen proved warm, especially when they'd stoked up the stove to boil a kettle on the hob. Michael pulled two chairs into optimum range while Harry banged about trying to find where the tea caddy and things like the spoons were kept.

How could he have been so blind? Naturally, he'd had no reason to doubt that Richard was Eric's child, even though the resemblance he'd observed in the supposed son's face couldn't really have been present. But people saw what they wanted to see, didn't they? The assumed similarity would have been accentuated by the shared habits—like the bird-like tip of the head—which must have been acquired by imitation rather than inheritance. Now that he knew the truth, and what to look for, Richard's similarity to Thomas was obvious.

Goode suddenly appeared at the kitchen door, politely enquiring if he could be of help and confessing his gratitude that they weren't burglars. The presence of a poker in his hand confirmed that he'd anticipated trouble.

"You can stand down," Harry said, graciously. "I had a nightmare—thought I was back on the ship—and managed to wake up poor old Michael here with my racket. He's doing his Florence Nightingale act."

Goode either took—or pretended to take—the explanation at face value, said that he hoped Harry would be able to settle, expressed the view that cocoa would be more likely to lead to a good night's sleep than tea or coffee, then tactfully removed himself.

Michael raised his eyebrows. "Does he know? About us? About you?"

"If he does, he won't give an opinion. Or let it affect his work. I'd rather go with tea than cocoa, though." Harry, frowning, stared at the kettle. "Will this thing never boil?"

"Leave it alone and it'll be fine. It knows you're watching." Michael settled himself on one of the chairs and pointed to the other. "Come on, sit down. We've got a lot to talk about. Like why I'm the last to find out."

"You're hardly last. I don't suppose anybody will rush to tell Eric. Or Richard. They won't hear from my lips, nor Caroline's. She made that plain to Tom."

"Did he tell you all this?"

"I think he told me just about everything. It was the night before he left to join the army. He was in a foul mood—had been for months, it seemed—and I wanted to know why. We took a bottle of claret down to the lake and the whole sorry story came out. Or at least half of it. The rest I learned later, when he was home on leave." Harry took a glance at the kettle; the thing still hadn't boiled. "He wasn't proud of what he'd done. An aberration, he said, in a moment of stress. He swore me to secrecy."

Michael wasn't ready to discuss Thomas and what might have been his motivation. "If that's the case, why did you assume I already knew?"

"Because I thought Thomas had told you. He said he had, and that he'd sworn *you* to silence, as well. He said that's why you'd argued."

"But we'd argued before that, in the spring. The dates don't work out, unless Richard was months overdue."

Harry leaped up to deal with the boiling kettle, leaving Michael to his thoughts again. Would he have to add *Thomas the liar* to *Thomas the unfaithful*? He surreptitiously pinched himself, wondering for a mad moment whether he was inhabiting a dream, but he was wide-awake.

Harry, who'd apparently been concentrating on making the tea, brought the pot and cups to the table. "All I can tell you is what he told me. I had no way of knowing if it's accurate."

"I don't recall him habitually telling lies." But maybe he hadn't known Thomas as well as he thought.

"Me neither." Harry poured the tea. "He must have had his reasons."

"Perhaps he was too ashamed of why we really quarrelled. It seems very petty, looking back."

"It often is. To start with, anyway." He passed Michael a cup. "I guess I should have suspected that the timings were all to pot, given that you'd not been around for a while. You didn't come to Porthkennack that summer, did you?"

"No. I determined never to come here again. I'm glad I changed my mind, though," Michael added, hastily. "I wouldn't have missed the last two days for the world."

"Really?" Harry stirred a spoon of sugar into his tea. "Even after this revelation?"

"That has rather knocked the gilt off the gingerbread." Michael shrugged, then blew on his tea. It was too hot to do more than sip, but cradling the cup brought much needed comfort. "But there was always a risk that I'd have found out some day. Better in these circumstances, I suppose."

"It's a lot for you to take in. And a burden to bear. I don't envy you returning to High Top tomorrow." Harry glanced up at the clock. "Today."

Michael shuddered; it would be worse than going into battle. He'd not only have to hide what he knew, but temper his facial expressions, be constantly wary of the slightest hint he might drop. Should he ask Harry what else he knew? Would finding out as much as possible make the situation easier or harder to deal with? He managed a long draught of tea—it had been made good and strong and reminded him of brews his batman had made—then took the plunge. "Tell me everything you can. The more I know, the better."

"As easy to hide a nest of secrets as one?"

"Something like that."

"If you're sure . . ." Harry laid his cup down. "Tom didn't know he'd sired a child, not at first. And why should he have suspected? I believe they only coupled once or twice. It was an unlucky chance."

Michael, who'd winced at the word *coupled*, bridled at *unlucky*. "No circumstance that produced Richard could be unlucky. He's a gem of a boy."

Harry raised his hand. "I apologise. A poor choice of words. None of this should reflect on Richard."

"Apology accepted." Michael forced a smile.

"Anyway, the next year Tom saw Richard's birth announcement in the *Times* and did his own sums. He knew there was a chance he was the boy's father and had to find out one way or another."

"Did he contact Caroline?"

"Yes. Rather out of the blue, given that they'd not been in contact after . . . after it happened."

Michael drained his tea, then poured them both another cup. "Go on."

"He wrote her a letter, but she insisted that Richard wasn't his. Said he was Eric's boy." Harry frowned. "She was furious at him suggesting there were problems within her marriage, and she insisted she had only ever loved her husband. I believe that to be true; you can see she still adores him."

"Which all begs the question of why she slept with Thomas? No." Michael rapped the table. "Unfair to ask you. Sorry."

"There's no need to apologise." Harry reached over to caress his hand. "I'd be asking the same things were the boot on the other foot."

"How could Thomas be sure Richard wasn't Eric's son?" Michael ignored for a moment what his eyes seemed to be telling him, now that they benefitted from hindsight.

"Clearly everything is circumstantial, although having seen the boy, the similarity between the two is unmistakable. Before you visited, I fished out some photographs of Tom as a child, and while he bears a strong likeness to our mother, there's enough of Richard about him." Harry took another swig of tea. "And there's the birthmark, of course."

"The . . . Oh, yes." Memories of his nephew as a baby flooded Michael's mind. "Richard had one on his forehead. It's almost faded now. Lily never had anything similar."

"That sounds right. Olivia doesn't seem to have one in her baby portraits." Harry pushed back the hair from his brow. "Mine's faded too. It only really shows up if the wind is beating a gale against my face, for some reason. Tom had a similar one, although it would have gone by the time he met you. Runs in our family, through the male line."

"And Thomas somehow found out that Richard had a similar birthmark?"

"Yes. He saw a photograph of the christening in the newspaper. It confirmed all his fears. Or hopes. I never did get to the bottom of whether he was secretly proud of what he'd done."

"For years I've wondered if Thomas joined up because of that argument we'd had. Was it because of the child?" That burden of guilt had hung about Michael for too long, and it would be good to lay it to rest once and for all.

"Your wits are addled. He'd enlisted long before Richard came along. The fling with Caroline might have been the tipping point, though. He felt like the worst sort of cad about it." Harry forced another half a cup each from the pot.

"Or so he must have said. I guess that may have given him the final shove, but if he felt such a heel, why did he want to be acknowledged as the child's father?"

Harry shrugged. "Pride? But when he realised he was never going to be allowed to have any connection with the child, I believe it changed him. He became a different man. Reckless."

"He joined the army because he no longer cared what happened to him?"

"Maybe. Or to forget what had happened that year."

Michael's conscience warred with his pride. He should feel a degree of sympathy for his old lover, but he couldn't. The betrayal—not just of him but of Eric, who was the most decent man Michael knew—cut too deep. "He chose what he did, always. Thomas was never pawn to fate."

Harry studied him sidelong. "I've long suspected he took that choice to its ultimate point. I met one of his fellow officers, who told me Tom was always at the forefront of operations, totally heedless of the danger he was in. They admired his bravery. I suppose dying for his country was easier than coming home to face the complications."

"So he left them for us to face? I call that cowardice, not bravery."

"I couldn't say." Harry paused in thought for what seemed an age before resuming. "I'd like you to know that I tried to get him to reconcile with you, but he wouldn't have it. He said he felt unworthy, given the circumstances."

"'Unworthy'?" That didn't sound like Thomas, more like something he'd have wanted people to believe of him. Any vestige of sympathy for his ex-lover was fast ebbing away. "He should have thought about that before he seduced Caroline."

"Or let her seduce him, which is always a possibility. I didn't ask for details." Harry's brow crinkled in distaste.

"I don't want to know them, either." Michael sipped on his tea, finding it lukewarm, stewed, and as unpleasant as this conversation. "You ought to be told the truth. About why we argued."

He explained the story of the practical joke gone wrong, only leaving out any reference to the finer details of his and Thomas's relationship. Mentioning that would leave a bitter taste in his mouth, given the night's revelations, and Harry must already have known that his brother and Michael had been lovers, or else why would he have been so confident in approaching him?

"It seems like we've both learned something tonight," Harry said, as the account came to its conclusion, blowing out his cheeks, then wrinkling his nose. "Thomas appears to have had a penchant for acting without thinking."

"And leaving the rest of us to pick up the pieces," Michael reminded him. "I have no idea how I'm going to face the family. I never could play poker."

Harry smiled. "Would you like me to come with you, back to High Top? Give you some moral support?"

Michael shook his head. "I appreciate the offer, but wouldn't it look rather odd?"

"Odd?"

"I'm not going to bolt through the door and start waving accusations around. I have to act as though nothing's happened, and your presence, as much as I'd value it, would only lead to questions. And questions are the one thing I don't need at present. I have to find time to take this all in. Oh Lord." He remembered the social pressure which would add to the moral one. "Richard is desperate to meet you again, and to visit here. When I get back, he'll be nagging at me about why we haven't fixed a date for the whole family to visit Broch."

"There's a simple solution to that. There's no point in making this more of a drama than it already is."

"'More of a drama'?" Michael bridled. "Harry, this is no laughing matter."

"I'm not laughing." Harry frowned. "I simply mean that if you want to pretend nothing has changed, then that's how you have to act. Not just in what you say but in everything, even the social niceties. I need to go to town tomorrow, but you can bring everyone over for luncheon the day after next. Eric and the boys can fish in the lake."

"And we all pretend things are as they were?"

Harry flapped his hand dismissively. "But that's what you want, isn't it? To carry on and 'smile, smile, smile'?"

The words of the familiar song, and its exhortation to light up a fag and stop worrying—as though either could provide solace in the face of a nightly bombardment—proved infuriating. "For God's sake. Don't fob me off with platitudes."

"Michael. Please." Harry held out his hand, but Michael ignored the gesture. "The situation is bad enough. Don't let it affect *us* too."

"Affect *us*? It's bound to affect us. Nothing's going to be the same anymore, is it?" Michael pushed away his cold and empty cup, then pushed himself out of his chair. He was horribly weary, unable to think straight, and knew that it would be madness to get into an argument now. This had the potential to end up as devastating a row as the one with Thomas had, but he couldn't resist picking at the scab of discontent. "Perhaps the only sensible solution would be to cut all ties between our families. We're clearly bad for each other."

"You're overreacting." Harry, on his feet now, reached for Michael's arm but was shaken away. "These sorts of events happen every day. People get over them. Life goes on."

"Do they?" Michael knew his voice was rising, and was likely to disturb Goode again, but he didn't care. "Does it? Maybe the Carter-Clemences are happy to just laugh matters off, but I'm not." He made for the door. "I'll sleep in my own bed here tonight. I'll be gone by the time you come down in the morning. Don't bother to see me off."

"Michael!" Harry's voice sounded behind him as he headed for the stairs, but he didn't want to listen. He'd had his fill of this family and this house. The dreadful thought that this house could have been the scene of Caroline and Thomas's adultery struck him halfway up the staircase, almost making him miss his footing. He paused, clutching the banister. Which room had they been in? Which bed had they used? Was it the one he was to sleep in tonight? Could they have been coupling in one of the places he'd always regarded as special to him and Thomas? Please God, not the boathouse.

He felt sick, sick to the core. The sooner he was away from Broch, the better. He might as well have been trampled in the mud of Flanders than return to something like this. Fate had taken his heart and rent it in twain, top to bottom.

CHAPTER ELEVEN

The early-rising birds were singing fit to burst as Michael pedalled past the gatehouse at Broch and out onto the road, headed not for High Top but for somewhere he could have breakfast. Arriving back there too early in the day—and unfed—would only lead to unwelcome questions. His head ached, lack of sleep and an excess of thinking having left it pounding. Life had changed, and this was the first day of that new existence; he would have to learn to cope with his burden as other men had learned to cope with leaving a limb in France. Although right now, dealing with the loss of a leg or arm seemed an easier prospect than coping with the loss of trust.

He knew of a good hotel in the middle of Porthkennack, one which would present little risk of him meeting anybody he knew. Maybe with a decent meal tucked away inside, he could find a fresh reserve of courage.

The bacon, eggs, and a good strong pot of tea he was served there appeared, at least temporarily, to make things slightly easier to face, although Michael had begun to wonder where the courage which had seen him through those war years had gone. As he called the waitress to ask for his bill, his eye was caught by something on the wall—a small painting in the style of Tissot, but not of the quality of the man himself. Probably this was one of the offerings from the local artists of whom he'd been so dismissive.

He remembered the discussion about art a few days previously, and Eric's remark that something's true worth was in the eyes of the beholder rather than in its provenance. Could he have been hinting that he knew his son wasn't his own? Eric was a good, decent man, no doubt the most decently behaved in this entire business, and he would be bound to do the right thing, as he counted it, by the boy.

Surely Eric couldn't know the truth, or Michael would have got wind of it. No doubt, with the benefit of hindsight and his freshly gained knowledge, Michael was seeing all sorts of stuff that hadn't really been there.

When it got to the point he could delay no longer, he set his wheels for High Top, although somewhat inevitably, given how fate seemed to be toying with him, the first person he saw as he cycled through the gate was Richard, knocking around a football with George. The easy grace of the boy's movement brought back memories of Thomas's uncomplicated athleticism.

"Uncle Michael!" The boy waved. "Do you want to join us?"

For a moment, the question seemed unanswerable, coloured as it was in Michael's mind by the revelations of the night before. What would he have done before he knew the great secret? Played without a second thought, and it would be best all round not to change his behaviour. "Of course. That sounds like a splendid idea!"

He propped up his bicycle and leaped into the game with a vengeance, burning off some of his frustrations, especially the disquieting notion that from henceforth he'd have to weigh every question and action.

"Play fair, Uncle!" Richard squeaked, after a particularly rough shoulder charge sent him tumbling.

"Sorry." Michael helped the lad to his feet. "I always forget that you're not fully grown."

"That's all right." Richard beamed at the compliment. "We just don't want you to be in trouble with Alice for getting me dirty."

"Indeed we don't. She rules that nursery with a rod of iron, George." Michael tipped a wink at their guest.

"I've noticed." George made a face. "She's worse than Clarissa, our nursery maid. She treats me like I'm only seven."

"They all do, I'm afraid. It's part of their job." Michael rolled his eyes, comically. "She treats *me* like I'm only five."

The boys giggled.

"It's cold trout for lunch," Richard confided, his mind obviously running on the usual boyish lines.

"Excellent." Why couldn't life's questions always be as simple as wondering what was to be on the table?

"And we're taking it down to the beach, for a full-blown picnic. All of us." Richard frowned. "Will you come?"

Michael knew a refusal would disappoint, and there were advantages to accepting. With lunch in a setting as stunning as the beach, there'd likely be less pressure to make small talk. "Certainly I'll come. Couldn't miss out on trout. Did your father catch it?" He wondered whether he'd put any untoward emphasis on the words *your father*, but if he had, the boys didn't appear to have noticed.

"He did. He's taking us fishing this evening." Richard bounced excitedly, as did his pal. "Just me and George. You can come too, if you'd like."

"I'll give that a miss, old man. Had a bad night's sleep and could do with catching up." Michael rubbed his hands. "The beach will be perfect, though. We can teach Lily how to count shells."

Richard frowned again, evidently put out. "She's not old enough yet," he stated, probably meaning that it was *their* game and not to be shared with mere girls. "She won't feel the benefit of it."

Michael suppressed a smile. That was one of Alice's favourite lines, telling her charges that they had to divest themselves of outer layers when indoors or they wouldn't feel the benefit when they went out again. "I suppose not."

"Keep it for when she's older, Uncle."

"I will."

"Next summer, maybe?" George suggested.

"Perhaps." If there was a next summer here. The thought of ever returning to Cornwall again and the associations it would always have, made another wave of nausea strike. "Right, I need to go and unpack, lads, or I'll not be allowed to come to the picnic. Alice will convict me of failing in my duty."

"Good plan." Richard consulted his watch. "Still time for another game, George."

Michael watched the lads run off, then righted his bike and headed for the house. Alice was by the door, fiddling with something on Lily's pram. She gave him a smile and asked whether he'd had a nice time staying with his friend.

"Yes, thank you. Lots to catch up on." He parked the bike and unhitched his bags. "You'll have to excuse me. Got to go and stow my kit."

"Please do." Alice smiled again. She was pretty, and pleasant, and did her job with an air of calm competence. Exactly the type of girl who'd make anyone a lovely partner, and clearly fond of *him*, even if she left Michael cold. He returned the smile, then set off for his room, thoughts stumbling down dark alleys into areas he didn't really want to visit. Of course, men like him had always entered into weddings of convenience, hiding behind their marriage lines and getting their particular pleasures away from home. Raising a family and fooling everyone. Would Thomas have done that if he'd survived? He patently hadn't found sex with a woman as daunting a prospect as Michael did.

Michael emptied out his bag, sorting dirty clothes from clean, then contemplated at his sketching case. The half-finished picture of Harry naked was in there, as was the completed one of him bare chested. Michael couldn't burn them in the grate, as that would risk suspicion of why anyone would light a fire on so warm a day. He didn't want to leave such potentially incriminating evidence lying around, though, so carefully removed them—avoiding looking at the subject matter—then hid the things amongst his clean underwear, where nobody would go rummaging.

He caught sight of his reflection in the dressing table mirror: the bags under his eyes spoke of lack of sleep; his drawn features reflected worry and confusion. His thoughts kept returning to Thomas, how the man had sworn he had the same view of sex as Michael, who'd vowed he'd never marry or have anything to do with women. Had that simply been another one of his lies?

Or did it just reflect the immaturity of opinion they'd had back in those days, a viewpoint that might or might not have changed as they grew, rather like Richard was bound to change his estimation of the opposite gender? Had Thomas been one of those men who would turn away from sex with his own kind as a natural part of his development? Perhaps he'd just liked men and women equally, as Jimmy had, and simply hadn't been presented with the opportunity of trying it with a girl until Caroline had come along.

How could Michael ever establish the truth, at this far a remove?

Harry might be able to offer some insight, but it seemed like he'd burned his bridges with Harry. Michael could pursue the other half of the tale, but could he in all conscience ask his own sister why his lover had slept with her? Or why she'd slept with *him*? But would that not break down any bonds of trust between them? The awful chance remained that not mentioning the subject at all would be far worse, with him burning with curiosity every time he was in her presence.

There was another danger to consider. If he pumped Caroline for the truth, that would surely risk the story coming out completely. That scenario would be fair to neither Richard nor Eric, making them suffer when it was Caroline and Thomas who deserved to. And given that Thomas wasn't in a position to accept his share of the blame, Caroline was likely going to have to face that burden alone.

Luncheon at the beach was delicious, despite the sand's tendency to invade any and everything it could. The glorious sunshine and pleasant breeze produced an atmosphere in which it was easy to place the peppering of questions about Broch. Michael gave an objective account of what had changed, or rather an account of how little things there had changed, and had to admit that he was no further forward in fixing a date for all the family to visit there. He put that down to the unrelenting pressure of estate business on Harry, which was tying the man up for hours and days on end, and hoped the mostly accurate excuse would be believed.

"Did they change the house much during the war?" Eric asked. "For its use as a convalescent home?"

"Not that much, as far as I could see." Not that Michael had gone looking, but nothing obvious had struck him. "Some changes to the outbuildings to accommodate more vehicles, although those might have been planned anyway, given that the automobile is making its presence felt everywhere. It's as though the place has been put in a glass case at a museum."

"I would imagine his mother had it all put back to the way it was, as soon as she could," Caroline speculated. "She'd have wanted to put the war and all its memories behind her."

"Yes." Michael, not wanting to catch his sister's eye, concentrated on a piece of pork pie. "Perhaps Eric will be able to spot what we laymen can't." He gave his brother-in-law a smile.

"I doubt that. You need a matron for those sorts of jobs. They don't miss anything." Eric launched into an entertaining story about some dragon-like woman who'd ruled her hospital and nurses with a rod of steel and a tongue of iron, but who could be moved to tears at the most mawkish tune, as had been witnessed by one of her ex-patients who'd spotted her at a music hall.

Michael was reminded of his evening with Harry out under the stars, the discussion about music, and how he'd boldly told himself he was beyond the pangs of jealousy now. He clearly wasn't. He cast a glance at his sister, and shivered.

Richard had obviously noticed. "Are you cold, Uncle? Or have you been drinking from a dirty glass again?"

"You little monkey!" Michael, glad of the opportunity for a diversion, got onto his feet. "I'll count to five, then I'm coming for you. George as well. You get caught, you get a handful of sand down your back."

Richard looked at his mother, got a nod of approval, then set off, squealing with delight, George close on his heels.

"You're worse than those boys!" Caroline shouted after Michael as he headed off across the sand. Maybe she was right, but at present he preferred the lads' innocent and honest company.

Once he'd caught the pair and administered the handfuls of sand—an easy task, given the boys' tendency to stick together—and they'd in their turn caught him, they rejoined the others for well-earned strawberries, cake, and a glass of dessert wine for the adults. The boys had to make do with lemonade.

Once the meal was finished and the remains packed away, the party began to disperse. Eric took the boys beachcombing, while Alice and Lily went off to make sandcastles. Caroline, who'd stated that she'd slept badly and needed a rest, was left alone with Michael, the pair of them slouched in deck chairs under the merciful shade of a large umbrella. Gaze firmly out to sea, Michael kept his voice light, talking of his visit to Broch and all the old memories it had evoked, before subtly changing the subject.

"Those pictures of you and Thomas. In the album Eric and the boys showed me. When were they taken?"

"Oh, years ago." Caroline waved her hand. "One of the times we were all at High Top and he came over for a game of tennis or something."

"I don't remember that. It must have been the year I was in the Lake District."

Caroline shrugged. "It could have been."

"Odd that Thomas should have still visited, though." Michael chose his words carefully. "I don't remember any other time he came over when I wasn't present. Or at least I don't recall being told about such a visit."

"He wasn't your exclusive property." Twin spots of red flared on Caroline's cheeks. "Sorry, that was too abrupt. I'm extremely tired, and I didn't mean to sound quite so tetchy."

"Then what did you mean?"

"That I always felt Thomas was friends with both of us—all of us—rather than your friend solely. The whole family was always pleased to see him."

"Thomas was my very best friend."

"I know." Caroline sighed. "Though you've not mentioned him in years, until these last few days. You never used to shut up about him back then. Until that spring, when you argued."

"That happens when you're young. People grow apart."

"Hmm."

Michael turned, sharply, at her disbelieving tone. "Sorry?"

The flushes of colour showed on her cheeks once more, and her reply suggested she, too, was weighing her words. "I was just thinking that whatever happened between you seemed awfully sudden, rather than the gradual change one might have expected if you'd grown in different directions."

"Perhaps we had good reason to argue." Michael left the question hanging in the air, but his sister didn't take the bait. Eventually, he probed again. "Did he mention anything, that summer I was in the Lakes? About what he'd done to make me so cross?"

Caroline flinched, then quickly regained her composure. "Can we not talk about this now? I'm so tired I can't think straight." She gave him what looked like a forced smile. "I'd like to try and get some sleep, please."

"I'll leave you to it, then." Michael rose, brushing the sand from his trousers. "But this conversation isn't at an end. There are things we need to discuss, Caroline."

Without waiting for a reply, he set off down the beach, to help Lily and Alice with their sandcastles. If that carried the risk of Alice believing he'd come to spend time with *her*, so be it. Michael had enough on his mind than worry about further social machinations. The anger he felt towards his sister had intertwined with the anger he felt towards Thomas. The man must have known that the act they'd shared had been a double betrayal, and Michael suspected Caroline knew as well. He ignored the voice of conscience which told him that he must have been happily bedding Laurie while his sister and his ex-lover had been having their fling. He needed to keep his wrath warm and his focus clear, or else he'd never find the courage to have this out and he couldn't live with the pretence.

"Spade, Nuncle!" Lily, who'd smiled delightedly at his approach, thrust the thing at him. "Dig, please?"

"Certainly. Let's make the biggest castle in the history of the world."

He dug madly, sending sand flying everywhere and Lily into fits of giggles. Soon the boys came over to lend a hand, clearly not wanting to miss out on the fun. Before long, great works were taking shape, with towers and moats and what started to look horribly like trenches, ditches with zigzags and corners. In his fragile state, even those lines in the sand stirred up unwanted memories.

"Let's smarten these lines up," Eric said, getting to work at straightening the ditches. "Lily should have the best castle we can make her, fit for a princess to live in with her prince rather than something for the King's Own Highlanders to defend."

Michael, grateful yet again for his brother-in-law's common sense, gave him a smile and received a nod in return. Eric might not have served abroad, but he'd done—still did—his country and his fellow men proud. "Your father's right, as ever," Michael averred. "I promised Lily the best castle we could make, and if you haven't yet found the prettiest shells to decorate it, you'll have to act smart about filling your pockets with them."

"Yes, sir!" Richard began a mock salute, clearly thought better of it, gave Michael a grin, then scampered off with George, saying over his shoulder, "We'll find the very best of the bunch."

"Those boys," Alice remarked, shaking her head, but neither man replied, simply sharing a conspiratorial smile instead.

"Dig, Nuncle." Lily tugged at his sleeve.

"You're a hard taskmistress," he replied, setting to work again on the elaborate bridge over the moat, although his thoughts didn't stray far. Richard had just shown remarkable discretion, evidently having gained such skills in diplomacy from nurture, rather than nature—Thomas hadn't possessed half the maturity or tact the boy had.

A moment's uncertainty crossed his mind. Could Harry be wrong? Could the business about the birthmark be nothing but coincidence? He looked up, to where the boys were walking slowly along the tide line, heads down to scour the sand for the finest offerings to lay at Lily's feet. Observing Richard, Michael knew that he'd seen that exact same walk and demeanour before, in Thomas as a young man. There could be little doubt that the familial connection was there; the boy could imitate Eric's habits and demeanour, but the natural language of his body came from elsewhere.

"Nuncle!" Lily tugged at his arm again. "Please."

"Sorry, old girl. I was miles away."

Lily shook her head, in clear imitation of Alice, another example of nurture influencing nature. But the dimpled smile which followed could only have come from Eric; at least there was no doubting the provenance of this small work of art.

The outing to the beach was followed by much furious cleaning of everything and everybody. Dinner was thankfully planned to be brief and informal, the boys invited to join the adults for a simple meal of soup and sandwiches, much to the annoyance of Lily, who was just beginning to understand that people were having fun without her.

Michael had never seen her produce such a display of petulance; he didn't envy Alice the task of calming the child.

Eric had arranged to take Richard and George for an evening's fishing, which both boys regarded as a huge treat. Michael declined to join them, determined to take the chance of talking to his sister on their own. He quickly dismissed the fleeting thought that Eric had got wind of something and had deliberately engineered an opportunity for the siblings to be alone, although that stratagem would have been typical of the man.

Once the fishing party had gone, Michael insisted he and Caroline take coffee in the drawing room, having to overcome a great deal of reluctance on his sister's part, ostensibly because she was still tired and wanted an early night. She eventually opted for ordering cocoa, rather than coffee, and an agreement that they wouldn't sit up too long.

"You didn't manage to steal a nap this afternoon, then?" Michael asked, once they'd settled themselves.

"I couldn't get off. I suspect I was overtired. I'm paying for it now, though." She stifled a yawn, somewhat theatrically.

"Any idea what caused your bad night's sleep? Lily's teeth playing up again?"

"No. She was a lamb, as far as I know. You were on my mind."

"Was I?" Michael almost dropped his cup, convinced that his sister would evade any talk concerning their relationship.

"Can you doubt it? I kept thinking of you, at Broch." Caroline avoided his gaze, something she usually did when dispensing only half the truth. "All the memories that place would evoke. I was worried you'd find it upsetting. Especially after you got so wound up about the book of war poems you found here."

"Hm." It was a cogent reply, but Michael didn't believe it. He would normally have taken his sister's hands at this point, forcing her to look at him and to be frank, but he couldn't bear to touch her. "Caroline. Be honest with me. Wouldn't those worries have affected you two nights ago, before I went over there for lunch, rather than on my second visit? You're either totally befuddled from lack of sleep or you're telling lies. I can't decide which."

She glanced up at that, smiling ruefully. "Why do you have to know me so well?"

"You need to correct that, my dear. I *thought* I knew you well. I'm not sure what to think now."

"I'm sorry?"

"I've found out things I wish I'd never found out." He took a deep breath, steeling himself. "Thomas. I know about you and Thomas."

All colour drained from Caroline's face, belying the words which followed. "Me and Thomas? What *are* you talking about?"

"You had a fling with Thomas. That summer I wasn't on holiday here. The summer those pictures were taken." That simple accusation hadn't proved so hard to say; the rest of the conversation would be the challenge. "There's no point in denying what happened. Thomas confessed to Harry, and Harry told me yesterday. I couldn't believe my ears."

Caroline looked as though she'd argue her innocence again, then laid her cup down, spreading her hands in defeat. "Then I have to admit it's true."

"Oh, Caroline, how could you let something like that happen?"

"I don't know, I swear. It was an act of folly." Caroline clasped her hands together, winding the fingers about each other. "He wasn't himself that summer. I'd never seen him so lost and lonely. He was clearly upset because you'd argued."

"Really?" Part of Michael didn't want to believe that, because it would make excuses for Thomas and he didn't want to excuse the man, but part of him was pleased to hear that he'd been so badly missed. "In that case wouldn't an easier solution to his loneliness have been to get the pair of us in a room and encourage us to patch things up? Rather than make matters ten times worse between us?"

"There's no doubt it would have, but Thomas wouldn't be persuaded. You remember how stubborn he was. He didn't want to come crawling to you for forgiveness and neither did he want you pleading with him. The pair of you were just too pigheaded to make things work, without a miracle."

"And did you decide that it was a hopeless cause before or after you slept with him?"

"Oh, for goodness sake!" She grasped the arms of her chair, knuckles white with strain. "Do you honestly think I'm that calculating?"

"Caroline, I have no idea what to think." Michael slumped forward, head in hands, trying to get his thoughts into some sort of order. He felt her hand on his shoulder—not a welcome gesture, but he resisted shrugging it off. They'd never get to the bottom of what had happened if they couldn't be civil with each other.

"I can't express how sorry I am for what happened. It was an aberration, a once-off. I was mad to have let myself do such a thing, I promise."

He believed her, no matter how much he wanted to cast her in the role of scarlet woman who'd led his erstwhile lover astray.

"And please don't mention any of this to Eric. He has no idea what went on and I don't ever want him to."

"I have no intention of telling Eric. Nor Richard." That matter had to be broached too. "I know about him, as well. I know who his father was."

"Thomas was not his father." Caroline had evidently spoken louder than she'd intended, and she leaned closer, voice an insistent whisper. "We slept together but he didn't . . ."

"Get you pregnant?"

"Must you put it so crudely?"

"It's a pretty crude business, my dear." Michael knew he was risking overstepping the bounds of decency but didn't care. "Do you want me to remind you of exactly what you and Thomas did?"

Caroline flinched but faced him out. "You needn't remind me. It's something I've tried to block from my memory."

"So you say." Maybe she had tried to eliminate that night—or nights, or afternoon, or whenever it had been—from remembrance, although that seemed anathema to Michael. The memories of coupling with Thomas were seared into his consciousness and would never be easy to eliminate, even if those memories were now tarnished. Perhaps Caroline and Thomas's lovemaking hadn't had the same dazzling effect; he'd cling to the small consolation that notion provided.

"And, as I told you," Caroline continued, "he's not Richard's father. Eric is."

"Oh, for goodness' sake." Michael sighed, frustrated. "You may try to fool yourself on that count but you can't fool me, or Harry. Once you know what to look for, it's plain to see that Richard's the image of Thomas. And what about his birthmark? All the Carter-Clemence boys bear that. Are you saying his having the same mark is a mere coincidence?"

Caroline, thin lipped, sat in silence, apparently unwilling or unable to reply to the accusation.

Michael wasn't going to let her evade him. "If you want to keep silent, then we're going to be sitting here for a long time, because I'm determined to have an answer. It's too important a matter to just ignore."

"It's possible Thomas was his father, given the timings and the birthmark," she agreed, at last. "But only his father in the barest biological terms. As far as everything else is concerned, Eric has been Richard's father since the day he was born, and will carry on being so until the day one or other of them is no longer with us."

"I don't dispute any of that. Eric's a model father, much more so than I guess Thomas would ever have been. He was obviously not the man we believed him to be." Funny how Michael had now begun so clearly to recognise his lover's feet of clay. He'd been too besotted previously by love—and then grief—to have any clarity. Now the scales had fallen from his eyes. "Even if he tried to stake his claim in the child, you were right not to let him. Don't look so horrified. Harry's told me everything he knows."

"If that's the case, then Harry's not the man I thought he was. Couldn't he have been decent enough to keep the secret?"

"He might have, but he thought I already knew." For all the hurt Harry had caused, Michael was determined to leap to his defence. Any anger he'd felt towards the man had faded, eased out by fond recollections of their making love.

Caroline's eyebrows shot up. "Why should he think that?"

"I don't know." Michael lied, unwilling to reveal all his cards. "I guess he believed that either Thomas or you had told me, given that we were all so close. Or that I'd have been bright enough to put together the evidence of my own eyes." Best not to dwell too much on exactly what had been said the night before. That would risk exposing the feelings which had been awakened for Harry, and his brain wasn't working efficiently enough—he was starting to pay for his lack of sleep—to think on his feet. All effort had to go to the matter in hand. "He's got a point. I can't believe I hadn't suspected before now, although I suppose it's only obvious when you know what to look for. The way Richard walks, the way he sometimes smiles—"

"Don't." Caroline pressed her fingers to her temples. "Please. Don't you think I know that? Don't you think I see it every day, no matter how hard I try not to? I have to focus on what he's got in him that comes from Eric," she stated defiantly. "The mannerisms, the things he says, his extraordinary maturity. They didn't come from Thomas."

"I know they didn't, and thank God for that. And not just because they obscure the evidence of his paternity," he clarified. "He's better off being Eric's creation than Thomas's."

"I'm well aware of that too." Caroline, hand pressed to her eyes, was evidently as upset by this as Michael was. Maybe he was being too hard on her. What if Jimmy had been a barmaid, rather than a barman, and Michael had paid for his few hours of pleasure with a lifelong reminder? He imagined a letter finding him in France some months later, informing him of impending fatherhood, but couldn't imagine what his reaction would have been.

He took his sister's hand. "What would you have done if Thomas had made it home? Contrived a way to ignore him for the rest of his life?"

"Yes, if that would have protected my son. I didn't want anything further to do with him." At last, she looked him in the eye. "He spoiled everything. He's still spoiling it."

She'd obviously seen Thomas's feet of clay too, probably long before Michael had. He suspected they'd both been used by somebody who probably hadn't valued them as much as they'd valued him. Thomas had always shown a desire to get what he wanted by any means, but Michael had been blind to the implications. He patted her hand.

"I was mad to sleep with him, Michael. Don't think I did it just because he was handsome and charming. He was a dear friend, always had been, and he slipped beneath my guard." She glanced at Michael, then away again. "When you and he argued, was it because of me?"

"What?" Michael, mind increasingly befuddled, shook his head. "No. Of course not. We argued before any of this happened, remember? What would we have had to argue about that concerned you?"

"His liking me. He'd always liked me. That summer wasn't the first time he'd made a pass."

Stunned, Michael opened his mouth and shut it again. He let go of her hands, suddenly disturbed by her touch and gasping for air as though he were under a gas attack. How many more revelations could he take?

"It was the previous summer. I laughed it off, naturally," Caroline continued, perhaps unaware just how deep a wound she was inflicting. "Told him I was a respectable married woman and that he was too tipsy to know what he was doing, which I think was the case. I wondered later whether he'd mentioned it to you and if that's why you'd cut off all relations with him."

"Our argument was nothing to do with you," Michael rallied at last, fighting to regain his equilibrium. "It was over a stupid practical joke he played. And you said he . . . you . . ." he struggled to find the words, again, "*it* happened because he was upset about our quarrel. That makes no sense if he'd been chasing you before."

"You never talked so crudely before you went to France." Caroline frowned.

"Before I went to France, I had no idea that my sister had slept with my best friend. And you keep changing the explanation for why it happened."

She took a while to respond, perhaps getting her story straight. "He *was* upset, that summer, and that's why I gave in to him at last, after all his persistence. I got to the point I couldn't bear to see him so miserable."

"So you compensated for his unhappiness by indulging in an act that was going to bring more unhappiness, and to those closer to you, as well?" Michael snorted. "Those you loved a damn sight better than you loved Thomas?"

"Don't you understand? Thomas was never more than a friend. I *never* loved him. Not like you loved him."

Michael flinched, as surely as if he'd been struck by a piece of shrapnel. "I beg your pardon?"

"Oh, Michael, what is the point of us prevaricating anymore? We might as well be entirely frank with each other." She tentatively reached for his hand, then stopped short, no doubt aware that the touch would be rejected again. "I'm not naive. I know what goes on in the world, that there are men who prefer men. And if you now assure me that you're not one of that sort, then I clearly don't understand your character at all." She paused to let him respond, although Michael couldn't manage anything but a nod. "So I was right?"

"You were right," he forced out. Somewhere in all the despair, the load had eased a little in sharing the truth with somebody who'd been so close for so long, even if that closeness was now under threat.

"You and Thomas were more devoted than any other pair of people I've ever known. I could tell what you meant to him just by observing you together."

"Were we that obvious?" Had everybody been able to see what they'd been trying so hard to hide?

"No. Or at least I'd say only to those who knew you really well, and caught you in unguarded moments. I saw you two in plenty of those, and the looks you shared were unmistakable."

"Does the whole family know? Did you discuss my love life while I was off serving my country?"

"Now you're being ridiculous."

"I'm sorry. I'm all on eggshells at the moment."

"I know." She patted his arm. "And, so far as I'm aware, I'm the only one who twigged. Although, given my experience with Richard and Lily, it wouldn't surprise me if Mother has known as long as I have. She'd never mention it, under any circumstances. And it wouldn't stop her loving you."

"So I would hope." Laurie had once said something similar—that mothers were the first to know and the last to be told, if ever told at all. How many of them must have taken their son's secrets to the grave because the matter could never be discussed? Like Caroline could never have discussed Richard's paternity with him.

Caroline continued, blithely. "Eric thinks you're just one of those types who aren't fussed about women. He knows one or two surgeons who've simply no time for settling down. Dedicated to their work."

"I'm not that. But if that's the impression I give people, all well and good."

"I wish it didn't have to be like this." She smiled, lightly touching his face. "All I wanted was for you to be truly content."

Michael grabbed her hand, removing it from his cheek. "I want to believe that, but how can I when you betrayed the love I had for Thomas by sleeping with him?"

"Betrayed you? As you've pointed out, you two had already parted brass rags." Caroline took out her handkerchief, then dabbed at her eyes. "Let me try to explain. Mother always used to bring an album of photographs—to show Mrs. Carter-Clemence—and she did so again that year."

"Some habits never change." It had become a summer tradition, both families meeting for lunch during the holiday and catching up on their news always played a part. Sometimes the exchanges bordered on uncomfortable, with both sets of parents vying for their offspring's most impressive achievement. "Go on."

"Thomas always seemed to be hanging round High Top that summer, though. I don't pretend he was hanging around to be with me. One day everybody else had gone out on a trip to Padstow, so I thought I had the house to myself, but I came in here and found him mooning over the photograph album."

"You hadn't arranged things so that you could be alone together?" He shouldn't doubt her, but he couldn't help himself. Too many certainties had turned out to be lies.

"No!" It sounded like the truth. "He got as much of a shock at seeing me as I at him. It was clear he'd been looking at snaps of you, and it was equally clear that he'd been crying. I suspect he thought he'd be all on his own and free to wallow in old memories without fear of being caught." She wrung the handkerchief in her fingers. "I got him some tea, and we started to talk. Really talk, as we'd never done before. He didn't say so in as many words, but I knew he was trying to get across how you'd been so close and how you were now lost to him. I didn't have to read too much between the lines to see you were the love of his life."

Michael's thoughts warred against each other. Perhaps he should be grateful that he'd still had Thomas's heart, but the betrayal couldn't but hurt like hell, as much as the fragments in his leg. "Is that when you took him to your bed? Even though you knew how we felt about each other?"

"Do I have to keep saying that I'm sorry? I was wrong."

"So you say. And is that why you brought the photograph albums this summer? So you could look at the pictures of you and him together and gloat?" Michael flinched as Caroline raised her hand, expecting her to slap him, but she held back.

"Don't be ridiculous. If it had been up to me, I wouldn't have brought those photos at all, but Eric and Richard were insistent that we kept up the family tradition, and I could hardly argue. I tried to object that they took up unnecessary room, but that was overcome, and I couldn't tell the truth, could I? That it would be too painful for me."

"Painful? What about the pain you've inflicted on the rest of us?" Michael leaped up, eager to be on the move—flight rather than fight. "I can't carry on this conversation."

"Michael, stop this. I'm not some trollop who deliberately set out to seduce the man you loved." She rose, trying to take his arm.

"Just leave me alone."

"No. You were the one who raised the subject, and you'll damn well hear me out."

He'd never heard his sister swear before; the shock stopped him in his tracks.

"Michael, what is it you want from me? If I apologised a hundred times it wouldn't make it not have happened. I can't change the past, only the present."

She was right. "I don't know what I want from you. That's the problem."

"You need a good night's sleep. We both do." She reached for his face, then drew her hand back. "Please forgive me. If not tonight, then at some point in the future."

"I can't promise that." He touched her hand, briefly. "I need time to think."

Michael left the drawing room and stumbled upstairs to his bedroom, petrified that Eric and the boys might return and find him in such a state. He doubted he had the inner resources to make a good fist of lying. Going through the process of washing and undressing like an automaton, he found his mind kept occupied with the latest revelations.

Irrespective of his tiredness, he couldn't yet face his bed, so sat on the windowsill, looking out on a glorious night, unseeing. No matter how he tried to clear his mind, a procession of faces passed through his brain, each one bringing a question. Why had Thomas done it if he'd still loved him? To get his own back because he'd blamed Michael for their splitting? And why had he made passes at Caroline before any split had occurred? Had it simply been that he'd needed to get his end away and Caroline had been convenient? The treasonous thought that *she* might have been the one he really wanted all along, and that Michael had been the dalliance, was too painful to consider. Thomas had surely never looked at Caroline the way he'd looked at *him*; she'd said as much.

The return of the fishing party, noisy enough as they came through the garden and audible throughout the house once they were inside, stirred him to action. He'd left the door of his room slightly ajar, and as he went to close it, heard Caroline greeting them, saying that she'd stayed up to celebrate the return of her fish-conquering heroes. Her ability to pretend all was as before proved stunning. An admirable quality or not? He didn't want to tackle such difficult questions any further.

Once in bed, he managed to get off quite quickly, body too exhausted to let his rambling thoughts keep sleep at bay, but he woke in the night streaming with sweat, unsure of where he was. He'd been having a nightmare in which he and Thomas had been out in no-man's-land, fighting not the Germans but each other. Rather than bayonet, they'd been using just fists and feet, Marquis of Queensberry rules discarded in the heat of their particular battle. He'd felt such hatred for the man during that dream, determined to punish him for all the pain he'd caused, not the least of which was going off and getting himself killed.

The voice of guilt—never far away—nagged at him again for his contribution to Thomas's death. If he'd only had the guts to talk to Thomas in the weeks after their argument, when they might have made up, then Caroline wouldn't have happened, and Thomas might have been less careless of his own skin. He might have survived to return home, and they could have resumed their relationship. That would have meant no coupling with Harry, of course. More importantly, it would have meant no Richard, or a different Richard, entirely Eric's child.

That prospect unsettled him most out of the what-ifs which whirred through his mind.

He should never have returned to Porthkennack; he should have forgotten about the place and all the memories it held. If he hadn't been on this holiday, they'd have never have met Harry and if he'd not slept with Harry, the great family secret might never have come into the open.

The crushing weight of responsibility kept further sleep at bay, until the first light appeared and the birds' dawn chorus lulled him off into an uneasy doze.

CHAPTER TWELVE

Next morning over breakfast, Michael had to admit that Caroline was still giving a creditable performance. He'd expected her to plead a migraine or some such, and take tea and toast in her bedroom instead, but she was present, correct, putting a brave face on things, and looking a sight less raddled than he was. The whole performance gave no clue that anything of import had happened, but then wouldn't she have become adept at hiding the truth by now?

He, on the other hand, felt distinctly out of sorts, barely managing more than some toast and tea. His head throbbed, his stomach felt as though an army had marched over it, and his thoughts couldn't settle on matters other than the events of the last thirty-six hours. Caroline was conspicuously considerate of and attentive to him—which made things worse—to the point where he had to apologise for not being fit company for anyone, excuse himself, and set off for the drawing room to be alone with a book and his own thoughts. Nobody tried to dissuade him, not even Richard, which showed everyone was wary of his mood.

Michael found a mystery book and tried to read it, but the story failed to keep his attention. He didn't fancy leaving the room so soon, not ready yet to face any other family members, so he rummaged out a pack of cards to lay out an elaborate game of patience, which would require just the right amount of concentration. He'd always had a deck with him in France, often relying on a game with colleagues or alone to bring relaxation and comfortable remembrances of home.

The cards worked their quiet magic, Michael immersing himself in the simple act of planning which one to place where, assessing the potential configurations and odds of success, in a way reminiscent of warfare. But then so much in life was now reminiscent of those days, and Michael was coming to the conclusion that he'd never shake off the effects of his time in France. To add to all his other woes, his leg was bad today; it hadn't given him jip like this in an age. Had he overdone it on the bicycle—or in Harry's bed—or was there a psychological effect coming into play, his body mirroring his mental state?

Whatever the cause, he could do without the pain.

A loud rap at the front door caught Michael's attention, although he assumed it was simply the postman or another such visitor. Only when Harry's deep, unmistakable tones sounded from the hall did he—literally—sit up and take notice. What did Harry want at High Top? If he'd come to rebuild burnt bridges with Michael, then Michael's raw nerves weren't ready to tackle such a tricky conversation. He wondered about making an escape, but that would have meant exiting through the window, and pretending to be asleep wouldn't convince anyone, so he grabbed a newspaper and tried to appear deeply interested in it as the door to the room opened.

"Look who's here," Caroline said, with no trace of forced geniality, entering the drawing room with Harry in her wake and wearing her friendliest smile.

"Hello." Michael rose to shake the visitor's hand; the normal rules had to be obeyed, even though they were all playing pretend.

"I came over to invite everyone to lunch, tomorrow. I realised I'd failed in my duty to return your hospitality." Harry smiled that smile, the effect of which went straight to Michael's trousers. The smile he'd worn—the only thing he'd worn—as he'd posed for his portrait. It, fuelled by memory of what had happened subsequently, was working again. Thank the Lord Michael had the newspaper in his hands to provide cover.

"That's very kind of you. I'm sure the lads will be delighted."

"They've been going on about Broch nonstop these last few days. They've almost driven us mad," Caroline confided, breezily.

Harry, too, did his part in keeping up the social pretences. "I hope it isn't a disappointment for them. They'll be expecting a cross between the Zoological Gardens and the White City, I suppose." His smile, now awkward rather than lascivious, was touching enough to breach Michael's defences. "Reality always pales compared to imagination."

At that—surely a reference to Thomas—Michael sat down again unsteadily, letting the newspaper drop.

"You don't look well, dear." Caroline touched his arm, solicitously.

"It's only a headache," Michael snapped. No wonder he didn't look well. Would anyone, if their world had changed irreparably and everybody around him seemed to be carrying on as normal?

"Steady on, old chap." Harry, turning his hat in his hands, frowned concernedly. "Is there anything we can do?"

Michael took a deep breath before touching his sister's hand; Harry needn't know they weren't seeing eye to eye. Not yet, anyway. "Sorry, Caroline. I've had this pounding head all morning. I could do with some fresh air to clear it."

"What about a walk by the sea?" Harry suggested. "A touch of the old ozone to work its wonders?"

Michael hesitated. To agree or not? Harry was bound to offer to accompany him on the walk, although that might be a more enticing prospect than sitting alone with his thoughts of having to make pleasant conversation with his family. At least with Harry he wouldn't need to pretend. He put on the heartiest voice he could manage. "Why not? Would you fancy keeping me company? Not that I seem to be decent company for anyone this morning."

"I will, then, as it'll clearly be doing the family a favour by removing you for an hour." Harry made Caroline an elaborate bow, said that he'd see her the next day, then accompanied Michael out of the room.

"Oh, well, yes, tomorrow it is." Caroline's voice sounded after them.

"Thanks for asking me along," Harry said, when they were out of earshot. "I wasn't sure you'd want to spend time with me again."

"Perhaps I'm only being polite. Or perhaps you're the lesser of two evils." They went out into the garden, taking the route down onto the beach, along the paths where Michael and Thomas had walked so often, although they'd never been as sombre or had such a weight hanging between them as he and Harry did. "And didn't you rather force my hand on that count, by inviting us all to lunch?"

Harry shrugged. "As you said, perhaps I was just being polite. You could find an excuse not to attend, if you feel so strongly about being with me."

"I don't know what I feel." Michael halted, as the full sweep of the bay came into sight. "Except for the obvious fact that I'm not sure I'm fit to be around today."

"I'm sorry if I've played a part in that." Harry stared out to sea. "The other reason I came here was to deliver my apology in person. I'm sorry for what I blurted out."

Michael studied him: the dark patches beneath Harry's eyes suggested he'd slept badly too. While Michael still struggled with the notion of forgiving Caroline, and Thomas had gone beyond the pale, pardoning Harry suddenly required no debate. "You're forgiven. I think." He walked on, but Harry didn't follow, still gazing out to sea. "Come on."

"Hold your horses. You get to see this every day." Harry took a sweeping view of the bay, then set off again. "The one disadvantage to Broch is that you can't see the ocean, except from the servants' quarters and only then a peep. Perhaps the place would benefit from that forced clarity of vista."

Michael, not daring to reply, led the way down to the beach. Best to keep the conversation on uncontroversial topics. "This is the first thing I used to do when we came here for holidays. Hare down to where I could glimpse the sea and sand. Get the smell, hear the gulls."

"I can understand that. There's a touch of magic in it."

"Yes." It *had* been magical back then, and clearly remained so for Richard and George. It even retained some of its wonder for Michael, no matter how much events seemed determined to tarnish his enjoyment. "I'd been reluctant to return here, but the first glimpse of the sea—untrammelled by being on a troop ship—changed my mind, at least for a while. You only came to High Top the once, as I recall."

"When you were staying here, yes. I also came the summer . . ." Harry paused. "Sorry. Me and my big gob again."

"You *can* talk about Thomas, and what happened that year, you know. I may not ever be able to reconcile myself to those events, and they've got me like a bear with a sore head today, but I refuse to let matters spoil the rest of my life." Brave words. Perhaps if he kept using them, he'd come to believe them.

Harry laid his hand on Michael's arm. "You're a good man. Better than any of my bloody family deserve to have as a friend."

Michael patted Harry's hand, then shook it free and walked on. "Don't be so hard on yourself. Thomas's actions are not your responsibility."

"Aren't they? I've been racking my conscience over it these last two nights. I sometimes feel as though me and my family wreck everything we touch."

"Isn't that rather overdramatising things?"

"You don't know the half of it. I didn't know the half of it until after my father died. All sorts of things are coming out of the woodwork."

Michael didn't probe. If Harry wanted to tell him, it would happen. "Really?"

"Yes. The house and estate and everything to do with them haven't moved with the times, for a start. Father was too obsessed with keeping Broch as it was, a bastion of prewar values, whatever they were supposed to be, rather than going along with worthwhile changes. Like better sanitation for the estate cottages, for a start." Harry sighed. "I wish he'd been bothered about the implications of what he was doing. There's a lot to be done, which is why I'm spending so much time trying to get together a sensible plan for doing it."

"I'd offer my help, but I'm not sure I have any relevant expertise."

"Would you? I may keep you to that, even if it's simply for moral support. Assuming the offer wasn't just you being polite."

"No, not at all," Michael lied.

"Thank you. It feels such an uphill task. Father became quite obsessed with fighting any changes. He wouldn't have let me do that work on the outbuildings, not approving of motor transport."

"Things move on. You can't resist them forever." Whether it was progress or the slow, steady emergence of the truth. "Begs the question of why he agreed to the place being turned into a convalescent home."

"He didn't. Mother wanted that, as soon as was decent after his death. Sooner than many people thought decent, although she had her reasons." Harry touched Michael's arm, making him turn to face him. "Mother didn't move only to be closer to Olivia. She's had enough of the place. Not all the memories she has of there are pleasant ones, and I'm not just referring to the loss of my brother."

"I'm not sure I follow you."

"There's no reason you should. We've not exactly washed the family's dirty linen in public, and what the Grays know is a small part of the whole. Thomas was, I'm afraid, his father's child, by nature and nurture. He wasn't the first to . . . um . . . take his pleasures where he shouldn't." Harry tapped his left palm with his right fist. "There's at least one by-blow of Father's in the area, and there could be more, for all I know. I have a half brother, never acknowledged except by the evidence of his features."

Michael recalled the conversation about the young man with the red hair, the resemblance he'd born to Thomas. "Not the lad who was a gardener here, for heaven's sake?"

"That's the one. He must have got the mop of hair from his mother, because that colour doesn't run in our family."

"It probably helped to blind *his* supposed father to his true provenance." Assuming his mother was married. "He served and was injured. Eric was talking to somebody and got all the gossip. He's still making a go of things. Handyman."

Harry kicked at a stone, sending a stream of sand flying. "I think he's always been a bit of a jack-of-all-trades. He came and worked for us sometimes, which distressed Mother terribly."

"Dear God." What further revelations were going to emerge? He'd always thought the Carter-Clemence family to be as happy as his own, although now he knew the Grays had a shared skeleton in the closet. "The old man was never flaunting his adultery?"

"I wouldn't put it past him. My father was an extremely calculating man."

Michael shivered, despite the sun's warmth. "How many more of his bastards are there?"

"I have no idea, and frankly I don't want to know." Harry shrugged. "I'm sorry. I guess I'm shattering your illusions about our family."

"You'd better tell me everything, if there *is* more to tell. Get all the shocks over and done with at once." Michael braced himself.

"I'm not sure there are many more, apart from the machinations of my father's mind. That by-blow of a gardener is younger than me, so no threat to the legitimate inheritance, and I wouldn't be at all surprised if that entered into the old man's calculations." Harry snorted. "He'd have expected Thomas to fulfil his part in continuing the line, and if that failed, he had me. It would have been a hell of a blow if he realised there was no chance of his younger son producing an heir."

"Why not? Just because your tastes run to men, that means nothing." Michael shrugged. "Plenty of marriages of convenience have produced an heir, then left the father free to pursue his own desires, whether they be male or female."

Harry studied him sidelong. "I'd never have believed you could sound so cynical."

"I've every right to. I didn't think Thomas could have done the deed with my sister, but I was wrong, wasn't I?"

Harry laid his hand on Michael's arm. He didn't shake it free this time. "You're not wrong as far as *I'm* concerned. The whole world would have to change for me to want to take a wife."

"Then we're in the same boat." Michael favoured his erstwhile lover with a smile. "If your father was so concerned for the family line, couldn't Olivia have obliged him legitimately, even if neither of his sons managed to? Did that not come into his so-called calculations?"

"I'm not sure poor Olivia came into his mind much at all. The Carter-Clemence men have never really had too much regard for the distaff side."

"No. I begin to see that now." As Michael had lain awake the night before, racking his memory for any signs of attraction between Thomas and Caroline that he might have seen had he not been blinded by love. But time and again he'd come back to the man's seeming indifference to and dislike for women. How could he have known him so well and not known him at all?

"Still, this is rather a moot point," Harry said. "Broch has a rightful heir, doesn't it? Your Richard."

"Very true. Was that why Thomas was so adamant to be recognised as Richard's father? To prove he'd secured the lineage for the estate?" And maybe let him return to pursuing men, if that really had been his preference.

"I think that would have played a part. Perhaps he'd already guessed that I wasn't likely to produce an heir." Harry bent, picked up some loose stones and sent them flying, one by one, onto the sand.

"Anyway, none of this is relevant." Michael sighed. "I doubt Richard will ever get the opportunity to explore his birthright. Not while Eric's still alive and maybe not after he's gone. Who'd tell him? He won't find out from me."

"Nor me. I've learned my lesson about blabbing." Harry shuddered. "You look awful by the way."

"Thank you so much. You do wonders for my ego." Michael grinned. "You look pretty dreadful yourself."

"Touché." Harry gathered up some more stones, and sent them flying. "If you want me to shower you with compliments, this is neither the place nor the time. I was concerned that you were still feeling the effects of your headache."

"Oh." Michael had forgotten he was supposed to be suffering. "No, the sea air's sorted that. Just as you said it would. The rest is the need for a decent night's sleep. You know, I could manage fine in France, grabbing shut-eye as and when, but now I've turned soft." He gazed up at the piercingly blue sky, at gulls swooping and mewing. Such a bright, sparkling day called for clearing the air completely. "Trouble is, I've made a pig's ear of things too. Yesterday, what little diplomacy I possessed deserted me."

Harry took his arm. "Let's find somewhere to sit and you can tell Uncle Harry all about it."

"That sounds a grand idea. There's a nice spot along here. Come on."

Not half a mile from High Top, a series of deep caverns ran back from the base of the cliffs. Michael's parents had always forbidden him and his sister to play there, and Caroline had put the same injunction on her son and his friend. If Richard was any part a Gray, and certainly any part a Carter-Clemence, he'd surely feel the same desire Michael had felt to explore the illicit caverns, and that appeared to be a damn sight more dangerous than it had been in the past. There'd been at least one landslip—possibly a series of them, given the nature of the jumble of rocks and earth—and the gaping maw of the cave was now largely fallen in. What had been an exciting exploration would now be perilous to the point of lunacy. Such a shame.

The caves had also been another place Michael and Thomas had explored—and where they'd explored each other on moonless summer evenings. Harry had wanted to tag along on their adventures, and never been allowed.

"I remember this old place," Harry said, coming to a halt by the tumble of stones. "Such a shame it's too dangerous to go investigating there now."

"I was thinking the same."

The large, flat rocks in front of the cave mouths were just out of range of any fallen debris, still providing a pleasant place to sit or to sunbathe, but they were empty of occupants, with people being wary, perhaps, of the rock falls. Michael found a comfortable place to plonk their backsides, with an upright stone to lean against as they sat.

"Your failure of diplomacy. What happened?"

"I couldn't keep my mouth shut, I'm afraid. You talked about espionage agents, but a fine bloody one I'd have made." Michael smiled, ruefully. Funny how a man who kept his love affairs discrete so efficiently hadn't even been able to manage twenty-four hours knowing the family secret without blabbing. "I confronted Caroline about what had happened."

"Ah. I see." Harry focussed on his fingers, drawing lazy lines on the surface of the rock as they'd once drawn lines on Michael's skin. "How did she take it?"

"How do you think?" Michael shut his eyes, wishing that he could find the words to even begin to explain his thoughts. He let the sea breeze wash over him, urging it to clear his mind, but it wasn't obliging. "She pretended she didn't know what I was talking about, then denied it. And all the rest."

"The rest?"

Michael sighed. "Sorry to be maddeningly evasive, but I'm not ready to go through the ins and outs of what she told me. Every time I think I understand what went on, I get a new insight and realise I know nothing at all. What you've just said about your father adds to my general feeling of confusion."

They lay back on the rocks, unspeaking, basking like seals in the sun.

Harry broke the silence. "You and Thomas were always poking about round here." Michael, shading his eyes, turned to face him. "We were. We loved it almost as much as the boathouse."

"They're the sort of places boys love. Secret places. Special places." Harry produced his alluring smile. "George and Richard will have the same."

"I hope they aren't exactly the same for them. Not yet, anyway." Michael snorted. "*Secret* and *special* are the words, though. We did it in both of these." He'd never told anyone that, not even Laurie when he'd provided a shoulder to cry on; liberating the secret felt cathartic. Maybe Harry had experienced something similar a few nights back, in which case perhaps Michael should try a little sympathy. "But then we did it wherever and whenever we could, as you can imagine."

Harry crinkled his brow, clearly puzzled. "I'm sorry? You've lost me now."

"The sun's addling your wits." Thank goodness there was nobody within earshot. "Thomas and I. Going at it hammer and tongs. Here. In the boathouse. In his bedroom."

Harry still frowned. "Arguing?"

"Are you being deliberately obtuse, to make me say it aloud? Going at *it*. What we did in your bed, only Thomas and I did it in a damn sight more places." Michael registered surprise and horror plastered across Harry's face. "Surely you knew Thomas and I were lovers? You must have known."

"Of course not." Harry's ashen face gave credence to his words. "I had no bloody idea."

Michael pressed his fingers to his forehead. Had he actually gone mad the last few days? Was this some delayed reaction to his experiences in France, manifesting itself in imagined conversations where everything he'd assumed was true was being stripped away? He glanced at Harry, who was all too real and all too evidently anxious. He'd received as great a shock as Michael had two days previously.

"But I thought you *must* have realised. All those hints when I came to lunch, about wondering what Thomas and I had got up to."

"That was just a coincidence, I swear. Do you truly think I could have let those secrets slip so casually if I'd been aware of the true extent of your feelings for him?"

That seemed to be the truth, as well. "Didn't you have your suspicions back in those days?"

"No. Honestly." Harry ran his hands through his hair, pulling it back from his forehead to reveal a hint of the old birthmark as the sun and wind hit his fair skin. "Thomas was so unlike me, for a start. I never dreamed he could feel as I do. And he seemed to like girls, given that he flirted with enough of them. The business with Caroline just went to prove it. No wonder you were so upset."

"Can you blame me?"

"Not at all. It's inexcusable that I should have let out the truth so inconsiderately. If I'd known . . ." Harry shrugged.

"You'd not have said anything?"

"Probably not. Although I might have been more confident about making a pass at you." Harry winked, although the sorrow in his eyes couldn't be easily hidden.

Michael, torn between the voice in his head which said he needed to tell Harry how much he'd hurt him and the other which told him to be kind, chose the latter. "That's another reason I thought you knew. Otherwise how had you come to the conclusion that my inclinations ran the way they do if you hadn't already suspected?"

"Like I do with any man I fancy. When I was a lad, I'd have had no idea, but now I can see the signs with the eyes of experience." Harry gently patted Michael's shoulder. "All I knew back then was that I liked you and that you appeared to be Thomas's private property. As a friend."

"That's the illusion we wanted to preserve," Michael conceded.

"It explains so much, with the benefit of hindsight. That's what riled him so much when I used to tag along after you two. Not wanting me to encroach on his territory. You, I mean."

"Not only that. Holidays were the only time we had the opportunity to be alone together, and we wanted to make the most of every opportunity to do it." Michael jerked his thumb over his shoulder, towards the cave. "Minds constantly in our trousers."

Harry chuckled. "*Plus ça change* in your case."

"Behave." Michael remembered what Caroline had said about anybody observing him and Thomas in an unguarded moment. Surely Harry had been witness to those. "If you could see that I was Thomas's 'private property' shouldn't you have guessed we were lovers?

And what about just now, when I said that I was surprised Thomas could have done the deed. What did you think I meant?"

"I thought you were talking about committing adultery. You'd referred to men pursuing their pleasures with either sex. I'm sorry to be so dim-witted, but while it may add up for you, it's taking me longer to grasp."

The question which had been forming in Michael's mind couldn't be restrained further. "When he told you about his affair with Caroline, didn't he mention me? I know he wasn't likely to confess all his . . . peccadilloes, but he might have hinted at something."

Harry gave him a sidelong glance, then shook his head. "He never mentioned anything about it, except for saying that he'd let you down, but I assumed that was about your friendship. And if I'd had any suspicions about your relationship, then that stuff about Caroline would have muddied the waters."

Renewed anger at Thomas was putting Michael on edge once more. "Men do have sex with both. And enjoy it."

"I know. I'm not stupid. Thomas liked girls well enough."

"So it appears." Michael snorted. "He always told me that was a smokescreen, because your father kept telling him he'd soon have to find the right girl and settle down. He said he'd been creating a pretence of following the man's wishes. I suppose the chances are that was a load of rot."

"I have an awful feeling you could be spot on. He managed to hide plenty from both of us."

Maybe from all three, if Caroline could be included. Michael gave Harry a smile, although the man seemed both tense and preoccupied.

"There's more to tell, isn't there?" Michael asked, forcing a brave smile. "I said I wanted to know everything."

"Am I so transparent?" Harry kept his eyes fixed on the rocks.

"I'm afraid so. More transparent than your brother, evidently."

"I'd rather not say anything. I don't want to see you hurt again."

"Bloody hell, man!" Michael slapped at the rocks, immediately regretting it as a sharp stab of pain shot up his arm. "I'm not a blushing maiden. I've seen and done stuff the last few years that would make anyone's hair stand on end."

"Don't make it so hard on us both. I'm only trying to do the honourable thing."

"'Honourable'?" Michael would have landed a punch on Harry's chin if his hand didn't already smart so much. "You can and you will tell me. If we have to sit here all day, waiting." A sudden, blinding revelation—what Michael's batman would have called a strike of the bleeding obvious—hit him. "Did Thomas have other women?"

"Whether he *had* them I genuinely couldn't say, but he had plenty hanging around him here during holidays or when he was on leave. One or two he seemed pretty keen on." Harry had at last found the courage to face him. "Caroline's the only one I know of that he bedded."

"There could have been more." Michael puffed out his cheeks. "There were plenty of obliging French mademoiselles to be found."

"I can't imagine him paying for the pleasure."

"Really? Given what we've learned, can either of us say that we know what Thomas would have done or thought?" Michael's understanding of the man was becoming increasingly fuzzy, as though seen through a glass, darkly and at a distance. "He's become a mystery to me. All I can say for certain is that we were lovers. And I thought we were in love."

"Perhaps you were. Perhaps you're reading far too much into things."

"What do you mean by that?" Michael's anger, never too far from the surface the last few days, blew fiercer.

"I'm trying to understand matters in the light of what I've only just found out. It's possible that it simply was a single indiscretion, a moment of madness between him and Caroline he later regretted because it was contrary to his true nature."

Michael bit his lip. Should he tell Harry what Caroline had alleged, about previous passes Thomas had made? What would be the point? "I'd like to believe that's true. I somehow doubt it," he said, when the silence was becoming uncomfortable.

"I'm so sorry." Harry pressed his fists to his eyes, like an upset child. "I'd say that a million times, but it wouldn't change the past, would it, no matter how much either of us want it to."

The unintended echo of Caroline's words touched a raw nerve.

"'Change the past'? My God, I want to tear it all down, moment by moment. I wish I'd never met your brother."

Harry looked across, eyes red from where he'd rubbed them. "You don't mean that. It's the anger talking."

"Don't tell me what I do or don't mean. You have no idea." Michael jumped down from the rock, brushing the sand from his trousers as the disciples had been told to brush the dust of an unfriendly village from their feet. "I can perhaps forgive you, if you truly didn't know that Thomas and I were lovers, but it's going to take a long time for me to forgive her, and I'm not sure I can ever absolve him. If he was here, now, I'd beat him to a pulp."

Harry stared, unspeaking, just shaking his head. That mute reaction proved as infuriating as a full-blown row.

"What are you gawping at?"

"I'm not gawping. I'm wondering how the hell we're going to get through tomorrow. I can't rescind the invitation, not now."

"I'm not expecting you to. I won't be there. I'll find some excuse— it won't reflect badly on you, so don't worry." Michael flicked a last speck of sand from his shirt.

"I don't care if it reflects badly on me or not." Harry, standing on the rock, towered over Michael in a manner both intimidating and exasperating. "I don't particularly care what anybody thinks. Only you. Your good opinion is the solitary one that counts."

Michael wanted to make a smart response, but words failed him just when they were most needed. He managed a pathetic, "Oh, fuck off, will you Harry?" before turning on his heels and heading back for High Top, ignoring the call of, "Michael. Michael!" behind him.

CHAPTER THIRTEEN

When Michael got back to High Top, still in a vile temper despite a long roundabout walk to try to calm down, the place was deserted, the family having all gone off to do some shopping in Porthkennack.

He found a note from Caroline explaining that they hadn't been able to wait for him, unsure of what his plans were, and that the cook would provide for him had he not lunched elsewhere. Another note, from Eric, which he found in his room when he went to change his shoes, asked if he'd be able to book transport to take them to Broch the next day. The joke that if they all tried to fit on his bicycle, somebody would fall off, couldn't hide his obvious underlying worry. He said he was taking Caroline and the boys for a jaunt as she seemed slightly out of sorts and he hoped she wasn't coming down with something, as he'd heard that scarlet fever was about and they'd never face Louise if they sent George back all spotty.

How much Eric knew or guessed about what had been going on remained a mystery, but Michael wouldn't have bet against his having a pretty shrewd idea that something was amiss or at the very least that brother and sister were not on the best of terms at present. Suddenly feeling the pangs of hunger, he pottered down to the kitchen, profusely apologetic for bothering the staff at such a time, and was presented with a collation of cold salmon, new potatoes, and fresh salad which was fit for a king.

He ate in the garden, the expanse of lawn and shrubs not feeling as empty as the dining room would have done, though he frankly had no desire to be with anyone—not even Richard and George—nor to risk facing questions about Broch or Harry or anything related to them.

It had certainly worked out well that he'd been left on his own for a few hours, to give his temper some chance of returning to an even keel, but his hands had been tied about tomorrow. Although, perhaps, he could book the vehicle before springing that reason to cry off that he'd promised himself. Perhaps he could feign illness, something that would get him out of both dinner that evening and the next day's expedition. What did the initial symptoms of scarlet fever consist of and would Eric spot he was feigning?

Michael returned his plate to the kitchen, refused the offer of cake, fetched his bicycle clips, and set off. There used to be a garage in Porthkennack that hired out horse-drawn carriages and was said to have advanced to a motor-powered char-a-banc or two, so that would be his first port of call. Right at the start of the holiday, Richard, who'd had to suffer the boasting from one of his pals earlier in the summer about the marvellous outings his family had taken in such a vehicle, had pleaded—most politely—if they might possibly take any opportunity to do the same. The mode of conveyance had seemed to have acquired as mythical a status as Broch itself.

Michael would do his very best to oblige his nephew, especially as the lad would have to cope with the disappointment of Michael not being there to enjoy the ride.

Having this quest to occupy his brain might help to keep some of the unwanted thoughts at bay, and if he ended up having to try two or three places, it would fill an afternoon that was beginning to look horribly bare. Harry had created a niche in his heart, a niche now empty. Michael recognised the first stages of falling in love—the aching yearning for the lover, that could only be satisfied by their presence—and just as with Thomas, the argument hadn't ended the longing. He tucked his trousers into his socks, aware that the cycle ride to the garage now had the potential to become morose, allowing Michael to wallow in thoughts which had gone from anger to sadness, but he focussed on the road; one accident, with its life-altering aftermath would be enough for one summer.

He came to a junction, then decided to take the long way round; he hadn't gone along this particular road since before the war, and the unexpected changes—new houses, what appeared to be a new cottage hospital—took him aback. As did the sight of a young man, hardly more than his age and clearly a veteran of the conflict, sitting in a wheelchair in the sunshine.

Michael had seen plenty of the maimed—and the mad—before, but the spectacle of this chap struck him to the core. He had a pinned-up sleeve and one leg of his trousers cut short at the knee, but he was managing to smile as he drank in the warmth of the sun on his face. Michael had rarely seen an injured man look so content, apart perhaps from when one of the men sustained a wound that destined him for Blighty, likely on a permanent basis.

That could be you. If that shell had landed a foot closer, or you'd been in a different part of the line. Yet he's happy and you're not. You have your health, a job, a loving family, and if you could only swallow your damn pride and forgive Caroline—not just in words but deep in your heart— then you can enjoy all of them. Your lover, as well.

All of it easier said than done, though.

He set his face for the garage and pedalled like the wind; if he stopped contemplating the problem, maybe his subconscious could find the right solution, because he had no sodding idea of what to do about the bloody business.

His return to High Top, job done, had something of the return of the prodigal about it, with Richard and George racing up to greet him, demanding if he'd been successful in hiring something, and could it possibly be a char-a-banc. His plan to avoid everyone would need revision, and quickly.

"Yes. Mission safely accomplished." Michael grinned. "Did you think I'd let you down?"

"Not you, Uncle!" Richard hooted, grabbing George's hands and spinning him round.

"You'll make yourselves so dizzy you'll be too sick to go on the outing." Michael tousled his nephew's hair once he'd come to a halt. "It'll be here at eleven o'clock tomorrow morning, so you better be ready, shoes shining, best bib and tucker and all the rest. Don't oversleep."

"I never oversleep." Richard sounded mortally offended.

"He'd miss breakfast for one thing," George chipped in, pinching his pal's arm.

"That would be an awful calamity to befall a chap." Michael ruffled his nephew's hair.

"You set your alarm too, Uncle." Richard's fleeting look of anxiety, soon hidden, pricked at Michael's conscience. How terribly upset his nephew would be if he excused himself the visit to Broch. The choice was clear: saving his pride and disappointing those he loved, or swallowing it and pleasing them.

"He won't stop talking about this place Broch." George rolled his eyes. "I've seen every picture of it and heard every story."

"Perhaps you should be a correspondent for the *Daily Mail*, Richard." Michael clapped his shoulder. "They're fond of hyperbole. Especially from people who've never experienced what they're talking about. I hope it lives up to all he's said, George."

Richard's offended frown had turned to uncertainty. "I've never even thought that about that. It won't be a disappointment, will it, Uncle?"

"No, I don't think it will. So long as the weather holds, you'll find plenty of things to amuse young men. Just be careful near that lake— it's not as shallow or as safe as it looks."

The boys' eyes widened in awe and gleeful apprehension. "Are there fish in it? Can we take our gear?" Richard enquired.

"There always used to be. And yes, I'd have thought so. So long as you've got an adult with you."

"Father can be with me, and you can be in charge of George." Richard nodded decisively, the matter evidently signed and sealed in his opinion. How could Michael refuse?

"It seems like I have the easier job, then. I'm sure George will be sensible." If this meant having to face Harry again, he would simply have to manage that, safe in the knowledge that he'd never have to repeat the experience if he didn't want to. His and Harry's paths hadn't crossed in these intervening years, and there was little risk of that happening in future.

"Hurray!" The boys whooped delightedly at the prospect of the next day's fun, earning a reprimand from Caroline—who was strolling towards them with Eric on her arm—and a warning that if they didn't learn to behave, they'd be the only ones of the party not going on the outing. Michael doubted that such a threat would ever be enacted, although it had the desired effect. Looking suitably ashamed of himself, Richard suggested he and George might go and play a nice safe board game until tea, a suggestion which won his mother's approval.

"We'll be in soon," she said. "I don't like that sky."

Eric glanced up at the darkening clouds. "We're in for a downpour. Just as well, perhaps. This muggy air needs clearing."

He didn't appear to be casting any aspersions on the atmosphere between brother and sister, so Michael took the remark at face value. "Yes. It's been horribly muggy."

"How's the head?" Caroline asked, once she'd watched the boys safely into the house and made sure they weren't off to cause mischief somewhere.

"Better than it was. If I go and put my feet up for an hour before dinner, I should be right as rain." And if it turned out that he couldn't face dinner, then the headache could get suddenly worse and he'd take beef tea in his room.

"I knew that walk with Harry would do you the world of good." Caroline's face remained unreadable, and the presence of Eric ensured that Michael couldn't ask her what she meant.

"The ozone," he averred, edging away. "Excuse me. I can hear forty winks calling my name."

Eric nodded. "Don't oversleep. It's fresh mackerel for dinner."

"I hope you won't pretend you caught them last evening, because I won't believe you." Michael waved airily and headed for the front door, keen to get inside before the heavens opened and before he could be nabbed for further conversation.

What *had* Caroline meant? Did she see the same signs between him and Harry that she'd seen between him and Thomas? Or was he reading too much into every sentence, looking for interpretations which weren't actually there?

He bounded up the stairs at the first rumble of thunder, reaching his bedroom just in time to shut the windows against the deluge. The chances were he'd not get any rest, as Lily found storms unsettling; he could hear rumblings from the nursery already, matching the ones outside. Poor Richard and George weren't likely to be able to play their game in peace, and they all needed to garner their energy for the next day.

Richard's obsession with Broch—part of his heritage, after all—was intriguing. Was it a sign of an element deeply ingrained within his breeding, the mark of Thomas lying within him as sure as the birthmark had been his father's external manifestation? Perhaps, again, he was reading too much into things, and it had another, simpler, explanation, the result of Richard and Eric's interest in old photographs and old stories. Richard was a bright, mature boy, so there was always a chance that he'd subconsciously detected something when his mother had discussed Broch, in a similar way to how he'd picked up on Caroline's wish for soldiers to return home from the war, or focussed, fascinated, on the picture of the man—Thomas—with the unruly hair.

It had to be possible that deep in his soul he had recognised a connection with the young man in the photograph. If so, given Richard's forthright personality, the family had to prepare itself to answer difficult questions in the years to come, especially if his resemblance to Thomas became apparent as he grew. That was hopefully far in the future, though—Michael had problems enough to deal with in the short term.

He threw himself on his bed, closed his eyes, but no matter how tired he felt, sleep refused to come. After ten minutes of tossing, turning, trying to get comfortable and failing miserably, he gave up. He'd get out his sketchbooks and have a look through; maybe the procession of images would gradually lull his brain into a torpid state. He told himself he'd simply work through the drawings he'd done of soldiers, knowing full well that he wouldn't be able to resist poring over the ones of lovers, past and present. Now that he'd rediscovered the pleasures of his craft, it was proving impossible to resist. He kept the pretence up, though, carefully studying pictures at random until he allowed himself to inspect the one of Harry by the pond.

The harsh black and grey lines on bright, bare, white paper couldn't mar the man's beauty. Michael drank it in like wine, soon unable to resist fishing out the other sketch, the one of Harry on the window seat. The image itself—let alone the memories it engendered—stimulated him, soul and body. Could he really give up any opportunity of sleeping with Harry again? Or the chance of developing the sort of relationship that he'd once thought he and Thomas might have? The idea he'd had about taking time to explore all the incarnations of love came back to haunt him. This morning, Harry had clearly been ready and willing to rebuild bridges, to try to make something good out of the present mess, to apologise where necessary and to forgive in the same measure. Why couldn't Michael ditch his damn pride and meet him halfway?

Michael looked out of the window, at places he and Thomas had walked and played, and kissed when the opportunity had presented itself. But that Thomas had been in part a creation of Michael's imagination, the ideal man rather than the actual one with feet of clay. Perhaps there had been pointers to the truth, but Michael had been too blinded by love—or simply too unwilling—to see them.

He's still here, trying to keep you for himself, his own personal property. Tell him to leave you alone. You've moved on.

Ay, there was the rub. He'd clearly not moved on from Thomas at all.

Michael decided he'd try to get through dinner with a stratagem of asking all the questions, deflecting any attention away from himself. How was the trip to Porthkennack? Did Eric know if there'd been a new cottage hospital built? Had Caroline treated herself to a new frock for the visit to Broch?

"I tried to persuade her," Eric confided, "but she wasn't having it."

"We're not visiting Windsor Castle!" Caroline replied, flapping her hand at her men folk. "My pastel-blue dress will be fine."

Eric grinned. "Those boys make it out to be better than Windsor Castle. A variation on Wonderland, but without a March Hare or Mad Hatter."

"Harry has his daft moment—" Michael stopped himself, before his treacherous mouth could let anything else slip unwontedly. The story of comparing Harry's anatomy to a cricket bat could never be told.

"Does he?" Eric's grin widened. "Glad to hear it. I've always thought that family too straitlaced for their own good."

"Straitlaced?" Michael snorted. "Only on the surface. Eric, you have no idea what goes on behind that idyllic, old-fashioned facade." He caught, from the corner of his eye, the change in his sister's expression, soon hidden. She was evidently steeling herself—would it be too cruel to let her stew longer? But no, that wouldn't be fair to Eric. "I heard some things today about Harry's father which would make your hair stand on end. It's given me quite a different view of that family."

"What do you mean?" Caroline's voice, quiet and tentative, carried an underlying hint of courage in the face of great fear. He'd heard a similar tone out in France.

"To put it crudely, that he was overfond of sewing his wild oats and didn't mind if his wife knew about it." Michael detailed what he'd learned that afternoon, about the gardener, alluding to Harry's views on the family inheritance, but skirting round the detail, for both his and his sister's sake. "And that's why Harry's mother doesn't want to live here anymore. I can't blame her."

"I know I run the risk of sounding horribly smug," Eric squeezed Caroline's hand, "but I've often suspected there was something rotten in the state of Broch. I couldn't put my finger on it, but now I see the heartache under the perfect surface. Looks can be deceptive."

"You've never mentioned any of this." Caroline smiled, returning the caress.

"I didn't feel it was my place. They're your friends."

"I understand." Caroline nodded. "Although the friendship between our two families has long hung by a thread. Thank goodness Harry came along to connect us again. Eh, Michael?"

"Yes." He managed a smile. "At least he has the decency to be open and above board about things, although I guess he has that prerogative now. Nobody left to offend or upset."

"He'd be a veritable Mad Hatter if he didn't employ some diplomacy along with his candour," Eric cautioned. "Openness is all very well, but there's a point at which common sense has to prevail. Did I ever tell you about the chap I had to treat when I was newly qualified? Shan't use his name, so no risk of breaking the old Hippocratic oath . . ."

Eric launched into a typically amusing and informative story about a patient whose prognosis had had to be kept from the rest of his family, not just because it would have upset them, but because he'd feared they might hasten his journey into the next world to ensure he couldn't change his will. Whether it was true—or embroidered truth—Michael couldn't tell, but it was certainly a timely intervention. Caroline relaxed once more, and if she'd heard the story previously, she gave no sign.

The conversation moved on past the dangerous corner and into a pragmatic discussion about arrangements for the next day. Michael was able to take his leave early, with the intention of getting a proper night's sleep. He'd anticipated another session of tossing and turning, but no sooner had his head hit the pillow than it was morning, with the sun streaming in through a gap in the curtains. A calm, dreamless night had left him refreshed and ready to face almost anything, including the butterfly of disquiet in his stomach which insisted on suggesting today would be momentous. One way or another.

CHAPTER FOURTEEN

The arrival of the char-a-banc produced an outbreak of whooping from Richard and George, which Lily joined in until Alice restrained their enthusiasm with a gentle reminder that if they exerted themselves too much now, they would have no energy left to enjoy the rest of the day. The children remained delighted at the prospect of the ride to Broch, though; no amount of adult common sense was going to change that. Michael suspected there could well be tears before bedtime, but so long as he wasn't the one producing them, he didn't care.

The day appeared to have been made for a jaunt along sun-dappled country lanes, with just enough breeze to keep the air fresh, yet plenty of warmth to promise a pleasant sojourn around the grounds. The storm had cleared the air, and the red sky which had followed it the previous evening promised fine weather ahead. Lily, almost growing from toddler to child before his eyes, seemed alive with anticipation, even though she didn't seem sure what the excitement was about. Caroline fretted every time the boys bounced about in their seats, clearly frightened that one of them would take a tumble off the vehicle, to the point where Eric—in sharper tones than he normally employed—insisted she shouldn't fuss so much and that no ill was likely to come to either of them with all the adults at hand.

The appearance of a herd of cows in the road, and an anxious farmhand trying to coax them back into their field, brought the char-a-banc to a halt and the children's excitement once more to fever pitch. Michael settled them—and his own nerves—by playing a game where he spotted something and they had to guess what it was from only the first letter of the rod. Starting with simple things such as *grass* or *gate*, which the lads said were so easy even Lily could guess them, he moved ever more ambitiously through *white cloud* and to *large rock* to *Oak tree with a dead branch*, which Richard said was a suitable challenge for their brains.

Cow whose face looks like Great-aunt Mary's was the hit of the game, although Caroline had objected to that one. As Michael averred, she couldn't argue against the fact that the placid, bovine quality of the expression had been exactly like their maternal aunt's.

"Just so long as the boys don't mention that when we next see her." Caroline shook her head. "You're a bad influence, brother mine."

"That's what uncles are supposed to be, sister." Despite his qualms regarding what the rest of the day would have in store, Michael's spirits were lifting, and when they got going again and he spotted Broch in the distance, he couldn't resist shouting delightedly, "There it is! Not long now," and firing the lads' high spirits again. By the time they turned through the gate, the boys' enthusiasm had reached little short of fever pitch.

"Cor!" Richard almost bounced off his seat. "It's huge!"

Alice frowned, and Caroline tapped his arm. "Language, young man. 'Cor' is no example to set Lily."

"Sorry, Mother." Richard put on a suitably chastened expression. "It's just such a lovely place. Isn't it, George?"

"It's smashing." He pointed towards the house. "Is that Harry?"

"It is indeed." An unexpected swell of pride coursed through Michael. Harry looked at his lovely best, smiling and waving.

I had him, he thought. *No. That's too crude a way to think of it. He was my lover. Could still be, were it not for this damn mess.* He joined his niece and nephew in returning the wave, trying to keep his expression as neutral as possible. Caroline's face gave very little away, although her body was tense.

"Welcome!" Harry shook Eric's hand as he got down from the char-a-banc. "I'm glad to be able to reciprocate your hospitality."

"We're all glad to be here. Especially the boys." Eric helped Caroline down, while the youngsters scrambled off the vehicle. "This place has become like somewhere out of a fairy tale as far as they're concerned. Good that they can see it's real, warts and all."

"Are there warts?" Michael felt mildly intoxicated, a light-headedness at being back with Harry in the place where they'd coupled.

"Let's get you a drink." Harry clapped Michael on the shoulder, gave him a smile, then took the boys' hands. "Ginger beer for you chaps."

Chairs and tables were laid out on the lawn; somebody—Harry or the superlative Goode—had also provided a rug and some toys for Lily, and a cricket bat and ball for the lads. Alice, blushing slightly in the light of Harry's dashing smile, thanked him for being so considerate of her charges.

"My pleasure." He bowed gallantly. "You need to enjoy a day out as well as everyone else."

"Hear, hear!" Michael took the glass of champagne offered him. "You've done us proud."

"Glad to hear it." Harry's fingers brushed against his, clearly extending the invitation to remake bridges. "Come and sit down, everyone. Unless you're tired of sitting after your journey, of course."

"I, for one. would be grateful to be in a seat which didn't continually bounce up and down." Caroline, on whom the champagne seemed to be working wonders, was obviously growing in confidence.

They settled themselves, Caroline remarking on how the shrubbery had developed since they'd last been at the house, and admiring the wonderful colours. Anybody observing the party would have been hard pushed to spot any underlying tensions, although an eagle eye might have seen the odd inquiring glance which Harry sent in Michael's direction, glances which were met with only a tight-lipped smile. If Michael was going to resume diplomatic relations, then he would do it on his own terms, and not give in easily to those come-to-bed eyes.

"Excuse me." Richard, who'd quickly knocked back his ginger beer and gone off to play, appeared at Harry's elbow. "I can't seem to find the stumps. George and I don't mind playing without them, but if we want to teach Lily, she needs to learn the game properly. I wondered if we were being a bit silly and couldn't see them for looking."

"Sorry, old chap. You're quite right." Harry, getting up, clapped the lad on the shoulder. "I was so busy with champagne and the rest,

I forgot the stumps entirely. I think I know where they are, though. Maybe your uncle could give me a hand getting them, as I have an awful feeling they've been stowed away underneath some old rubbish and it'll need four hands."

"Oh, please don't go to any trouble," Caroline said.

"It's no trouble. We can't have Lily getting the wrong idea about something so important." He favoured Caroline with a dazzling smile. "You were always a dab hand at cricket. Perhaps she'll show the same talent." He jerked his thumb over his shoulder. "Can you come and help, Michael?"

"Certainly." Michael laid down his glass and followed in his host's wake. If he'd been a betting man, he'd have placed ten bob on Harry having somehow planned this—perhaps intending to make a thing about his having forgotten the stumps if the lads hadn't notice—in order to get Michael alone should he need to. If so, the strategy was effective.

They made their way to one of the outhouses, where sports equipment had been stored since time immemorial; even the cobwebs looked as they had years before.

"I didn't think you'd be coming here," Harry remarked once they were inside and he'd started to rummage in a pile of discarded golf clubs and the like.

"*I* didn't think I'd be here." Michael took the items handed to him and stacked them neatly against the wall. "But I had to do my avuncular duty. Couldn't let Richard and Lily down. Or George."

Harry, frowning, kept his eyes fixed on the task, and said airily. "Oh, yes. They're a lovely bunch of children. The nursery maid—Alice, was it?—must have an easy time of things."

"Except when Lily's teething." Michael tidied away an old tennis racket. He could see the objects of their search plainly, but it was taking Harry an inordinate amount of time to reach them. If he had something to say why didn't he just come out with it?

At last Harry stood up, three stumps and a couple of fly-blown bails in hand. "Is avuncular duty your sole reason for being here?"

Michael, light-headed from knocking champagne back on an empty stomach, tried tempering his response, principally because he was consumed by an urge to push Harry against the wall and kiss him.

"No. We have some unfinished business, although I suppose we won't get the chance to talk about it today."

Harry smiled, clearly relieved. "Not with me being on hosting duty. You could always return. You're welcome here at any time. You know that."

"I know." Michael sighed. They stood, silent, seemingly unable to make progress, although the fact they weren't arguing must have been a small step forward.

"We should get back," Harry said, eventually. "They'll be wondering what's keeping us."

"We'd better have our excuses ready." Michael swept up a mass of cobwebs in his hand, dabbing some onto his hair.

"What's that for? Playing Miss Havisham?"

"Wait and see. It's what the army would call a diversionary tactic."

When they rejoined the company, Eric was trying to teach Lily how to hold a bat properly, while George appeared to be coaching Alice in the art of spin, for which the nurse had far too slender fingers.

"What on earth have you been doing?" Caroline rose to brush the mess from Michael's hair.

"Getting these," Harry said over his shoulder as he went to present them to Richard.

"We had to give them a jolly good clean." Michael nodded, sending the last bit of web flying. "Veritable army of spiders stationed there."

"You appear to be wearing most of them," his sister responded, drily.

"Oh!" Alice gave a shudder. "Thank you for getting rid of the things."

Michael, temporarily distracted by the sight of Harry's trim backside as he bent to knock in the stumps, made a bow. As if that weren't enough, the lads practicing their batting stances brought back memories of those awful bat-related jokes he and Harry had made in the bedroom. Given his suspicions about the stumps episode, Michael wouldn't have been surprised if cricket, as opposed to croquet or clock golf, had been deliberately chosen by Harry to evoke those recollections. He was inclined to show the bloke that the plan had worked.

"You should get Harry to give you a display after lunch," he shouted to Richard. "He's renowned for his skill with the bat."

To his delight, Harry blushed, clearly trying to conceal the fact by leaping up and grabbing the cricket ball.

"Let's have an over or two before lunch. You lads can bat, and Michael can keep wicket as punishment for his cheek."

"Keep wicket?" Michael pointed at his legs. "What about pads? Or gloves, come to that?"

"We're not at Lord's, for goodness sake." Harry dismissed his concerns with an airy wave. "Don't be a sissy."

Naturally the boys were ecstatic at the prospect of cricket, dragooning Eric in to help in the field. Lily, for the moment, would have to watch with the ladies of the party, out of harm's way. Nobody could be quite sure just how well the boys were going to connect and if Harry went in to bat, everybody would have to take cover. Once they were all set, Harry obliged with an over of donkey drops which George could easily hit away for a run or two.

"Pitch them up a bit," Richard snorted from the covers. "He's a good batsman."

"Like Ranjitsinhji?" Harry picked up a bit of speed, which George dealt with efficiently enough until one particularly pacy delivery reared off a small hummock of grass, fizzed past the lad's bat, and caught Michael on the arm.

"Sorry!" Harry came racing up, hands outstretched in apology and white as a sheet. "Forgot myself for a minute. George is so good a bat I thought I was playing a first-class game."

"That's all right." George clearly didn't understand the danger he'd been in had the ball reared a foot higher. "It was good practice for when I'm older."

"We'll find a more level bit to play on after lunch. I think the moles have been here." Harry, colour only gradually returning, glanced at Michael's arm. "You'll have a corker of a bruise there tomorrow. If Richard and George are anything like I was at that age, they'll count every bump as a badge of honour."

"I'd gladly donate it to them." Michael rubbed his arm, glad to find that nothing appeared to be broken. "I'm not batting against you unless I do have pads."

"You can wear the old suit of armour." Harry looked at the bruise again, winced, then casually put his arm round Michael's shoulder to draw him in the direction of the table. "Come on. It's time for luncheon. Goode will be out fussing over us in a minute."

The arm had felt a touch proprietorial; Michael suspected the others would read nothing into it apart from friendship, although given that they seemed to have eyes only for the feast laid out for them, he wasn't sure anyone apart from him had noticed. He gave Harry a brief smile, then slipped out of his grasp.

Lunch—served out on the terrace on a table well tucked into the shade—was excellent. Probably the skills of the woman who'd made the cassoulet had been called on once more, and the menu she'd produced was the perfect blend of items suitable for all ages. Lily loved the tiny little sandwiches, which were like something from *Alice in Wonderland* and a perfect fit for her hands, while the boys appreciated sausage rolls and cheese straws and what they'd no doubt regard as other masculine items. Michael was simply grateful for something to soak up the champagne and an activity to take his mind off Harry's presence.

Harry was appropriately attentive towards his female guests all through the meal, ensuring they had plates and glasses well topped up. Alice bloomed under the attention, although the smiles he gave her didn't match the occasional one he threw at Michael.

They'd come to the point where nobody could manage a scrap more, and were planning the afternoon's activities—Caroline and Alice trying to insist the children take a rest and the gentlemen making the argument that they shouldn't waste the fine weather—when Goode, apologetic, appeared in order to inform Harry that he was wanted urgently by his mother on the telephone.

Harry, rising, spread his hands apologetically. "Make yourselves at home. I have no idea how long I'll be."

"We'll wait here for you," Eric averred. "It won't do these young savages an ounce of harm to take a rest after all their running around."

"Can we go fishing in the lake later?" Richard asked, as Harry edged away. "Uncle Michael said it might be possible."

"Then I mustn't disoblige Uncle Michael." Harry replied flirtatiously, dashing off to answer his mother.

Michael, hiding a grin, made conventional comments about hoping he wasn't going to be hearing bad news, to which Eric equally conventionally responded that it would be a shame on such a fine day. Caroline suggested that finding a bit of shade in which to have forty winks would be an excellent idea. Despite Richard's and George's submission, the plans came to very little, the two boys too keen to be up and doing. Michael volunteered to take them down to the boathouse while the others had a rest, in return for which perhaps he could be let off fishing duties. Eric readily agreed, as did the ladies, Lily already dozing off on her mother's lap and Caroline looking like she'd soon join her.

They wandered down the path, Michael pointing out some of the places he'd played and recounting those adventures which were suitable for young ears. Inevitably the boys wanted to see inside the boathouse; one unexpected advantage of the revelations concerning Thomas was that Michael could face that without qualms, something he'd have struggled with previously. His change in attitude towards his ex-lover had changed his attitude towards Broch and its memories, as well.

The boys seemed to enjoy poking about in the half-light, seeking out hidden treasures of oars and half-rotted cushions.

"Can we take a boat onto the lake?" George asked.

Michael frowned. "You'll have to check with Harry. The lake always used to be a bit tricky, being pretty deep, but it was safe so long as you didn't horse around. I've a feeling it's not quite as easy to navigate as it was, though."

"We're both good swimmers. And you'll be here to keep an eye on us, won't you?" Richard placed his hands together entreatingly.

"I will, but your mother would have my guts for garters if anything befell you. Wait till the rest of the grown-ups are here and then we'll see." Michael cast his eyes about for something to offer instead. "Do you know how to canoe?"

"No," the boys chimed in unison.

"We used to take this old green one out. One of you could sit in it here and I'll show you how to use the paddle." He couldn't have suggested such a thing previously, but Thomas's fall from grace had affected this precious object as well.

"Thank you!" Richard let George have the first go, the pair enjoying getting to grips with the feel of the paddle and making measured strokes. There might not have been any water, but imaginative nine-year-olds can find pleasure even in dumb show.

Voices outside announced the imminent arrival of the rest of the party, and the three emerged from the boathouse—only slightly dirty—to greet them. Harry, who'd clearly been released early from filial duty, and Eric were laden with the fishing gear.

"Oh, smashing!" Richard ran up to his father to help him with the tackle. "Thank *you* for letting us." He beamed at Harry.

"I said we shouldn't disoblige your uncle. One must always obey the wishes of one's elders." Harry grinned at Michael.

"Steady on. I'm not that much older than you." Michael returned the flirtatious smile, wondering if Caroline's eagle eye would recognise the true nature of the exchange. "Perhaps I should turn back the years and give you a walloping, like you used to get when you were being a nuisance."

Harry slapped his shoulder. "No setting the boys a bad example! Come and help get them set up."

Michael led the way onto a small jetty which they'd traditionally fished from. "I was telling the lads that the lake's dangerous. They'll have to take care."

"They will. Dangerous waters, I'm afraid." Harry addressed the boys, but Michael had an inkling the words were also meant for him. Dangerous waters indeed, given all the hidden currents below the surface of this apparently typical social grouping.

"Everything sorted with your mother?" Michael asked, casually. Harry seemed happy enough, but Michael was now wary of facades.

Harry shrugged. "Just a bit of business with her solicitor she wanted advice about and that really could have waited, except that for Mother, waiting is something she no longer does well."

"Couldn't Olivia have sorted it, being closer at hand?"

"Of course she could," Harry rolled his eyes, "but Mother's convinced that only a man can handle this kind of thing." He glanced down at Lily, who'd attached herself to his side. "Don't you grow up with those sorts of attitudes. This is a brave new world, and I, for one, would like to see womenkind taking a brave new attitude."

Alice clicked her tongue disapprovingly at the sentiment, but Caroline nodded. "Good thing too. If there were women in positions of power, maybe we wouldn't have got into that awful mess of a war. Sorry," she added, red-faced, "perhaps you think I'm just a silly chit of a thing who doesn't know what she's talking about."

"Not at all." Harry rested his hand on her arm, setting off an unexpected pang of jealousy in Michael. In such a way would Thomas have touched her. "I believe you're speaking a load of sense. Eric's lucky to have such a levelheaded wife."

"I certainly am," Eric said, with a smile. "And when Lily's prime minister, I'll be the proudest father in the world."

"What about Richard?" Caroline enquired. Michael flinched at her sharp tone.

Eric turned to his son. "Tell your mother what I said when we went night fishing."

"May I?" Richard seemed unperturbed. "I thought George and I were sworn to secrecy."

"It's an appropriate time to revoke the requirement." Eric grinned.

"I cast, all on my own, for the first time." Richard beamed. "And Father said he was the proudest father in the world only we weren't to mention it in front of Lily in case it upset her, and once she'd done something equally amazing, then he'd be equally proud of her too."

Michael, who hadn't realised he'd been holding his breath until he suddenly felt it release, shared a relieved glance with Harry as Caroline said, "Oh, Eric. You soppy thing," and pecked her husband's cheek.

Richard and George shared their own glance—one of evident distaste at such a show of affection in public—while Lily squealed, "Kiss!" and giggled uncontrollably. Caroline took her hand, then went to busy herself laying down blankets and cushions for Alice, herself, and her overexcited daughter well away from the water's edge, although she seemed to be keeping an anxious eye on their activities, despite the calming presence of Eric and the other men. She had a point, given that a moment's inattention could lead to a lifetime of regret, but boys had to be allowed to be boys. The females of the party set to making daisy chains and persuading Lily to turn away from what her brother was doing, while the lads started out with their nets and buckets to dip for strange creatures in the lake before they went in search of larger quarry.

Michael and Harry helped them clear the jetty of some of the unwanted "presents" the ducks had left on it so the lads could settle themselves without risk of ending up covered in bird mess. Eric's skills were soon called on to identify one or two of the more peculiar items the boys caught, although even Michael could name a water boatman or pond skipper. Hawker dragonflies, like small aircraft, flashed brightly across the surface, while a startled moorhen—flushed from the reeds—departed with as much dignity as it could muster.

Soon the boys grew tired of annoying invertebrates and turned to fishing; Eric set up their rods but insisted they bait their own hooks, using some of the fruits of their pond-dipping. He helped them to cast, then left them to it, slipping off his shoes and socks, rolling up his trousers, and dangling his toes in the water, for all the world like a schoolboy himself. Except for the pipe he lit up. Michael considered joining him, but—suddenly conscious of his scarred leg, which neither Alice nor George had seen—just sat on the jetty.

Harry clearly harboured no such inhibitions, joining Eric in splashing his feet in the cool water. "What do you think of the place now you've seen it?" he asked Richard.

"Smashing." The boy beamed. "I prefer High Top's location, being so near the beach, but the gardens here are much nicer. And there's no lake at High Top. Or boathouse."

"Thank you for your gracious estimation. We aim to please." Harry inclined his head. "The boy has taste, Michael."

"Of course he does. He's a marvellous lad."

"Oh, Uncle!" Richard had flushed scarlet. "Lucky it's George here. Any of the other lads from school might have ragged me all term if they'd heard that."

"Sorry. I'll restrain myself. It's the sun making me silly," Michael confided, giving George a nudge. "I promise I won't say anything like it in front of your other friends. I'll tell them you're an awful stinker."

"That's the sort of thing you'd do." Harry leaped to his feet, brushing the seat of his pants. "I'll just check on the ladies. See if they're comfortable or need more lemonade."

"Do you like Harry as much as you liked Thomas?" Richard remarked, once Harry was out of earshot.

Michael, glad that Harry had gone, said, "I think so. He's very different to his brother, though."

"Yes, I suppose he is." Richard nodded. "I guess it's like us and the Cooper-Wooley boys. If you want to play cricket, you'd want to be with Jacob, wouldn't you, George?"

"Oh yes," the lad replied. "But he's no use at making a den, so you'd want Alex for that. Ooh, I've got a bite!" He jerked the tip of his rod up.

"You'll lose it, doing that," Michael said. "Got to be gentle. Take a lead from Eric—he always has a soft but firm touch."

"Eh?" Eric jerked out of his reverie. "What's that?"

"George is having trouble with a bite."

"Too late." George, frowning, flipped up the rod, with its empty hook. "Lost him."

"You'll learn. It's as much an art as Michael's sketching is," Eric averred. "Coax the fish in. Don't force it." He gave the lads a demonstration of the best way to gently reel in one's catch.

Michael, watching inattentively, welcomed the change of subject. One day Richard would realise that all his uncle's assertions about why he'd never married were just so much eyewash, and then he'd be asking for the truth, assuming he hadn't already worked it out for himself by then. Or, indeed, already.

"No luck?" Harry's voice, soft and mellow, heralded the return of the man himself.

"Not with the fish." Michael gave him a quick smile. "Eric's trying to put them right."

"Is there anything he can't do?"

"If there is, I've yet to discover it. All round Renaissance man."

"Steady on!" Eric remarked. "You'll make my head swell."

"Uncle Michael's right," Richard confirmed, "you're the best father any boy could have."

"I think we'd better get you two fishing again before I turn red." Eric, evidently pleased, got the boys' hooks baited and cast.

"Your nephew's spot on," Harry murmured, low enough that only Michael could hear. "It's all a mess, but it's turned out for the best."

"You've never said a truer word." Michael lay back against the grassy slope, while Eric joined them. Conversation centred idly around Porthkennack gossip, punctuated with gaps in which Michael's eyes insisted on shutting themselves, encouraged by the soporific sunshine. He cast a glance out of the side of his eye to find Eric already dozing and Harry not far behind. He should stay awake, but the arms of Morpheus were entwining themselves around him.

He woke with a shock, at the sound of a splash and a cry which had penetrated his sleep. In his dream it had been a young subaltern falling in a rain-sodden shell hole, but reality showed it to have been Richard, flailing in the lake with George beside him. Eric was already on the jetty, slipping into the water, Harry scrambling to join him.

Caroline, screaming, came stumbling down the bank. "He's gone under again. He'll be drowned."

Michael grabbed her arm. "Don't you go and join them. Leave it to the men."

"No!" Caroline, shaking herself out of his grip, dashed to the jetty. Michael pursued.

"Caroline." He enfolded her in his grasp, pulling her back. "It's under control. The water's not too deep here, but further out it's dangerous. If you go meddling, it could make things worse."

Harry already had Richard in his grasp, the pair of them swimming strongly for the bank, while Eric and George steadily doggy paddled the short distance to safety.

Alice, blankets in one hand and a fretful Lily in the other, threw the covers down to Michael, who used them to wrap the boys.

"What happened?" Caroline asked, fussing over her son.

"We slipped." Richard's teeth chattered. "The jetty had got a bit wet and slimy, from the weed we'd dragged up."

"I slipped," George confessed. "Richard came in to save me. We got tangled in something. More weeds, I guess." He glanced down at his legs, where a layer of green slime supported his story. "I'm sorry. I should have been more careful."

"I'll have this lake cleared properly." Harry, shivering, flapped his arms for warmth. "Get some signs put up to stop people going out on it. We don't want anybody else to be at risk, even if they're trespassers."

"Signs won't stop people if they're intent on mischief." Eric was—ineffectively—trying to dry himself on a small towel from his fishing bag. "And when I was a boy, being told I couldn't do something was a great incentive to do it."

"Will you all stop it?" Caroline, voice cracking, had both boys firmly enfolded in her arms.

"Stop what?" Michael asked.

"Pretending nothing untoward happened. They could have been killed."

"Caroline, they're fine," Eric assured her. "No bones broken, only a bit of dented pride and a lesson learned to be more careful."

Caroline wouldn't be mollified. "It could have been worse."

Eric put his arm round her shoulder. "It could, but we didn't let it be. We were all here to look after them. Me and Michael and Harry. As we'll always be."

"We certainly will," Harry agreed, while Michael nodded. For as long as the lads needed caring for, they'd fill that role, although how would Caroline feel when Richard was a grown man? She couldn't wrap him up in tissue then. And what on earth would she do should another war ever break out?

"I'll give them a check over if you want," Eric added, "but I suspect that all they need is a swift change of clothes and a small medicinal glass of port, if Harry could rustle up either of those. The cold and the shock are the worst risk they face at present."

"I can oblige with both," Harry said. "And a change for us too, so long as none of us are fussy about fit. Caroline, you'll have to excuse us looking like tramps."

Caroline managed a smile. "As long as you're all well, you can look like Fred Karno's army for all I care."

Goode, who must have spotted the commotion and met them halfway back to the house, was put in charge of organising a pot of tea, some biscuits—and a medicinal drink or two—after getting the ladies settled in the sunshine, it being warmer outdoors than in.

"I'll take Eric upstairs to find him the nearest thing to shirts and trousers which fit," Harry said, as they neared the house. "Michael, could you see what you can find for Richard and George in Thomas's old room? Mother always was a terrible hoarder, and there are clothes going back years there."

"Of course."

Caroline, still clinging to the lads, said, "If it'll be a bother to find clothes the right size, why not get the char-a-banc driver to go back to High Top and get them something from there? Or take us all home, now."

Michael studied his sister sidelong. Was she as reluctant as he was to see Richard in Thomas's clothes?

"Nonsense, my dear," Eric said, briskly. "They need to get changed now. The breeze on that char-a-banc would chill me to death, let alone them."

A fresh outbreak of teeth chattering settled the matter.

Michael placed his hands on the boys' shoulders. "I'm taking them straight indoors and getting them dry. A bit of activity should warm them up. Race you." He set off at a pace, the boys in his wake. Perhaps if he could take all of this at a run, it would be manageable. He'd not been back in Thomas's room since their quarrel, and the place would be full of associations, but if he concentrated on the task in hand, surely it wouldn't be that hard?

The boys beat him to the house, overtaking him at the last moment, then halted at the door, too well brought up to run indoors. They processed up the stairs, stopping now and again to get their breath back, then headed for the bedroom. It felt like entering a museum exhibit, hardly anything changed since Michael had last tumbled on that bed. The room was clean and tidy, although a sad emptiness pervaded it, which even the boys seemed to detect, lowering their voices as they came through the door.

"I think this must be the closet," Michael remarked, knowing full well where the doors he was heading for led.

"Coo," Richard said, as they stepped in. Thomas had always liked his clothes, as the serried ranks of hanging shirts and trousers, and the shelves of neatly folded underwear and the like, testified.

"He kept his things tidier than his hair, didn't he?" Michael gingerly picked up a sweater, then replaced it. "All this is far too large, even for well-grown lads like you two. Let's see if there's some older stuff stored away."

Below the shelves sat old cases, a light sheen of dust over them indicating they might not have seen a duster since Harry's mother moved away, taking her insistence on venerating the past with her. Michael drew one out and opened it to find old, albeit clean, sports clothes—school rugby shirts and shorts, a cricket sweater, hideously ugly items that Michael remembered he and his schoolmates being forced to wear in the gymnasium. He gently rummaged out a pair of flannel shirts, but could only find one pair of decent shorts.

"One of you will have to wear long trousers. And roll the bottoms up if need be." He laid out the fruits of his search and left the boys to get changed. To his surprise, the clothes proved a much better fit for George than for Richard, the latter being clearly a different shape to his real father.

"We seem rather silly, don't we?" Richard said, as they paraded in front of a long mirror.

"Speak for yourself." George grinned.

"At least you're dry." Michael grabbed a large shirt, bundled up their wet clothes in it, then ushered them to the door. "Come and stun the ladies with your elegance."

Eric and Harry must still have been getting changed, but Caroline and Alice were being served tea by Goode, who'd made them comfortable. The brew was delicious—and very welcome—Michael knocking back an entire cup before his host appeared, looking stunningly fresh, with Eric carrying off a rather natty cricket outfit which he, too, had had to roll at the ankles.

"For I'm to be Queen o' the May, Mother, I'm to be Queen o' the May!" he said, doffing an imaginary hat and bowing.

Lily, giggling, scampered over to him, raising her arms to be picked up.

"Shall I pour you soon some tea?" Caroline offered, smiling.

Harry gave Michael a smile. "I think Goode's on the way with something a bit stronger."

Goode was indeed on the way, making his entrance bearing decanters of brandy and port. Harry insisted upon Richard and George being allowed a small glass each for strictly therapeutic purposes, to which Caroline agreed so long as George didn't report it to his mother until *she'd* explained to Louise precisely what had happened to earn him such a treat. Harry and Michael kept tipping them a wink about indulging in such naughtiness, although the lads clearly found the drink stronger than expected, if deliciously sweet. They began to giggle, at which point Eric suggested it might be as well to get them home before any drunken carousing ensued.

Michael sent for the char-a-banc driver, then got together all their stuff, Alice ensuring that nothing was left behind. Except regrets, naturally, Michael wishing he'd had more time to talk to Harry, although exactly what he could have said with the others present, he didn't know.

"We'll send the clothes back to you when they're washed and aired," Caroline promised, as Harry handed her up onto her seat.

"Oh, don't go to any trouble," he said, with a wave of his hand. "You're on holiday."

"I could cycle over with them," Michael suggested, airily.

"If you're sure." There was an edge of excitement in Harry's voice, which Michael hoped nobody but he had registered. "I won't be here tomorrow, though. Bring them the next day, if you're free."

"I'll do that."

"I'll see they're washed," Caroline promised.

"No. Bring them as they are and they'll go into the laundry here. Caroline," Harry raised his hand to forestall any argument, "I insist. It was our lake that did the damage, so I should pick up the pieces."

Caroline, eyes narrowed, simply nodded and said, "As you wish. And despite the calamity, I've had a lovely day here. Thank you for being such a wonderful host."

"Yes, thank you very much," Richard echoed.

An outbreak of gratitude and handshaking erupted again, before the char-a-banc set off. Michael twisted round, to better watch Harry waving, and returned the gesture with a salute of his own. He'd come back the day after tomorrow, and things would be all right, wouldn't they? He turned back to see Richard in his father's clothes once more; the icy prickles on his neck reminded him that it would take a great deal to put everything right.

CHAPTER FIFTEEN

The rest of the day passed in a whirl of hot baths, clean clothes, hot soup, and early nights. Michael slept well, a restful, dreamless sleep—or at least with no dreams that he could remember. He woke in a pleasant haze to another day that promised sunshine and warmth, as idyllic as any he could remember from childhood.

When Michael at last left the house, Richard and George had set up the croquet things, determined to teach Lily to play the game now that she'd been introduced to cricket. Alice had them under her watchful eye while Eric had retreated to the hammock with his pipe and a book.

Michael fancied nothing more than taking himself, his sketchbook and his thoughts down to the beach, but Caroline asked if he'd like to go for a walk. Something had happened during the visit to Broch, he felt certain, some change to her as subtle as that prompted in him by his interaction with Harry. So he took her arm, and set off for a stroll through the shaded lanes. At first, conversation sailed through the safe topic of Broch and how little it appeared to have changed, until Michael steered into rougher waters.

"Right at the start of this holiday," which seemed an age ago, now, "Richard said that if you had a wish, you'd want all the soldiers to come home, unharmed. Remember telling him that?"

"How can I forget?"

"My friend Laurie," if she read between the lines that he had been more than a friend, it didn't matter anymore, "used to say 'beware of what you wish for.' If Thomas had survived, wouldn't that have complicated matters?"

Caroline tightened her grip on his arm. "We both know it would. And no matter how many times I've told myself that I'd rather deal with complications and have Thomas—and all those other poor souls—alive, deep within me there's a deeply uncharitable streak that says I'm relieved things turned out as they did. I'm sorry if that hurts you."

"Why should it hurt me in particular?"

"If Thomas had returned, you and he could have been reconciled."

Michael halted, turning her to face him. "I might have wanted that a week ago, but now I know it could never have worked. I don't think he'd still have wanted me. Perhaps he'd have preferred you."

Bright colour flared on her cheeks. "He could prefer all he wanted; he'd never have had me."

"Then perhaps he'd have chosen another woman. The Thomas who'd have returned wouldn't have been the man I've been thinking of all these years." He gently caressed his sister's hand. "It's time for me to stop living with memories and get on with life as it is."

"That's the only way." She folded his hand in hers. "I was on tenterhooks all day yesterday, convinced that something awful was going to happen to Richard. It seemed like fate."

"But it was all fine. In the end."

"I know. Although I'd rather not have seen him in Thomas's clothes. Thank goodness they fitted so badly. He looked like a clown."

"I'm glad I wasn't the only person worried about that." Michael sighed. "It wasn't pleasant going through Thomas's things, I can tell you. I don't know why Mrs. Carter-Clemence hasn't just given them all away. There are plenty of local lads who'd have benefited."

"Perhaps, given what you told us regarding her husband, she was petrified of seeing some poor unfortunate local child in her son's clothes and been unwittingly looking at her husband's son or her own grandson, I suppose." She wrinkled her nose. "Does that make any sense?"

"It does. What an awful thought." They walked on. "Although it could be simply a case of keeping alive the memory of a departed loved one by keeping their things as they were."

"As though they might walk back through the door to collect them?" Caroline nodded. "What would Harry do if he had the opportunity to chuck them out?"

"I haven't asked him." It might be a safe topic to explore the next day. Bland enough not to be offensive but personal enough to help with mending bridges. "He doesn't strike me as a sentimental type. He appears to be coping pretty well with the fact of Thomas's death."

Caroline nodded. "You learn to live with it, don't you? As I live with the knowledge of Richard's parentage every day. If I beat myself about the head with it, I'd go mad."

"You've coped well." Michael halted again, by the entrance to a field whose gate provided an excellent place to lean, enjoy the view, and share confidences. "I wish I had half your courage to just go on. I can't see clearly where the road ahead leads."

"Nonsense." She squeezed his arm. "You're as brave as anyone. You'll see the path, so long as you carry on going forward. You need to move on, make something good out of the bad."

"That's sounds horribly easy."

"It isn't, I assure you, but it's worth the effort." She rubbed his cheek with the back of her hand. "My little brother. You've seen how protective Richard is of Lily? Well, that's how I feel about you. And at the risk of you telling me to mind my own business, or worse, I'm going to ask you a question."

"That sounds ominous." Michael couldn't help but smile at the grave expression on his sister's face. "Do I need to brace myself?"

"I hope not." She narrowed her eyes, seemed to weigh him up for a moment, then asked, "Do you like Harry? And does he like you?"

"We rubbed along together fine. Until—" He was going to say, *Until your indiscretion got in the way*, but that would have been too harsh. It wasn't Caroline's fault they'd quarrelled. "Until we had a bit of a bust up about Thomas and Richard and everything."

"I thought he appeared a touch awkward when he came round to invite us to lunch."

"Yes. You see quite a lot, don't you?" He smiled. "Unfortunately, we managed to get into another argument during that walk along the beach. I nearly didn't come yesterday; it was only not wanting to disappoint Richard that changed my mind."

"I'm glad you came. The way Harry looks at you; it's how Thomas used to. No," she put her finger to his lips. "Don't say anything, simply listen. If there's a chance that you and Harry could be happy together, then please don't miss it just because of something that neither of you did. This is my burden, not yours. Move on and make something good."

She had a point, a very good one. She'd not let Thomas ruin her life, nor that of her loved ones. "Even when all my certainties have gone?" It was a weak last sally, one he didn't quite believe himself.

"All of them? Is that really true?" She'd sounded like that when he'd been a small boy and she'd caught him telling some tall tale.

"I suppose not. Come on," he took her hand. "Let's get back. They'll be wondering what we're getting up to."

When they arrived back at High Top, Eric swung himself out of the hammock at their approach. "You two look unusually serious."

"Do we?" Their appearance must be contrasting with Michael's mood, which was lighter than it had been for days. "That must be because Caroline's been giving me much-needed advice."

Eric jabbed with the stem of his pipe. "Was it good advice?"

"Probably." Michael rubbed the back of his neck. "I'll have to go away and think about it."

"Hm." Eric glanced from brother to sister, then took out from his pocket a strange-looking device with which he began to clean the bowl of his pipe. "I'd say that as families go, we're not such a bad bunch. Especially when I hear about the Carter-Clemence antics."

"Sorry?" Michael frowned, confused at the turn the conversation had taken.

"I was just thinking, lying in my hammock, that I've been an extremely lucky man, one way or another. Not every husband likes his in-laws. Nor his children, come to that."

Caroline, smiling sweetly, appeared as captivated by her husband as when they'd first met. "You're very deep today."

"I am. That tumble the lads took in the water yesterday has come back to haunt me. I realised how awful life would be without Richard." Eric kept his gaze fixed on his pipe. "There must be fathers up and down the country who know that sense of loss, and I've been thanking

God I'm not in their band. Even though he isn't my son in terms of the biology of the matter."

Caroline gasped, putting her hand to her chest with a wince.

"Don't look so startled. I've known a long time, and I suspect Michael knows by now, so we might as well have it in the open. It makes not a jot of difference. I love him and I love you." And with that remark, as matter of fact as, *Those stitches need to come out, matron*, he lit up his pipe.

Caroline, colour slowly returning to her face, watched him. "You've never given me the slightest hint," she said eventually. "All those times I've worried that you'd find out, and you knew. Why didn't you say before now?"

"Because Eric's the most decent gentleman I know," Michael answered for him, then wished he hadn't. Husband and wife needed time alone. "He'll have had his reasons, which he'll no doubt explain. I'll go and see what the boys are up to."

"Thank you. I think we'll toddle off for a while too," Eric said, before taking his wife's arm, and leading her off for a walk. Michael watched them go, wondering when Eric had found out about Richard and what had been going on in his head since. It would be just like him to form a theory that Caroline herself might be sure of her son's paternity, and to have kept quiet to avoid hurting her. From a distance, Michael couldn't make out what his sister and brother-in-law were saying, but if he needed to know, he'd find out. In the meantime, the revelation took a huge burden off his shoulders.

"Is Mother all right?" Richard's voice sounding at Michael's side made him jump.

"She's fine. Just having a moment with your father. Old married couple sort of thing." Michael hoped his nephew wouldn't notice the tangled emotions in his own voice.

"Oh, I see." Richard rolled his eyes at George. "Lily's got tired of croquet. Do you fancy a game?"

"Why not? We'd best leave your parents to it. They might get very soppy."

"Ugh." Richard took Michael's hand, no doubt to lead him to a place of safety away from such unseemly shows of sentiment.

"Perhaps we should go indoors," Michael suggested. "Would you like to play whist, George?"

"Yes, please." George grinned. "You'll have to teach me, though. Mother doesn't approve of children playing card games."

"Playing whist is almost playing bridge. Terribly respectable, really. Just the thing to take us through to lunch."

And after lunch he'd try to nab Eric. He had questions to ask.

Someone "upstairs" was clearly smiling on him, given that Caroline—who was wonderfully serene over lunch—announced that she and Alice were taking the children to buy them new summer hats, the present ones being not fit for public display. Michael had a fleeting thought that the stratagem might have been produced specifically to allow him and his brother-in-law the opportunity to talk, but he dismissed it. He was still reading too much into everything.

Eric proposed an afternoon fishing, on the same principle of getting back onto a horse once you'd had a fall, and Michael—no angler, but welcoming the opportunity—asked to tag along. Eric would surely have some word of wisdom about how to forgive.

Michael had intended to bide his time, waiting for the right moment, but he hadn't accounted for Eric's forthright nature.

"You'll be wondering about this morning," Eric remarked, as he retried a cast which hadn't been perfect the first time.

"It did rather come out of the blue." Michael cast out his own line. "Not the knowledge about Richard, by the way. Harry let that slip when I visited Broch."

"Hmm." Eric didn't appear surprised. "You wouldn't have expected me to know. I understand that."

"I never suspected for a moment, and I had no intention of rocking the boat. He's so clearly your pride and joy."

"Of course he is." Eric gave Michael a sidelong smile before concentrating on his fly as it danced over the surface of the lake. "As is Lily, and she will be more so when she's old enough to take fishing or any of the other things one does with the little 'uns."

"Not all fathers take such an interest."

"More fool them, then." Eric pulled in his line and recast. "I'm going to tell you something that not even Caroline knows. I'd be grateful if you keep it in strictest confidence."

"You have my word," Michael promised, determined to do a better job than he had previously with family secrets.

"I've told her that my knowing about Richard's . . . um . . . provenance, was to do with his birthmark. How I'd seen pictures of Thomas as a boy, when we were previously down here on holiday and that I'd put two and two together. It's a plausible tale, and the one I'd like you to adhere to, if she mentions it."

"I will," Michael reassured him, then waited.

"What actually happened was that Thomas wrote to me. At least he had the discretion to address the letter to the hospital." Eric winced, distaste creasing his handsome features. "I suspect that was the extent of any discretion he possessed."

Michael sniffed. "I'm rapidly arriving at the same conclusion. How could we have all been so blind to the man's faults?"

"Because he was charming." Eric frowned, pulling back his line and flicking it onto the water again. "He proceeded to tell me all the business with the birthmark—that's really where I first got to hear about it—then he told me about what had happened with Caroline."

"The swine." How could the man have had such brass neck? "Eric, I'm stunned."

"So was I." He managed a smile though. "I was a bit dim at first, wondering where all the birthmark stuff was going. Perhaps he was trying a gentle lead up in order to soften the eventual blow."

"I think you do Thomas too much credit." Layer after layer was being peeled away to expose somebody entirely different, somebody who'd created an image of himself that was different for each person he was close to: lover, brother, mistress. "Did you reply to the letter?"

"I did. I told him that I'd never regard Richard as anything else but mine, because that's what he was and always would be. That everyone made mistakes, and while Thomas could and should suffer the consequences, I wouldn't have my son suffering with him. These things are no great deal unless one is willing to let them be."

"Is that truly how you felt? If so, you're a little short of a saint."

"A saint?" Eric grinned, shamefacedly. "I'm hardly that. Saints don't . . . um . . . manoeuvre people the way I manoeuvred Thomas."

"Go on." This story was taking unexpected turns.

"I told him that if he wanted to establish the child's paternity I'd arrange a test to be held. And I assured him that I'd also arrange for the test to show quite unequivocally that I was Richard's father. There *is* no such procedure, of course, but my colleagues and I could have persuaded him otherwise."

"I bet you could." The prospective sleight of hand gave Michael new respect for his brother-in-law. No saint, thank goodness, but a pragmatic and fiercely protective man. There was no doubt he saw Richard to be kept as his own. "You amaze me, Eric. I don't have half your capacity to forgive and forget."

"Oh, I couldn't forget, old boy. That would make me superhuman." Eric wrinkled up his face, pulled in his line, and began to adjust it prior to another cast. "I'm not sure I've ever forgiven Thomas, either."

"But Caroline? You've forgiven her?"

"Yes. Strangely enough, I have." He deftly pitched his fly onto the water once more. "Think of what I've seen working with servicemen. I know I'm a bones man, but I'm not blind to the implications of what soldiers get up to outside of battle. There are diseases you can catch however careful you are. You know the sort I mean—the brothels of France were infested with them."

"So I understand."

"It wasn't just out there that men were desperate. It happened at home, that last fling before embarkation. Men—and women—lost their moral compass. They did things in the shadow of death that they would never have done otherwise."

"But—" Michael hesitated. Caroline and Thomas's affair hadn't been a snatched night of passion on the very eve of war.

"But that wasn't the case with them?" Eric kept his eyes fixed on the water. "No. Indeed. Thomas was a desperate man, though. His father once told me he'd joined the army because he was both selfish and a coward. Odd, isn't it?" At last he faced Michael. "Not the qualities one would expect in an officer."

Michael pulled in his own line, all appetite for sport gone. "What did he mean by that?"

"That Thomas had always wanted to have his own way, irrespective of the consequence to others. Chip off the old block, if what you've said is true."

"Yes." That trick he'd played on Michael back at Cambridge was evidence of that.

"I believe he was fond of you. And after your friendship turned sour, he set his sights on Caroline. She tells me he'd been bothering her for a long while. I'd already guessed something of the kind." Eric reeled in his line once more. "Looks like they're not biting on this fly today."

"Let's try another." Michael watched as Eric expertly dealt with the hooks. "If Mr. Carter-Clemence felt his son a coward, which is not a term to be used lightly given recent events, why was Thomas so determined to claim paternity? A coward would surely have shirked his responsibilities."

"It was to do with Broch, of course. Nobody could guarantee another male heir would appear, and if Richard could be produced, there'd have been no pressure to produce another."

Michael nodded. Yes, that could very well be the truth. "Will you ever tell Richard that Broch could rightfully be his?"

"I might, when he's a man. He's showing every sign of having the maturity of mind to take it in his stride. His obsession with Broch won't hurt, either." Eric gave him a sidelong glance. "Harry might have something to say about it."

"Harry's as pragmatic as you are. There'd be a workable solution." Michael gazed at the water, where the fish were rising for midges but signally avoiding the artificial flies on offer. "And there's no guarantee he'll have any. You know that not everyone came home with his ability to father a child intact, and he's not mentioned looking for a wife." That was an excuse he'd stored up for his own use, should he find himself being pressured into marrying.

Eric nodded, either taking this at face value or pretending to.

"What if Richard asks before then?" Michael continued. "He's not daft, and you know how obsessed he is with photographs. What if he happens to see a picture of Thomas—or Harry—as a child and compares it to his own baby pictures, what then?"

"Then I'll jump that fence in the best fashion I can. When it happens and not before. I've lived the last nine years on a day-to-day basis. You get used to it."

"True." That's how they'd lived in France, knowing that they'd have to deal with whatever turned up, one way or the other. Eventually they stopped trying to plan for a future that had no guarantee of arriving. "These last few years must have been hard on you."

"Not hard. You might say it's been simple. I could have made a fuss, but I love Caroline and I love Richard, and I couldn't risk losing either of them. Better to swallow the pill, forgive, and move on. The knowledge that only I'm aware of Thomas's letter helps, somehow. *My* secret, to set against Caroline's. Aha!" Eric leaped into action as his fly jerked below the water. "That's better." He expertly landed the fish, put it into the keep net, and prepared to cast again.

"Is forgiveness as easy as all that? No more effort than landing that trout?"

"Certainly not. Like anything worthwhile in life, you have to work on it. But plenty of men have had a lot worse to deal with."

"Yes." Michael remembered the man he'd seen as he'd cycled into Porthkennack. That could so easily have been *him*, sitting with the leg of his suit pinned up.

"And I could focus my anger—because believe me I was furious at first—on Thomas. I might have been deluding myself to put all the blame on him, but as a pragmatic strategy, it got me through." Eric flipped his rod up. "And another! Trout pâté for lunch tomorrow."

"Shame I'll probably miss it." Michael fussed over his own rod and line. "As we're being so very frank, may I ask if you'd rather Caroline had told you, years ago?" The terrible thought that Eric might have been as cruel as Thomas had proved to be, nagged at him. Might he even have cut off any opportunity to have it all in the open so she'd have to live with her secret as a punishment for what she'd done?

"I do," Eric replied at last. "I hoped I wouldn't have to be the one to raise it."

"And now? That accident changed your mind so decisively?"

"Yes. If anything had happened, how could we ever have broached the topic? Richard's ghost would have stood between us, forever condemning us for cowardice." Eric had never sounded quite so deep.

"True." Like Thomas's ghost had wanted to stand between Michael and Harry. "That mishap touched me too. I never for a moment thought they were in real danger, but who knows what might happen another time. I promised Richard I'd sketch him when he was older, but I'm inclined to bring that forward. I'd like you and Caroline to have the finished item."

"Thank you." An streak of emotion almost broke Eric's voice. "Could you make it of the two lads, though? It might seem a little pointed otherwise."

Michael nodded. "Good thinking. It'll help me to save face when I change my mind. I can say it's a memento of the holiday. I'll do one for Louise, as well. Just so long as she won't then expect one of George's sisters."

Eric raised his eyebrows in sympathy and got back to tempting the fish.

Michael caught his nephew over tea in the nursery, much to the delight of both Alice and Lily, who continued to find him a source of hilarity.

"That sketch I promised to do of you when you're eleven. Remember?"

"Ye-es." Richard swallowed hard, evidently preparing himself for news good or bad.

"Would it be a pain if I did something of the sort this summer? Of you and George?"

Richard beamed. "It wouldn't be a pain at all. Thank you." He leaped up, running over to hug Michael, a rare privilege and not one he lightly bestowed.

"I'll do two of them. One for your mother, George."

"Ooh." George almost capered with delight. "My sisters will be so jealous."

"They'll be able to see how handsome Richard is. Takes after his uncle, naturally," he added, with a wink at Lily. His prophetic soul could just imagine his nephew marrying one of those girls. Michael could only hope *he* lived long enough to make a speech at the wedding—whoever Richard chose to spend his life with—to embarrass him with some of the adventures and conversations they'd had.

Lily clambered up onto his lap. "I love you, Nuncle."

"I love you too, tiddler. And your father. And your mother." There, he could say it. And it felt like the truth once more. "And your brother. Even though he's got a funny face."

"You said he looked like you!" George pointed out, at which they all chortled.

Normal family life had resumed.

CHAPTER SIXTEEN

Next day, Michael cycled to Broch in a peculiar mood—half trepidation, half elation, all nerves—still unsure whether to just return the borrowed clothes and go home again. As before, the sight of Harry drove those plans from his head. The man must have been waiting and watching from one of the windows, as he was at the door ready to greet Michael as he pulled up.

"Back again?" he called, holding out his hand to be shaken.

Michael couldn't help a grin; no matter how intimate they'd been, the proper social practices had to be observed. He resisted saying something like, *Isn't that bleeding obvious?* settling instead for shaking hands, loading Harry with the clothes, and saying, "I'm afraid so. No matter how painful, I always return when I say I will."

Harry winced. "Is it still that bad?"

"I wasn't just thinking about memories." Michael grinned. "I've got a bruise the size of a hen's egg from that cricket ball. Were you aiming at me? The more I think about it, the more I'm sure you'd never have risked hurting George. That ball was always going to go straight past him."

Harry held up a hand. "Guilty as charged, at least concerning intention. It went closer to the lad than I'd meant it to."

"But why?"

"I wanted to get your attention. I wanted you to react to me. To stop pussyfooting about and playing polite. I wouldn't have minded if you'd laid me out with a punch, so long as it wasn't simply something social and civil."

"I can't decide if you're an evil bastard or just a silly sod."

"Silly sod. That's me. I'd rather you told me you hated me and shouted at me to bugger off than leave me in this terribly polite and agonising limbo."

"I don't hate you." *I don't want you to bugger off. I want to take you upstairs and roger you stupid, right now.* But that would be too straightforward, discounting the depths of his hurt and redeeming it too cheaply. Except, of course, it wasn't Harry who had a ransom to pay. "The only thing I hate is hypocrisy. Tom had two faces. One for us and one for you, I guess."

Harry shrugged. "He had one for everybody."

"How many faces do you have, Harry?"

"Only the one." Harry, smiling, gently stroked Michael's arm, then withdrew his hand as though he'd overstepped the line. "As I've said, I'm too candid for my own good. I could never hold my own at the gaming tables, as I'd wear my hand on my face. I'm not my father's son, not in terms of his nature, anyway."

"Just as well." If there was something Michael had learned the last few days, it was that a man wasn't necessarily made by his bloodline, but by the standards with which he was raised. Harry had done well not to be tainted by the malevolent Carter-Clemence influence.

"I promise you I'll never deceive or trick. All my sins will be in the open."

"Really? Doesn't that risk getting arrested for exposure?"

"Shame that cave of yours is too dangerous now. No risk of exposing oneself to the world there." Harry flashed him a dangerous glance.

"There's always the boathouse," Michael replied, eyes racking Harry from crow's nest to keel. "If you don't fancy your bedroom."

"I'd fancy you anywhere." Harry returned the appraising look. "But I've never done it in the boathouse. Lots of places here I haven't done it, actually."

"Then you've plenty of scope for exploration." Michael slipped his arm through Harry's, and they set off for the lake. With the cave out of bounds, the boathouse was the right place—symbolically—in which to lay the ghost of Thomas, and his pernicious influence on Michael's life, once and for all.

"Did you and Thomas have this as one of your places?" Harry asked, as they reached the door. "Or is that a stupid question? I suppose you did it every and anywhere."

"That's about the size of it." Michael grinned. "In that green canoe for a start."

"Really?" Harry's eyebrows shot up. "That can't be physically possible."

"Want a bet?" Michael tugged Harry into the boathouse, then forced him against the door, kissing him intensely as they pushed it to.

"I never bet against what I suspect will be a racing certainty," Harry remarked hoarsely, as they broke for air. "Even if I can't imagine how it was done." He took a sideways glance to where the canoe was partially visible in the half-light from the dirty window. "Unless one of you was standing and the other on your knees?"

"How prosaic. We were much more inventive than that." Taking Harry's hand, Michael steered him to where the cushions and rugs had always been kept. If Broch ran true to form, they'd still be there. "Ah. Exactly what we need."

The cushions were moth-eaten but two were useable, and the rugs only needed a good shake—outside the door—to rid them of the dust of years. The canoe, securely stored within a wooden stand, was easy to pad out and make comfortable; if narrow, at least all the hard edges would be cushioned.

Harry nodded, approvingly. "I like the cut of your jib."

Michael pulled him closer for a kiss or three. "Seems like your jib is raised and ready for action."

Harry groaned, in what sounded like a mixture of pleasure and exasperation. "It was cricket jokes last time. Are you going to run through all the naval ones this time?"

"Oh, no." Michael's groin thrust gently against Harry's. "I'm keeping plenty of them for the next occasion."

"If that canoe isn't as comfy as you promised, there may not be another occasion."

Michael didn't believe that; what man in his right mind would turn down the chance of intimacy? Except that *he* nearly had done, being so wrapped up in his stubborn pride. Not trusting himself to speak, he kissed Harry again, pulling him over to the canoe. Actions would be better than words, which was almost how the old saying went. Except, as he realised with horror, they had nothing to hand to facilitate them doing what he and Thomas had done here and what he'd hoped to repeat. Where was a jar of Vaseline when you needed it?

"Have you forgotten something?" Harry asked, just as Michael had got him pinned against the framework. "Are you thinking of oiling the machinery?"

"How do you know what I'm thinking of?"

"The contents of your trousers are giving it away." Harry stroked the parts under discussion. "Lucky for you that one of us is prepared." He drew a small container from his pocket.

"You swine." Michael grinned. "How long have you had that in there?"

"Since I got dressed. You know sailors—ever the optimists."

"And thank goodness for that." It didn't take long to reach the point where the jar of salve was needed, both of them too eager to share their bodies again to linger over the preliminaries. They could take things slowly another day—many other days.

Their coupling was surprisingly comfortable, Michael relieved that his memory hadn't been playing tricks on him. The restricted space produced an atmosphere of consolation and reassurance, the sensation of being swaddled and kept safe. In the past he'd enjoyed sex for the sheer enjoyment of it, for the excitement of breaking the rules, for the snatched pleasure when death might be waiting round the corner, but never before had he found such solace or healing.

Afterwards they lay together in the canoe, feeling they'd claimed it for themselves, smoking in sweet silence until Harry asked, "What's happened these last few days? You seem more at peace."

"I am. There's been a bit of air clearing." Michael described his conversations with Caroline and Eric, and his brother-in-law's revelations.

Harry, who'd been nodding approvingly during the account, whistled as it reached the end. "Who'd have guessed he could be so deep? Or so devious?"

"Not me. He's a dark horse. And, as I've long suspected, he's a better man than I am." Michael took a pull on his cigarette.

"He's a better man than most people. You're lucky to have him in the family."

"Don't I know it? This whole thing could have gone belly up were it not for him. Back then, and now, and all the years in between." He snuggled closer.

"Have you forgiven Caroline?"

Michael exhaled a thin stream of smoke. "I'm about halfway there. Ask me again at Christmas."

"And Tom?" Harry turned up his face to look Michael in the eye. "Can you forgive him?"

"Is there any point in forgiving someone who can't benefit from it?"

"I wasn't thinking so much of the benefit to him as the benefit to you. You're a different man—understandably so but that doesn't alter the fact—since I nearly ran you over."

"For the worse?"

"You could never take a turn for the worse. Not in my eyes." Harry stubbed out his cigarette, then grazed his hand along Michael's cheek. "You've had a tinge of sadness about you since we first met again, although at least I now comprehend why. But sadness isn't dangerous the way that anger is. To nurse your wrath against Thomas can't be doing you any good."

"I know. I know." Michael sighed. "They say that time is a great healer, although if that's so, it's being tardy about it. Or perhaps I'm just being impatient. Maybe by next summer I'll feel different. Assessed what's important and what's not."

"Will you come back here then?"

"If invited. I thought it would be hell on earth, but I've found such unexpected happiness."

"I should damn well hope so." Harry cuffed Michael's arm. "We can know a lot of happiness in London too. You've seen how discreet Goode can be. We won't have to hide too much once we're behind the closed doors of my flat."

"How could I refuse an offer like that?" Michael stubbed out his cigarette, which had burned dangerously low, then leaned in for a kiss.

"What is it you really value, above all else, Michael?" Harry asked, once the kiss had been completed to their satisfaction. "And don't say your sketching, or I might be forced to punch you."

"Shame. I do value it, not least because it was the catalyst for us first making love. Ow."

"Don't be a baby. I didn't punch you as hard as I could have. What else?"

"The fact I got home in one piece. Richard, and Eric, and the affection I feel for them. Sex with you in a cool, clean bed." The counting of blessings struck a chord in his memory. "When we were looking for the cricket stumps, did I see a bag of old seashells?"

"Seashells?" Harry, puzzled, wrinkled his nose. "You might have done. That place is full of old rubbish. Why?"

"You'll see." Michael eased himself out of the canoe. "Once we've made ourselves decent. Goode may be discreet, but one wouldn't want to scandalise him."

Cleaned and tidied—or as clean and tidy as they could manage—they wandered up to the outbuilding where the sports gear was still stacked.

"What is all this about?"

"As you pointed out, Broch's too far from the beach. I'm making do." Michael set to work clearing away some old hockey kit, uncovering a large bucket full of dry and dusty shells, which he showed to his host.

"I had no idea those were there. Did you and Thomas collect them? Olivia was never keen on beachcombing."

"These could well be the ones we got. They look old and dirty enough." He took the bucket by the handle. "Let's take these out onto the lawn."

"What *are* you up to?"

"You'll see."

"Whatever it is, I'll get Goode to bring us a little preprandial stiffener to fortify us." Harry rolled his eyes. "I have a feeling I'll need it."

Once they were settled on a blanket on the lawn, with a glass of sherry in hand, Michael tipped out the contents of the bucket, then singled out a collection of the less-disgusting shells. He laid the first one in front of him. "*Un*, the first, that's Thomas. I used to think he was the best, the ideal. I'm a wiser man now."

Harry nodded, sipped his sherry, and waited.

"*Deux*, that's Laurie."

"Ah, I see." Harry grinned. "Just how many shells have you got hidden away in that hand of yours? Will you need the entire bucketful?"

"I shall ignore that. This isn't about boasting over my conquests." He cast Harry a glance, but the man looked suitably sober. "Richard loves it when I count shells for him, in as many languages as I can manage. But I've never had the chance to enumerate aloud what they signify for me."

"Sorry." Harry touched his arm. "Go on."

Michael pointed to the second shell again. "Laurie was the chap I went to the Lake District with *that* summer. Not long after, he was taken ill, rowing. Dead when they got him out of the boat."

"Dear God. You've not had a lot of luck, have you?"

"So it seems. Not until now." He gave Harry a smile, then laid down another shell. "*Trois*. Freddie. Not a lot to say about him, really. Fleeting but fun."

"Sounds like some of the ones I've known."

"Are you the one who'd need the whole bucket?" Michael placed a slightly crumbling oyster shell on the lawn. "*Quatre*. Jimmy. I liked him. I liked him a lot."

"Where is he now?"

"Gone the way of all flesh. Freddie's the only one who may have survived. Unlike," he added a mussel shell to the row, "*cinq*. Wilfred. The war took him too." He laid down a fine scallop shell, the best he'd been able to find among the bucket's contents. "*Six*."

"Me?"

"You."

Harry picked the shell up, turning it between his fingers. "Would it be too bloody soppy to say that I hope there's not a *sept*? Not for a long time to come anyway?"

"It would be too bloody soppy by half, but that's the trouble with you sailors. Load of sentimental softies."

"I'd show you who's soft, right now, but it would horrify Goode. It'll have to wait until we're alone again." Harry laid his hand on Michael's to briefly squeeze it. "There must be more places here where you've done it and I haven't. You could lead me astray."

"I'd be glad to." Michael upended the bucket. "We could catalogue them all using these."

"Would there be enough shells in that pile?"

Michael put his arm round Harry's shoulders. "There might not be enough on the whole beach."

Explore more of the *Porthkennack* universe:
riptidepublishing.com/titles/universe/porthkennack

a PORTHKENNACK HISTORICAL

A Gathering Storm
Joanna Chambers

a PORTHKENNACK CONTEMPORARY

Wake Up Call
JL Merrow

Broke Deep
Charlie Cochrane

House of Cards
Garrett Leigh

Foxglove Copse
Alex Beecroft

Junkyard Heart
Garrett Leigh

Tribute Act
Joanna Chambers

Dear Reader,

Thank you for reading Charlie Cochrane's *Count the Shells*!

We know your time is precious and you have many, many entertainment options, so it means a lot that you've chosen to spend your time reading. We really hope you enjoyed it.

We'd be honored if you'd consider posting a review—good or bad—on sites like **Amazon, Barnes & Noble, Kobo, Goodreads, Twitter, Facebook, Tumblr,** and your blog or website. We'd also be honored if you told your friends and family about this book. Word of mouth is a book's lifeblood!

For more information on upcoming releases, author interviews, blog tours, contests, giveaways, and more, please sign up for our weekly, spam-free newsletter and visit us around the web:

Newsletter: tinyurl.com/RiptideSignup
Twitter: twitter.com/RiptideBooks
Facebook: facebook.com/RiptidePublishing
Goodreads: tinyurl.com/RiptideOnGoodreads
Tumblr: riptidepublishing.tumblr.com

Thank you so much for Reading the Rainbow!

RiptidePublishing.com

ALSO BY CHARLIE COCHRANE

For a complete book list, visit: charliecochrane.co.uk